Let's Dance

FRANCES FYFIELD

BALLANTINE BOOKS

A Division of Random House of Canada

BALLANTINE BOOKS

All rights reserved under International and
Pan American Copyright Conventions. Published in
Canada in 1996 by Ballantine Books, a division of Random
House of Canada Limited, Toronto. First published in hardcover in
Canada by Alfred A. Knopf Canada, Toronto. Originally published
in Great Britain by Penguin Books Limited, London, in 1995.
Distributed by Random House of Canada Limited, Toronto.

Canadian Cataloguing in Publication Data

Fyfield, Frances
Let's dance

ISBN: 0-345-39838-6

I. Title

PR6057.Y74L4 1997   823 .914   C96-932011-6

Printed and bound in Canada

To Angela Nightingale,
for being alive

Chapter One

THERE WAS NO OTHER WAY TO DESCRIBE IT. A perfectly beautiful house which also managed to be ugly. There was a glory in its pretence to be a truly grand house whilst being, in reality, a mansionette masquerading as a mansion. There was no spitting of gravel as a car turned into the drive, since the gravel was half submerged into the weedy earth, leaving a smooth tread and puddles. The tennis court was similar, erupting with moss, the pond to the side choked with weed and a haven for frogs, while the lawn resembled a green lunar landscape, spongy to the feet, riddled with mole-holes. Round the back, where the red brick of decaying outhouses met the pitted surface of the stable yard, a berry tree was shedding an early autumn crop so plentiful it was ignored even by the birds. The grounds were sweet smelling, as edible as the house. Like good rich food, a blessing and a curse.

The front was a two-storey elevation, mostly glass window set in sandstone below a shallow pitched roof of dull but definite grey. The front door had altered with the generations, undecided about fate, looked temporary, far too small and cheap between a pair of fat columns. These had once been surmounted by stone lions, added and then taken away at the same time as the stone globes on the gateposts. Humility followed pretension.

The out-of-scale Corinthian columns alone appeared to announce not only a huge reception hall, but also twenty bedrooms of liberty hall, instead of the mere five. As it was, a small vestibule was flanked by two fine front rooms with enormous windows, one living room, one dining room, each with fifteen huge panes of old glass in elegant, thin frames, currently dirty but none the less magnificent. It was the kind of hospitable, slightly blowzy house which invited the colourful domination of virginia creeper and weeds, never the sinister overtones of ivy. But the creeper had been killed: there were trails of it growing up against the mellow gold stone, like a trail of debris on a handkerchief, holes in the upper slabs where foliage had been held if not controlled. Each brick of this perfect example of English eccentricity, *folie de grandeur* and sheer, if muddled, taste, came from the valley landscape where the house stood as if growing out of it, unable to live elsewhere, insulted by the suggestion. Invisible from the road, the house withstood all weathers, and was perfectly isolated.

There were one and a half bathrooms for all those rooms, one lavatory in the servants' quarters. Three servants at one time, plus gardener and stable lad, plus any assistance needed from the village, now hamlet, lying one mile away and the town, five miles beyond and visible from the hill. Some gentlewoman had once considered it a struggle to manage with a staff of five. Those were the days.

Serena Burley lived in it alone. A man called George, who was not paid for his labours, drove each day from the town to look after her and her dog. No one knew where he came from or why he had done this for the three years of Serena's erratically developing dementia. Janice, who was paid, although not handsomely, also attended. Robert and Isabel, Serena's far-distant children, visited for frantically busy weekends in which they mended things and went away, saddened, appalled and relieved. George was such a Godsend, they never questioned either his identity or his motives.

They worried about their mother while half tolerating, half detesting one another. Most of the time, the detestation won. Robert was a bully and Isabel was weak. He regarded her with all the contempt held by the strong for the meek who had also managed, by no effort of their own, to inherit the earth. Robert would inherit little from his mother: the house was held on some obscure leasehold arrangement. Isabel's inheritance came from someone else. Neither of them could quite believe Serena's diagnosis, since the rude health of both of them made them deny the existence of anything incurable. And because Serena Burley had been such a password for magnificence, it was impossible to imagine that she would not, somehow, reemerge from this senile chrysalis and laugh at them.

"It can't go on," Robert kept repeating. "It simply can't. She'll have to go into a home. You'll have to make her. Or go and look after her for a while until we decide what to do."

"Go and look after her? Why can't you go and look after her? What's the difference between your responsibility as a son and mine as a daughter, and besides, you're the one she adores ..." Isabel would feel the lump of tears whenever the conversation got to this point, which it did on every telephone call. However would she acquire a family of her own if she went home to her mother? Almost on cue, as if someone was squeezing them for effect, there would be the sound of screaming children in the background of Robert's home.

"That's why," he would hiss triumphantly, a stage-whisper of a hiss, intended to be heard by his sensible wife who loathed her sister-in-law as much as she envied her. "*We* have no power to shove her into a home, because she's still just about sane, and I couldn't possibly go and look after her because I have family responsibilities . . . "

"That was your choice!" Isabel would yell at this point, also intending to be heard, but the guilt crept up into her throat at the same time and made her voice tremble on the edge of petulant hysteria.

" . . . I have kids and no money and a tough job, none of which applies to you . . . "

The words "you lazy slut" were never quite announced: they hovered there, over the wires, to be repeated at supper by Mrs Robert Burley, but they still entered the iron of Isabel's soul. A son is a son till he takes him a wife: my daughter's my daughter for all of her life.

"She's fine as she is. She's got help . . . "

This was Isabel, avoiding confrontation as she usually did, denying her mother's example, that of her aunt as well. She was unequal to it at the best of times, which was never like this, hampered by guilt and the luck of life which evaded her brother, hampered even more at the moment by the denouement of yet another love affair. All Robert could do was moan about the responsibility of having kids: all she could dream about was the utter privilege of what he claimed as an affliction. Whether it was love or babies that formed the subject matter of dreams, she could no longer distinguish and was not about to try. Her own mother had told her not to come home and, apart from brief visitations, she had done her best to comply.

"How can you say everything's fine? The house is falling down."

"All you care about are the things inside the house!" Isabel screamed this time, despite herself, the high notes of her shrill voice warbling like a raucous jungle bird.

"Better than caring about nothing but yourself. Like you."

Staring into space after such family chats, Isabel imagined her beloved mother, her eyes which grew paler and paler with age and the arms outstretched in the great big greeting which would be Serena's welcome. No one else had ever inspired such huge and unrequited love. Or such pride.

There was a series of photographs in tarnished silver frames on top of Serena's desk. Some of them talked, some did not. The one of Mab, Serena's sister, for instance, showed the solid, uncommunicative face of a woman to whom life had been scrupulously unfair, right from the day when her mother had decided to call her Mabel, because of that Mabel Lucy Atwell look: deliciously fat cheeks, snub nose, eyelashes to kill for. Later Mab was still best seen in profile, because even as an adult that plumpness resembled the moon, with features set uncertainly in a squashed circle, a currant bun of a face with a frizz of hair.

Next to Aunt Mab were Isabel and Robert, clinging to her fat thighs. Serena had taken that photo herself: no one showed to advantage. She featured alongside, inside a better frame, wearing a black ballgown, with husband on arm, receiving adoration. That was preferable. Serena had been venerated wherever she went, the subject of a thousand schoolgirl crushes and a hundred leering men, while her sister Mab blossomed into the kind of child people called bonny, or so she had explained to Isabel, leaving her niece to wonder what it might have been like to be sibling to a younger sister so beautiful she made men and

5

women alike catch their breath. She was not aptly named. Her name suggested tranquillity, whereas all her life Serena had howled at the moon. There were more than vestiges of a former, sensual beauty about her eyes, her hair, her carriage.

The photograph of fat, capable Mab began to talk. Well, Mab said, cheerfully, I had to develop in other ways. And I was, I am, happier than my sister, in the long run. My sister is not going to like being old, you know, but for me it makes no difference. No one will notice. Serena turned the photo down so she could not see Mab, smiling.

"Bedlam!" Serena shrieked. "What rhymes with bedlam, George?"

"I dunno. Can't you think of something easier than that?"

"Tart."

"Part?"

"Fart!"

"Oh, very funny. Better write it down quickly. Where's your pen?"

Sitting at her desk, Serena was suddenly protective. She leant forward over a pile of paper, shielding it from view. "You'd better not look at what I'm writing, George. Secrets."

"I know, I know, but I can scarce read, remember?"

"Don't believe you. You're a clever fucker. A right smart *bugger!*"

He chuckled, good-natured in the face of an outburst. "Language, Mrs Burley, my lovely sweetheart, you gotta watch that language."

She relaxed, put her head in her hands. "Language is the root of all good and evil, George. Which is a shame, because I can't remember the verbs." She looked round, wildly. "What do I mean, George. Verbs? Words?"

"I think you mean words," he said gently. "And never you mind. You got plenty of words left."

"What's happening to me, George?"

"You need feeding, that's all."

He plodded out of the room, making an effort to behave as if he had no right in there and she had not called him in in the first place. As far as anyone else was concerned, he never went further than the kitchen. He had a place by the fire, along with the dog. He was not paid to do what he did. He was not supposed to do anything for Serena: he did what he did for the dog. Or that was the way it had started out.

The house had a strange and lopsided magnificence, certainly in comparison with any he had ever known, although he had never been familiar with a wide variety of houses. At home he could not have kept a hamster: the rules, imposed by the authorities, the lack of air and the neighbours, did not allow. Here the place smelled blissfully of animal and warmth. There were falling-down outhouses outside, a coalhouse where a boy could keep a rabbit, a backyard and a whole acre of land. He saw it as a kind of flawed heaven and inside it he had this strange sensation of vitality. Mrs Burley was a good woman and she needed him when no one else did. She was mad only in other people's estimation. There was no one else he would rather obey.

"Things she does!" he informed the dog, as well as anyone else who would listen. "Course she isn't mad. She's sane as you and I. You know what? I got there this afternoon and how do you think she was doing? On her hands and knees, she was, planting plastic flowers outside. I said to her, I said, you shouldn't be doing that, you'll get your knees muddy. Fuck off, she says to me, why not? There's fuck-all else growing here. If I put these lovely things here, then the others will know they should grow. Makes sense, don't it?"

And that was the fact of it. So much of what Serena did made sense. To Serena and also to George. They shared a common and secret logic which did not require even the effort of mutual tolerance. George, Serena and, to some extent, Janice, conspired to maintain a façade and to keep Mrs Burley where she belonged, and, although Janice did not know it, to preserve George in relative safety.

He was back in the kitchen. There was a fuel-burning stove of indeterminate age at one end, with a sweet nursing chair in front of it, the sink at the other end and a badly done, uphill sloping quarry-tiled floor uniting the two. There was also a refrigerator, an electric cooker and a series of old kitchen units littered against the walls, a couple of deep, walk-in cupboards built into the fabric of huge sandstone walls and a series of doors which had once puzzled him until he knew better. One led to a pantry, a miserable little room, full of fuse boxes, a washing machine, what still passed for a freezer and shelves full of stores, all dusty and deficient, the place a masterpiece of bad design. Something called Fablon, a kind of stick-on polythene, coated the pantry shelves, curled at the edges, making fingers stick and grime collect. Looking out from the pantry window there was a spinney, beginning with a small bank on which he had seen the ferret play last summer, both of them enchanted with the sunlight.

The wood had been cut back and now took revenge by crawling forwards in a thicket of sycamore. Nearest the window were the purple autumn crocuses which he could call his own, the bulbs he had planted signalling a new ownership of this wild territory. George watched the ginger cat crawl among them, pause where he had planted out the Christmas tree the winter before, willing permanence on both its withered branches and his tenure in this blessed house. The cat strove to survive, just as he did. Serena said it would grow up to be handsome, which was more than anyone would ever say about him. George had done his growing in another world, and in this one acquired a new skin and an identity which, for the first time ever, pleased him.

The other door, aside from the one that led into the corridor, an avenue that bore signs of Serena's eclectic taste, led down to the cellar. In saner moments Mrs Burley had told him about people keeping food down there before the advent of the refrigerator, why didn't he go and look? He had looked, closely, once or twice and never again. Janice said there was a cheese press made out of half a ton of stone, because it had once been a dairy. Stone shelves, a back cellar full of junk, a little window covered with dank weed, a place where things were put and left for ever. Until Serena had a party, magicked glasses, knives, forks, out of there. Oh, really? There had been no parties here in three years: George would have hated a crowd. It was the look of the steps down which so appalled him. They were stone, but so worn that each of them lisped into the centre, lethally slippery, the outward edge forming a wavy line, glistening with damp. It was the thought of how many people, how many hundreds of thousands of footsteps, had created that effect by constant traffic that had unnerved him. George did not like darkness, or servitude.

The dog got up out of her basket, cautiously enthusiastic. She seemed, like her mistress, to lose the capacity for barking in the afternoon, made a noise only for those she liked.

"Fine bloody watchdog you are," he grumbled. "C'mon, ol' girl. You and me against the world. C'mon."

She moved her fat rump, thudded her tail, looked up beseechingly. Cold, outside.

"Walkies," he said. "You'll feel better for it after."

They went out the back. Past the pump that no longer worked, over the fence into the park, her paws clipping on the remnant of concrete by the stable yard. There was a fine powdering of frost on the grass: the cattle had been taken indoors, so the land was theirs. In the distance was the treadmill of the town. He raised a fist to it.

In all of the vexed, fifty-odd years of his life, George had never been this happy. He needed this status quo, and without giving it much thought was determined it should remain exactly as it was.

Janice did an evening shift after George had gone, four hours a day. She was a comfortable woman and a natural diplomat, a necessary talent for one who pursued a patient career in looking after the elderly, albeit one that was founded on her nervousness about doing anything else, except clean things, which was what she had once done here. Patience was certainly a virtue. What did these poor old dears have to do with jargon about being mentally challenged? She looked at Serena Burley over the rim of her spectacles and then averted her eyes. Serena would have responded better to a man: Serena lit up in the presence of the male sex, but for a woman Janice did better than most when it came to persuading her to eat. People who had not entirely lost their table manners, but were still aware enough to know they were doing something not quite right, were embarrassed to be watched, although Mrs Burley used mealtimes as a great attention-seeking exercise. It was as if she wished to prove her frugality by never admitting to hunger. She lived on chocolate, and the only thing she could cook, albeit with maximum labour, was fish and chips. As one who had cooked for two fussy children and one bottomless pit of a husband for what seemed like endless years, Janice did not think this diet a sign of madness in itself, in fact it seemed a sign of sanity. All the same, these antics over a meal could be irritating to anyone else, who had failed to eradicate impatience as Janice had, leaving a vacuum filled with nothing but endless affection, loyalty governed by prudence and a fear for what she held dear.

"Too hot," Serena complained. "Ooh, far too hot. I can't eat this. Why is it so hot?"

It was not hot: Janice had ensured it was merely warm, so that Mrs Burley would do what she usually did, which was tear off chunks of fish and feed them under the table to the ever-waiting dog. It was *de rigueur* that half the meal would be given away: proof to herself, in some benighted way, that Mrs Burley was a civilized, delicate and far from greedy woman. Janice kept quiet, apart from saying, mmm, this is nice, by way of encouragement. A bit like running water making people want to pee. She did not like the thought of Mrs Burley's fingers, covered in dog saliva, putting chips into her own mouth, but there was nothing she could do about that and it was better than the old girl eating nothing at all. Janice supposed that owner and dog must be immune to each other's germs after all this time. It was the dog looked poorly. That was the daftest thing the daughter had done, buy that dog which had grown into a fat and indiscriminately friendly bitch, as pleased with male strangers as Serena was herself. Janice cleared the plates.

"Would you like some ice-cream?"

"Too cold," said Serena. "Isn't it?"

The sky outside was black, that time of year when darkness began to rule and daylight in the evening faded into a memory. The days had been grey and cold, limiting the mean allowance of light to a few hours of indifferent illumination per diem. Would Mrs Burley still be here in the spring? Janice dreaded winter. The house had begun to unnerve her after dark: she had dreams about it. She looked with longing at the outline of her red car, blurred by the wavy lines of the glass on the kitchen door. Should have put it away in the dilapidated garage round the back, where the sight of it would not fill Serena with envy. She patted her pocket for the keys, which the old dear kept trying to pinch; still wanted to drive, poor old duck. Janice did four until eight, Mondays, Wednesdays and Fridays, and it was almost time to go, but Mrs Burley always began to talk when they were both on the downward run, and then she did not quite have the heart. Tonight she was going to be bold, strike for freedom ten minutes early. There was something oppressive, intense and mischievous about her charge this evening, and her own movements around the sink became brisk.

"I've got one son and one daughter," Serena began, "and they don't love me any more because of the words."

"Never, Mrs. B.," said Janice, making her chatter into a parody of cleaning-lady talk because Mrs Burley liked it that way. "They love you a lot, but they got to work, you know. And they live a long way away."

Janice did not believe that sons and daughters owed it to their elders to interrupt their lives and turn themselves to the ignominy of the kind of service that was her livelihood. Only those who did not know what it was like would ever expect that, and she would have killed herself rather than have her children do for her what she did. They could do it for someone else, but they were never going to do it for her. They were never going to see her eat with open jaws and suck her fingers as she gave chips to the dogs. You had to have your compassion paid for to do this job.

"Don't go," said Serena. "Please don't go. I'm frightened."

There's a ritual, see? Janice would tell her husband. A black-mail ritual, when she tries to stop me going, only it doesn't cor-respond with my hours.

"Course you aren't frightened. You don't know the meaning of the word."

"What verb?" Serena was suddenly angry; terribly angry. Janice paused with her hand on the door latch, looking out to the comfort of her red car. In that, home soon. Sooner the better.

"A bit cross, maybe. Never frightened, not you. Don't worry about it, love. See you soon."

That was a ritual too, the use of simple words and simpler promises. She remembered closing the door on that sullen and disappointed face with its sharp features, big soft eyes hinting at the splendour of all that former beauty, blowing kisses as she got in the driving seat and went hell for leather out of the rutted drive and on to the road across the fields. By the time she was halfway to the church, the music blared, making a cocoon of the car, making her relax too much. She missed one of the biggest potholes, bounced into another, felt a thump on the bottom of the still new car.

The wages of guilt. She was not only ten minutes under time, but fifteen and that included getting out of the house. She stopped by the church, got out to examine the car in the thin light of the winter sky, bending and squinting beneath it as if what she might see could make any difference. Really, daughter or son had no cause to come back and take on this old lady, but, supposing there was any money in the till, they should fill in the potholes in the road so that other people, on their wages, did not have to ruin their cars when they happened to be in a temper themselves. Then she relaxed, let her breath out: there was nothing she could do. Why rush home anyway? Home was where the heart was, but it meant more demands. Home was halfway sustained by Mrs Burley's cash: she could not afford to feel churlish, or wish for the end of this era.

So she stood by the graveyard in the dark, smoking the cigarette that was mandatory in the Burley household, forbidden in her own, watching the sky. Outside the sky was a different creature from the sky observed longingly from the inside of window panes. It was lighter and brighter, full of comforting mystery, not really dark at all. Hope in October; must have been the crocuses out of the pantry window, made her think that way.

At the end of that lumpy drive over the fields, where the track met the car park next to the church, she faced a cottage. Nice couple with absent children moving about in there, and nothing else but her smoke and the dim knowledge that she should not, in this sudden delirium of free time, lean against the other car parked alongside. There was movement behind the cottage windows. Horrible curtains, she thought. Cheap.

She remembered, with a slight and guilty amusement, the relations between these worthy neighbours and Mrs Burley after the latter had written off their motor car in a head-on collision. Mrs Burley did not like giving way. End of Serena's driving licence; end of neighbourly goodwill, since she had not seen fit to apologize. Difficult to forgive someone who wrote off your car: she could see it now, all over their front lawn. She sniggered silently at the thought. Then there was a soft crunching of footsteps, which made her freeze without real fear. Bloody George. Appearing behind her as if she needed supporting.

"You shouldn't smoke," he said. "Bad for your health."

"So is sneaking up on people in the dark, you silly bugger. What you doing here?"

Only George, the harmless one who had given her the creeps at first, until she found they got on fine, running the place comfortably between them, provided George was given the illusion of being in charge and also given his manly credit for being the only one who could possibly make Serena obey an order she did not already see the advantage of obeying.

"Dunno. Coming back to the car. Don't it feel like midnight, and we haven't even reached the news on the radio?" There was a mute accusation in that, a reminder of the time, five minutes over eight, but twenty since she had left the house.

"Serena told me her husband's buried in this graveyard. She told me a while back, so I planted this crocus. Thought I'd tend it, so I went to see Sal at the end of the road, to get some water in case they needed it."

Janice wondered how it was that George always got to know everyone's name. She must have been coming here a good many years, but George, in his three, knew the names for all the faces she had ever seen. It was not a mere semblance of control, she realized; it was complete.

"Then I thought, you can't have weeds on a grave. I'll have to go on tending Edward's grave, I thought. Not that anything's growing, apart from the crocus. Funny, innit? You and me here. No one else."

Glory be, thought Janice, listening with admiration and a

faint sense of outrage: he's on first-name terms with the dead as well.

"I bumped my car, George. Be an angel and have a look at it for me, will you? I don't understand these things."

He had turned away from her, not that he ever came close, hands in his pockets; harmless, a bolshie little man, short of leg, squat, powerful and utterly benign, keeping a good distance. "Look at them stars," he said. "Better than my crocuses, and longer lasting."

He had a torch, ever well-equipped, lay on the ground and pulled himself under the car without a word of protest. She could hear his breathing, a grunting that turned to humming as the light played. The humming stilled her conscience that he should be so willing, but she was still pleased when he emerged, stood and dusted himself off. George never seemed to feel the cold and nothing was ever too much trouble.

"Nothing," he said. She doubted if he knew anything more about cars than she did, but allowed herself to be reassured.

She moved within three feet of him, never going closer. The sky was clear as water, dark while luminous. They pivoted together, noticed of one accord. A flickering light from the house half a mile away, nothing more than an unnatural glow.

"George," said Janice, querulously, "what's that?"

"She's on fire," said George, almost admiringly. "That silly old love is on fire."

The fire had taken hold of the outhouse nearest the kitchen door. It had a back wall made of brick, wooden beams which burst and splintered. Serena, who had put the ash from the fire into the bin designated for that purpose, did not think of her own actions as being the cause. She had found the first burst of flame, from the lawn-mower petrol, also stored in there along with a mercifully short supply of coal, slightly alarming, but now the sheer sound was exhilarating. She had trailed across the yard from the back door to within three yards of the heat, repeatedly carrying a mug of water which she flung half-heartedly towards the inferno. Wind blew the smoke away from herself and the house: she knew no sensation of fear, but the work tired her, so she stood and watched. Then went indoors to her desk, looked for paper to burn, all those letters, all those useless words, but when she reached the door of the dining room she forgot what her errand had been, went back and got that thing that played tapes from the kitchen. The flames died so quickly: it seemed such a shame that this vision of heat and light should be so short-lived.

When the fire brigade arrived, Serena was dancing. The tape machine was bellowing forth a military march, to which she waltzed and smiled, and invited them to join in. Serena had fond memories of bonfires. And dances.

"Isn't it lovely?" she asked them. "Will you dance?"

They stared at her, bewildered, themselves distracted from this fire, full of mild anti-climax. The coals glowed in the dark: it was more like a cheery blaze, a frivolous waste of household fuel and the beams that had once supported a roof. Then, while others unloaded the hose and went to work, George took Serena in his arms, and waltzed her slowly across the overgrown lawn.

Janice watched them laughing and felt sick, with a feeling of terror she could not define. It was not so much that she knew she could not bring herself to work for a pyromaniac because she was afraid of fire, but it was a tide of frightful premonition. It sounded so well, Serena and George: it was a combination of

17

will-power and victim and she could not work out for the life of her which way round it was.

Then she went indoors and screamed down the phone to Mrs Burley's daughter a litany of recriminations she did not feel, accusations that were unjust, warnings that were a reaction to shock and a situation she could suddenly see was untenable. She did not look for a result. She was not searching for fairness, justice, resolution. She was screaming against the fire which could have engulfed her and might not have happened if she had left on time. Your mother will die here, she shouted.

And that was how Isabel Burley came home to look after her mother. Because the appeal to do so came not from a bullying brother, but from someone else, who could no longer pick up the pieces. And, of course, because of her own agenda.

The flames had been fun, but it was no good trying to be clever. Difficult enough to concentrate on being good.

It was never as bad in the very middle of the night like this, when there was nothing to see but darkness and she could imagine that tomorrow everything would be back to normal. She was energized by the dark, like the evil spirits fostered by Bibles and fairy stories, but Serena Burley did not hold with God, never had. No merciful God would ever do this to her. Only a sadistic creator, motivated by malice, could first tease his servant with the irritations of age and then exercise this power for terror. It was the work of malevolence, and although she would address respectful pleadings towards any handsome deity of the male sex who would give her back her mind, she would not curtsy towards a psychopathic dictator.

"Damn, bloody, bloody hell."

In the early hours of the morning, her mind was as clear as a bell. She could think in whole sentences and could even tell herself what a shame it was to have no belief, because it would be exquisite to pray in words and have the illusion of someone reading the despair. The fact that her mind was clear for as long as this in the hours before dawn could be construed as a gesture towards mercy from her cretinous creator, she supposed. During this time, designated as the darkest for the soul, but in reality the only time when there was no distraction at all, the words did as she asked and turned into phrases. Perhaps this God kept different hours. On second thoughts, she considered it was a refinement of heavenly cruelty to give her spells of clarity like this, at these invariable times of day, when she could remember who she was and what she had done. Serena adored these interludes and dreaded them.

She called for pen and paper, snapping her fingers towards the imaginary servant in the corner; the pen appeared in her hand and the paper on her lap. She wrote, furiously.

Who was she, then? Serena Burley, aged seventy-five, one-time intellect and beauty of this and other parishes, citizen of the wider world where she had travelled with her husband as the culture and the foil to his grand but limited mind. He dug oil wells and gave lectures on petroleum science: she filled houses with books, flowers, letters and charm, because that was her vocation. She provided en route the statutory two babies, who were not a vocation at all.

"I quite forget how we did it," Serena remarked out loud, shaking her head, laughing. Her hand paused; she rubbed her wrist. The paper was curiously blank for all those words. She continued the record. Speaking out loud assisted the business of writing.

A goodish life, she wrote, in which she had been well served by long-suffering people. Her sister in particular, plus others. They had chosen to love Serena and all who belonged to her with a level of self-sacrifice that had been vital to her growing children, and a source of excruciating irritation to herself.

That was what charm had achieved for her. Enormous charm. She thought with a brief smile of self-admiration how it was she could define guilt, but had no experience of it.

What a joy it had been to use her witty talent with words to threaten, cajole, flatter, achieve. So few had the skill to communicate: she was one of them. Words made demand meet supply. She wrote laboriously: "I . . . absolutely . . . adore men and I love the poetry of words."

Shitting, miserable, fucking arseholes . . . Spit. Cunt. Rats.

The writing seemed to have slipped on to her wrist. She shook the Biro and spoke to it sternly.

If she had a tape recorder, like the one she'd used for Edward's lectures, she would be able to say exactly what this condition was like. It was the nightmare of an operation where the patient is merely drugged, not anaesthetized, rendered immobile and helpless in the face of hideous pain and the knowledge that the surgeon is removing the wrong leg. Or trying to push the baby back in. The image made her cry and giggle at the same time and reminded her that there was no time for crying. Crying only served to eclipse this hour into more of the bumbling confusion that filled the day, apart from those crucial minutes, sometimes a whole thirty at a time, when she could control the clouds and make them move away from the sun.

"TTT. Tutt Tutt!"

The moments of reprieve were never long enough for her to do the things that were imperative. Such as phone Isabel and tell her never to come home again; make her promise faithfully she would do no such thing, the less she saw, the better. Tell her that she had not been a good mother to her daughter in that awful, pious sense people meant and she had no expectation of the silly child being a good daughter either, so there. She had never been a good wife either. She had never learned to cook, but could drive with all the aplomb of a chauffeur. How good she was at organizing parties. She hummed to the tune of a dance. Mantra words, lovely words. Rabbits, cats, dogs lavatory poo and big fat pricks . . .

"Crabb'd age and youth, Cannot live together." Who said that? Crabbed age cannot live with anything. Serena felt as if her breath would kill a plant: only the plastic variety would survive. It was no good luxuriating in all these words; there was the real business to be done. Crabbed age should die.

Oh, for one of those recorder things, simply to prove to someone in the morning that she could still articulate. She could go downstairs now, telling them all about it at the same time. Such grand facts to record for posterity. Such as, this floor is very cold, these stairs grow steeper and longer, this carpet is rough and someone has stolen my shoes. She paused for the black moment by the living-room door when she did not know where she was and the terror hit in waves, and then, in a flood of perspiration, it passed when she saw familiar objects, waltzed round them, touching and nodding, saying hallo. The hallway leading from the stairs at the front of the house to the back was colder still and the floor in the kitchen was a chill that burned. Someone had stolen her shoes.

Bitch, cunt on wheels.

So cold, she would tell them: the light of the moon, coming into my kitchen like a damn thief and if George had hidden the knives again, she would fillet the man with a fork. Empty threats. This was the place where she started to fail. Serena had always been less at home in kitchens than living rooms or any place where she had been hostess, dispensing of herself. Talking, flirting, listening, touching. It seemed that darling George had begun to trust her again since she had become more careful. There were knives in a wooden block, standing upright like exclamation marks. What she should really be doing now was what those Japanese men of honour were supposed to do and that silly bitch Madame Butterfly did. Kneel, thrust the thing into the breast-bone, yell something final. The thought of the pain was frightening, and anyway, the dog would laugh. Not a bad thing, perhaps; she would have given her back teeth to make someone laugh out loud instead of that sometimes respectful, sometimes insolent stare, tinged with puzzled sadness, which she got if she was lucky.

God was an arsehole.

Hari-kari, whoever he was, had no fucking business in a kitchen; she would be deafened by the whimpering for a start, herself, the dog or the cat, made no difference. Back upstairs then, colder and colder, the cat in her arms. Although she protested, cat had cold steel against her throat. Nothing could be colder than her feet. Serena spoke softly to Ginger, explaining that this was not selfish; it was just too bad she was needed for practice. Serena had always loved cats, admiring the way they refused to heed a single social obligation, but, all the same, something had to die first to make sure she got it right.

She nodded, regally, at the grandfather clock on the way upstairs.

Back on her couch, concentration failed while she wondered what to relinquish in order to get the full use of her hands. Fur or knife, knife or fur, find the slippers, get feet warm, don't let go of anything, although the wretch wailed, knowing she wanted her throat. Cats were always feminine, to Serena's mind, regardless of sex. Females should be stoical about life as well as death.

And then she coughed, big, explosive spasms, out of control, too many cigarettes, too much age, and the knife lunged into the pillow and Ginger was off like greased lightning. She howled, shook her fist, but the cat stayed on top of the wardrobe, licking to get rid of the taste of Serena, just like everyone else did. Look, she said, we were in this together. The cat had no imagination.

"No bollocks!" she yelled.

Bums, cunts and bums. Fucking bums.

Back to the writing-paper then, restless.

There was another thing to do with the knife. She would stick it right up her private bits, turn it round and round and round, dig it in. Killing herself this way might be no worse than a big bleed and certainly better than having a baby. That was tomorrow's plan, then: she would get ice from downstairs; something to put on top and dull the pain while she bled away slowly from below. Three hours at least before anyone would find her, six if she said she was tired, and by then half her vital fluids would be in the mattress.

Tomorrow, promise?

First she wanted to tell them, so that when they found her she could point to the paper. The sounds she made these days were so ugly. Dawn edged prettily round the window with the promise of a fine October day. She wrote busily.

Fucking bloody arseholes, fucking cunts. Bums, bums, bums. It's all on that paper, there; her whole life history on the paper which she put under the pillow for transferring to the desk.

She even told them how dawn had looked before another day of horror.

Grey, colour, shot with light, streaked with excrement.

Curious.

Chapter Two

ISABEL BURLEY began most conversations by saying she was sorry. It was not always clear why, but she was usually in a state of apology about something. She was thirty-three years old and honed into fitness and a slenderness she wore well without anyone remarking how extreme it was. The joints were too big for the body: experts would notice a closet anorexia; the rest were either bewitched or bewildered by the long legs, ballerina features and gauche lack of grace, as if life had frozen her adolescent years into the stance of either a frightened gazelle or a clumsy foal. She had a nervous laugh and was widely perceived as reliable, if stupid. If she turned up for an appointment damp, breathless and late, she still turned up without fail. Poor little semi-rich girl, sometime acrobics teacher, sometime cosmetics saleswoman, sometime student, victim to her own good looks, her own incessant concern about them and a constant anxiety to please. There was more than an element of the dizzy blonde, except she was dark. Whenever she passed a mirror, she checked her long hair.

The riches, such as they were, consisted of Aunt Mab's inheritance, received with bewildered gratitude over a decade before, to the fury of Mab's nephew Robert, who received nothing. Aunt Mab had been a schoolteacher who knew very well how to invest her stipend, so the fruits of her prudence and her pretty cottage had been enough for Isabel to buy a London flat and thus avoid the need to earn more than a modest living. Isabel always served her notice, but she preferred jobs she could leave. What others spent on mortgages, she spent on clothes. Her brother Robert said it was amazing she had never tried drugs, since she was extravagant and they were not fattening. The riches were not of the endless sort, but they were sufficient to set her apart from striving contemporaries. What was left of her inheritance, Robert said, was all for pissing downwind, like the fool she was. This was not entirely true: Isabel had invested carefully, and although she knew where the bottom of the barrel was, she was never going to scrape it.

Men loved Isabel, who had been brought up never to be a nuisance and rarely was. Despite the feeling of inadequacy that made her twist her mouth in front of a mirror in the morning, telling herself over and over, "I am not silly, I am not silly," a practice learned from a self-help manual and rendering at least one lover paralysed with laughter, she could never quite encompass the truth of her own denials. Isabel Burley was not, after all, a fool, but she had two inhibiting agents to that hidden, mental chemistry which was not brilliance, but certainly intelligence. Firstly, education had centred around dancing class, whatever Aunt Mab had done to redeem the lack in school holidays; and secondly, she loved her mother in an unconsolable way. She had always hoped to emulate Serena when she finally grew up; she had never lived up to the image.

The ability to drink men under the table was only one of the characteristics they admired; another was her constant availability. She was good at delivering men back to their own doorsteps, or taking them to hers, where they lay, impotent and groaning, for twenty-four hours and she, sweet thing, did not mind. Later they would translate this experience into the memory of a good time, remember her with affection, while not quite recalling anything she said. "I love Isabel Burley," was not a sentiment shouted from rooftops. She dispensed enough kindness to deserve greater loyalty, but she did it without either thought or finesse.

As for the friendship of women, that was difficult. There were waifs and broken-hearted strays, but otherwise women could not see Isabel as either safe or unenviable.

"I love you Issy... You know how much I love you."

"No, I don't know. If you loved me, you'd be married to me and not to someone else."

It was Joe who caused the problems by being really mad about her. Married, of course, engaged initially on the first sight of Bella in leotard. He had a couple of nights out on the town with Issy, simply to relieve tension, which it did, before she sent him home to his nuptials. Despite his marital bed, Joe could not get her out of his mind and after six months came back howling at the windows of her posh flat for all the heart he had found there once. She had let him in, and two years of passionate vacillation followed.

"How could I leave her? She would never manage without me..."

On the evening of the night when Isabel received the phone call about her mother and the fire, Isabel had bitten Joe, on the thigh. The bite was ugly, and a perfect reverse pattern of Isabel's teeth. It drew minimal blood, although the scratches to his chest and the head wound from the edge of a jug, thrown across the room with considerable force, bled furiously. This occurred in the interval between after-work hours and going home, the traditional time for a married man to call upon his mistress. By ten that night, Isabel was contemplating the wreckage of her blood-stained bedclothes and her whole, loveless existence. It was not the first time her occasional propensity to violence had horrified her as much as what she had become and what little she had ever achieved. Bimbo. Airhead. Cheap. Everything her mother had never been, let alone what Aunt Mab would have wanted for her. She was in a state of self-hating chaos. Her love for her mother, Robert's endless chastisement, and the reservoir of guilt which always lapped against her backbone, made her a soft enough touch already.

Life had never thrown Isabel in close conjunction with any form of mental ailment except that encountered in the street. In the midst of her desultory packing, she remembered briefly what she had once known with uncomfortable clarity, namely that Serena had never approved of her, was one of the majority who considered her a fool. She put the realization back inside a box and into the attic store room of her thoughts.

The thought of Mother's flesh, roasted rare, black on the outside, pink in the middle, tipped an unwary balance poised on the cliff of a wasted life. By midnight, going home to look after Serena seemed the only thing left to do. And the only thing that might redeem her pride. It was her mother who was the one who might give love and want it back and it was for both the privileges, the getting and the giving, that she went home.

"Love you, Mum. Now, what are we going to do about your hair?" Isabel had entered a world far distant from the anonymity of London and it was difficult to call it familiar. Yet ten days later the place she thought of as home had reclaimed her, made her forget how anxious she had been to leave it in the first place: how nothing between the ages of eighteen and twenty-one had ever worked; how miserable she had been. All she could recall now was her arrival. No sign of Serena. No greeting. Instead a clash of sound from the tape deck in the long living room, reverberating and echoing over the whole house, shivering the timbers in a series of violent discords. Mother shouting above it, "I don't need you, I need words!" thumping the wall to make the kind of row that drowned thought. Isabel had paused, then rushed towards the noise, which stopped before she reached it. Serena's eyes, defiant, met hers.

"The words are over there," she had begun, looking towards the desk, before a big beatific smile dawned in that stretched, ugly-attractive face and she had sprung towards her daughter with an energy that defied her years. Her hair was dull and her make-up odd: thick, pale foundation, brilliant blue paste over the eyelids. There were subtle changes in the mouth since Isabel's last, fleeting, visit. Now she was here to stay. Make things better; do something properly.

"Darling! You're so thin! My lovely child!"

There was the strange sensation of being greeted by a duchess. A hostess who hid the fact she was expecting this guest and had been anticipating the arrival for some time.

Isabel had melted into her embrace, drowned herself in it. "Shh," she had said, "shh, Mummy. It's all right now." Saying the words and making the gestures she wanted for herself.

"I do love you," Serena had said. "I do, I do."

Had she ever said that before? Isabel could not remember, only knew how sweet it was to hear.

"I know you do. What a big hug! You never used to like hugging."

They had swayed together, Serena's soft bosom surrendering the smell of lavender, her arms surprisingly strong.

"You never used to like music so much, either, sweetheart. What's got into you?"

Serena had withdrawn slightly, to arms' length. Enough distance to look into Isabel's face, caress her cheek, pinch it playfully, but in a way which hurt a little. Isabel had a dim memory of scratches over her buttocks from a lover. Affection carried scars. She had not flinched. The analogy of a lover continued, with her mother's delicate hands on her own slim hips, the swelling stomach of the older woman pushing forward with great insistency, spreading against her own waist, the voice urgent with whispered confidence.

"Darling, you've come home at last. Let me tell you things . . ."

Today, the wind blew.

"Let me tell you something," George said to the dog as they plodded back across the fields. "Number one is that there's far worse things than being on your own. Serena and I know that, don't we? Believe me. And there's worse things a dog can do than run sheep, or a man chase women, but I'm glad you've lost the habit."

The dog squatted, strained with total concentration. George looked at her with concern: trouble with bowels was a sign of age in a retriever, so he'd heard. Serena should stop feeding her pap. He thought how he would break up into little pieces if anything happened to this old bitch, and not only because she was the formal *raison d'être* for his being in Mrs Burley's house. There would be far less reason for him to be there on a daily basis if there was no dog to walk: he could hardly take out that vicious little ginger cat which needed no guardian and already ate, slept and ran where it pleased.

"The worst thing you can ever be," George told the dog as they resumed progress uphill, "is too crowded. Penned up with a hundred other people, never left by yourself for a minute. Not when you squat, not when you sleep, not when you eat. I didn't know what hell was, but I'm telling you now, that's exactly what it is. And if that's hell, this is heaven."

The wind gusted strongly in their faces. George challenged himself not to walk slower in the face of such force and an uphill gradient: it was a discipline to walk at the same pace at all times. Get the heartbeat going, set a steady pace and keep it up for at least an hour, make a bit of a sweat, but not too much, and just keep going, enjoying the sensation of muscles at work. Once he had established a pace, then he could look around. See nothing but the fields, feel the mud beneath his boots, catch from the corner of his eye the fungus on that tree, the squirrel leaping from one bare branch to another, the fat blackbirds near the house. When the dog lumbered away in comic and futile pursuit of a rabbit, George almost doubled up with pleasure. "You can't explain it to no one else," he told her. "Not to no one who doesn't know what you mean already, why you should chase that thing, and I should be so happy. I doubt if Mrs Burley knows it either, but at least she never asks questions. You can't explain being happy, that's for sure."

He had the dreamer's knack of forgetting. Out here, or in the garden with the dog who was the receptacle for all his secrets, George could think of his own home with less revulsion. Not a home, more of a billet, a bed-sit in a hostel for so-called hopeful cases, people from abnormal lives on their way to what passed for normality. He had lived there for four years, a half-way house in a new town which had become home. Get a job, they said, ha, ha, ha. Should be easy for a well-built man like you, factories around here not fussy about a record as long as you work: amazing, but it's still difficult to find someone willing to put in the hours and besides, you won't have much opportunity for your little game among all the heavy machinery. He had stuck it for a month, then gone berserk, run out of there screaming, sacked next day. We don't mind the record, the boss told his social worker, but he can't stand being crowded and we can't be doing with the disabled. Which George somehow dimly knew himself to be. Despite his physical strength.

"And how did you get to be here?" That was Janice asking. He could laugh at the memory of her curiosity, the affront to her of something happening without her knowing.

"Oh, I was just walking by. Saw Mrs Burley trying to trim that bush outside the gate. She couldn't do it, so I said, give us those shears, Missus, I'll do it for you."

Something like that, a lifetime ago. He did not mention the lassitude of those long walks before Serena had found him. Long walks in the countryside reached in his battered car, the only solace he knew for despair. Those empty days before Serena had asked him in for tea and behaved as if she had known him for ever, no questions, no judgement, simply acceptance.

Greyer clouds rolled forward over an already grey sky, the beginning of the afternoon darkness, and George marvelled at how much of these mean days he was able to spend with the light on his back. His red hair was thin on top, his ears stuck out, but he refused the benefit of hat and gloves which Serena pressed on him. Makes me too hot, Missus. He swung his legs over the gate and marched round the back of the house. There was the familiar smell of homecoming, and also, in the sight of Isabel's jaunty little car, the sulphurous smell of a crowd, and the whiff of danger. He frowned. He was trying to extend towards Isabel Burley some of the vast affection he felt for her mother, but he could not. All right: he hated her and she disliked him. She was not a patch on her mother: she had no class, and she made him tremble with the old, familiar shame.

He could hear the murmur of voices from the living room. On the kitchen sideboard there were letters waiting for the postman, at least two letters a day. He always took them, posted them in town. He had collected the post, too, from Sal at the end of the road, but now, he supposed, Isabel would object, once she noticed. Fear clutched at his lungs. Already he was relegated to the kitchen as if he had never gone beyond; Isabel's rule prevailed. He saw the erosion of his tasks and also saw, with contempt, that there was one envelope addressed in a clear hand, larger but similar to Serena's microscopic script. Her own were important letters, Serena said. He looked at them as he scooped them up in one large paw, ready to leave without a word, sick with a kind of envy. George wanted his house back. He was also waiting for an accusation from Isabel. She gave me those things, he would say. Gave them me. I never took them.

"Serena Burley has Alzheimer's disease," John Cornell told his son, with a slight satisfaction he found difficult to hide. "She's on her own," he added unnecessarily, "and going barmy. Now that isn't a good thing."

"She might not have Alzheimer's," said his son, looking up from the catalogue. "Rumour has it she's been getting very strange and eccentric, that's all."

"I know what I'm talking about. I had several drinks with

Doc Reilly. It's not eccentric to set your own coalhouse on fire: it's mad. The doc says it can only get worse."

"Well, I think that's very sad, because she's always been a charming woman, and anyway, I don't always believe in Dr Reilly's diagnoses."

What an unholy alliance they were, his father and Doc Reilly.

Cornell senior snorted into his coffee mug and kicked the rostrum where Andrew sat.

"Just as you don't really approve of the good doctor. Or filthy commerce, or earning a living. What do you approve of, Andy?"

Better to shrug, pretend he was not paying attention, distract Father with something else, to stop an early-evening conversation, at that time of day when Dad needed a drink, from escalating into the kind of destructive exchange of words that was more a swapping of insults than a row which achieved something. Not even a clearing of the air, since the air between them was always thick with misunderstanding, beyond the curing of either of them. Andrew did indeed struggle with the unpicturesque partnership of Doc Reilly and his own dear old Dad. It had begun over the years while Father graduated from wheelchair to sticks: from fallen glory to wily strength. He and the Doc were a pair of smalltown, clever rogues in a constant process of graduation to something worse. If they had lived in a Wild West town, Dad would have been an undertaker and they would have carved up business between them. Doc Reilly, for instance, did not abide by any code of confidentiality when one of his patients was dying, especially a patient who might possibly have a house to sell and furniture for the picking. The auction room in which they sat contained three sets of deceaseds' effects, all of them erstwhile visitors to Doc's surgery, asking for him in particular, and while most of the stuff was reasonable rubbish, some of it was always far better. Andrew could see his father now, hovering over Serena Burley's ugly house and exquisite furniture like a fat vulture unable to wait for the victim to be entirely without movement, too impatient for the last sign of breath. Nearly dead was as good as dead.

"Too early for fog," John grumbled.

He did not even look like a Steptoe; that was the problem. He looked like an old gent.

It was a rich little conurbation in which they lived, prosperous market town on the one hand, ugly on the other, full of Midlands contempt for anything fancy. The ugly end had made John Cornell his money after he had built the two cheap estates in the sixties, houses that still changed hands with monotonous regularity. Were people so easily fooled, both then and now, when houses were so lacking in quality but full of gimmicks, Andrew wondered? He was equally amazed at his father's level of business cunning, which diversified his empire entirely as fashion dictated, but always slightly ahead of it. Cornell had once pandered to the overwhelming desire for something new, while never forgetting the dual gods of nostalgia and greed. First, the new houses with an old look, then old furniture made palatable.

"We've got a good lot of stuff coming in this week. There'll be more after Christmas."

Because the elderly died in winter. Andrew had spent almost eight years of his life nursing his father after a car smash which had never curtailed the drinking or dulled the old man's wits. Doc Reilly said that this was how the boy had learned his love of a good antique. Both of them had resented it. John was not made kinder by disablement and the youthful Andrew had been poised for flight, which now felt too late for the prematurely middle-aged man he had become. He had never possessed an ounce of his father's wildness, weighted as he was with the absence of his father's conscience.

"What kind of a reserve price do we put on Mrs Jones's sideboard?"

"I don't know. A lot, I would. It's handsome, like she was, once. It won't go first time round unless a dealer buys it."

Strange the way his father leered over furniture the way he lusted after women and yet, in a public way, was so capable of appearing to treat both with respect. A façade, while his son felt a frisson of pure affection when his blunt fingers ran over polished wood, sorrow when he examined something damaged. Andrew would feel the fracture in a fine chair leg with all the sensitivity of a vet with a favourite lame horse, the Doc said, while with women he was useless: tongue-tied and shy. A clod of a boy, his father confided; a man to waste all his hormones stroking inanimate objects.

John Cornell lumbered to his feet, leant heavily on his stick and made for the door of the disused church that served as an auction room. He had never had time for the clergy, but he had to admit the buggers could build. The door alone would stop a tank, and if his son's docility was going to deny him the satisfaction of shouting, then he might as well leave.

Andrew was fingering a blue vase. Put it back in the cabinet where small items, some they had bought, some for sale on commission, remained.

"Dad?"

"What?"

"Don't you think you should have asked a few more questions about this?"

"That was three weeks ago, son. And he seemed a harmless enough fellow: friend of Derek's. Been in before with the odd bit and piece. Puts his cash in his sock."

"Yes, I know, you said. A few small items over a few weeks. Nothing he would ever own himself. How do we know where he got them?"

"Nothing very valuable. Why worry about fifty quid's worth? Friend of Derek's. Bound to be OK."

"For Christ sake, since when was being a friend of Derek a recommendation from the Queen?"

"You know what, son? You've got homophobia, that's your problem."

He was halfway to the door, nonchalant about getting the boy to react after all. Good to see him there, stiff with righteous rage.

"Dad . . . Another thing. . ."

"What now?" He loved this door, so difficult to shift, a challenge.

"You won't get your hands on Serena's stuff for a while, you know. Her daughter's come home to look after her. Your lovely old Mrs Burley could go on for ever."

Triumph indeed. John Cornell's shoulders shook with the kind of mirth that could only be created by knowing more than someone else. It was a source of solace he had perfected in illness. He changed tack, looked at his son sorrowfully.

"I know, son, I know. Don't ever think you're first with the news. And her brother's asked us to do a valuation. When you've time, that is."

"He what?"

"You heard. It's only me with licence to go deaf, you know. Not you, at your age."

He went, the door left open behind him, the suggestion of scorn and restrained laughter heavy in the air. Inside this church there was no odour of sanctity, and much of desecration. Andrew Cornell sat at the rostrum, once a pulpit, staring at a room full of old furniture. He did not bother his head with thoughts of where his life had gone wrong, how on earth it had diverted itself up this avenue of exploitation and discontent. He thought about Isabel Burley, imagined her beauty against his plainness, then thought with less intensity about her mother, and what an inestimable pleasure it must be to lose one's memory, provided it included the forgetting of all those times one had been either coward or fool.

Do you love me, dear parent?

Home is where the heart is. The homes of Isabel's childhood had been in other houses, before Father's affluence and Mother's wish had landed them in this place. Father had lived for present splendour and ignored his pension plan. He had died on his one last trip abroad after Isabel had left this house. Her memory of him was blurred.

Do you like me?

It seemed an urgent question to ask as they sat by the fire, but she could not bring herself to put it into words. "Do you love me, Mother? Do you? Did you ever?" She did not ask it: it was impertinent, she knew, but in the face of Serena's studied indifference it seemed a worthwhile query. Isabel wanted a reward for what she was doing; wanted her mother, forgetful as she was, to remember that her daughter's presence in this remote house might have involved some kind of sacrifice, might even have been seen as noble enough to be worth someone saying, Thank you, well done, that child. But no one had, Mother least of all.

Over the first week Isabel had met the butcher, baker, vicar, George and Janice. The latter two seemed to resent her presence, Janice to the tune of downing tools altogether, while others took it for granted with amazing speed, as if they were suddenly relieved of a burden themselves. Isabel had come to realize that there had been an informal but efficient network that looked after her mother's interests and that, frankly, the whole gang was sick and tired of the task, except daft George. Serena's wider circle of party-going friends seemed to have disappeared. Perhaps it was the fear inspired by people who were ill to the point of madness, as if they were contagious, and this made Isabel indignant, deflected her thoughts. She could not yet begin to understand that aversion. Her mother was simply a case of warped magnificence, not in the same category as anyone else.

"Who are you writing to, Mum?" Isabel was careful; tried to be sensitive. Mother's desk was private and she was never going to try to look inside it. Privacy was sacred: she must not invade it. A pause, a guttural reply. "People. Lots of people."

"Do you remember writing to me?"

"Oh no, darling, I never wrote to you. Did I?"

The image slipped out of focus.

Isabel felt an overwhelming sadness. Where was the creature of power and beauty, bending to kiss her in a waft of perfume before leaving to go somewhere else? The writer of the great wad of exciting letters, sent from all over the world, displayed with pride to friends as the product of the fairest hand on earth?

"Mum, I think we should have a party. What do you think?"

There was no reply. The darkness outside was complete. Serena sat in her armchair by the fire, a writing pad on the table in front of her, one hand shielding what she wrote, her eyes squinting through her glasses at the page in the light of the standard lamp behind her. Her fountain pen scratched across the paper with a sound which had begun to irritate, like the distant sound of a dripping tap. Isabel noticed how her mother's glasses were scratched and dirty: the sight made her feel deficient. Ten days here, busy with reorganization and novelty, bathed in the glow of her own virtue and she had not noticed that her mother's spectacles were less than useless. Or that what her mother wrote in these evenings and afternoons was likely to be scribble.

"A party, Mum! What do you think?"

Serena sighed and put down the pen.

"A what?"

"A party!" Isabel found herself yelling. Ashamed of it, she lowered her voice. "A party, Mum, for your friends. You know."

Realization dawned on Serena's face. "A party? You mean a party?"

Isabel found herself shouting again. She was looking at the paper Mother covered with writing, remembering the wonderful letters received at school, her own window on foreign worlds, the borrowed sophistication she had felt on receiving them, thinking at the same time of the letter she had written to Joe this week, the craven apology and all the anger dead. Do you love me? Does anyone to whom I have surrendered myself love me?

"I said, a party! I meant a party!!"

Mother smiled, then shook her head.

"Lovely. But we couldn't have a party without George. And George wouldn't like it."

"What does George matter?"

"George wouldn't like it."

"I'd like it."

The eyes behind the scratched glass looked preternaturally calm and magnified into an owlish wisdom. The face was transfixed into a wide smile of artificial politeness as she picked up her pen again and spoke with dismissive precision out of the corner of her mouth.

"You'd like it? But you don't matter at all."

Isabel counted to ten, slowly. It was not the first of the insults, only the neatest and, even in the euphoria inherent in the knowledge of doing good, being for once in her life Virtuous with a capital V, she had noticed them all. She dismissed them as she guessed she was meant to dismiss them, as part of Mother's little insecurities. Less than that, in fact, simply a form of teasing, meaning nothing, surely, characteristic of the way her mother had always teased. The wounds and the hugs were synchronized.

"Love you," Serena said, without looking up from her writing, murmuring with the sighing distinction that only occurred in the evenings. "Love you lots. Do you love me?"

Isabel did not reply. Then, "We need some more coal for the fire," she said.

"George got the coal in earlier. He brought it from the new place where the coal lives now. Bucket by the back door."

George did everything. He was polite, coyly deferential to Isabel, and did not flaunt his indispensability. He scuttled away when he saw her, but he still did everything. It was he who understood this domain, he upon whom Serena relied.

No. She needs me.

The kitchen smelled, of stove and dishcloth and chips and warm dog. Beyond that door, the evening was bleak. Winter glowered. She did not like leaves drifting against the back door, the constant domination of the vast garden, the mud which clung to shoes and the silence of the stars at night. Hush, child: things done in the name of love are well worth doing. Loving and being loved; that was life. By the time she came back from the kitchen with the bucket of coal, the living room was full of sound. Mother's tape deck was turned up high and Mother's plump body blocked the fire, swaying to the sound. She clutched her skirts to reveal her stockings and wiggled her hips.

"Did you say party?" she asked. Beamed.

"Pretend you're a man," she said. "Let's dance."

Chapter Three

*H*OME, SWEET HOME. People are looking at me.

George felt the cold sweat of panic. Not the rage of his claustrophobia, the panic of guilty conscience.

I wanted a friend, he told himself; someone to talk to, but people like Derek can only be enemies. Who loves ya, George?

George knew he should not have left those letters in his room, not for a minute. Nothing could be left in the hostel rooms, unless it was old clothing no one else would want. Dirty socks, even underwear, walked away from the washing machine in the basement. The laces from George's training shoes had gone. And so had the letters, probably for the sake of the first-class stamps. Inside prison walls there had been some code of manners. Here there was none. He could see Derek, laughing.

But then anything, even a piece of paper, was currency to small, skinny Derek. George found the envelopes, less the stamps and the contents, in the waste bin under the kitchen sink, along with the remnants of Chinese takeaways and polystyrene containers for hamburgers. Derek might return the letters, but he would want to barter, and any material that he could glean from the letters, such as the address from where they were written, would already have been absorbed. George hoped against hope that Derek's erratic concentration did not make any connection between the address in the letters and his own daily destination. He also hoped the information had not been shared. Derek had the morals and the curiosity of a cat. George had befriended him before realizing the pathetic mewing was the preliminary to a scratch.

The prevailing smell in the kitchen was soap and nicotine. George did not drink or smoke, the others' single largest expenditures, and he cooked proper food. They called him Miss Tiggy Winkle. He was the only one who brought inside what he called proper food, namely the raw materials, meat and vegetables, bread that failed to stick to the roof of the mouth, ingredients that required preparation. The length of time he took making his evening meal made him the object of some derision, deflected in part by the element of admiration maintained for anyone who persisted in eccentricities, and the fact that he left what he did not eat, including apple pies and cakes, which were more popular than stew made from scrag-end of lamb or vegetable soup. George earned himself peace and an element of anonymity with the deliberate leftovers of his solid, nutritious food. He flexed his muscles round the kitchen sink, just to let them see he was guarding his back.

The kitchen was as far removed from Serena's as any kitchen could be. Galvanized steel cupboards, an industrial cooker with eight stern gas rings, an oven big enough to roast an ox. Two sets of utilitarian formica-topped tables flanked by stacking chairs, set on a grey-and-white lino floor, always indifferently clean. Bright neon lights to illuminate the spartan comfort and show up all the faces as they set about the business of eating. Attempts had been made towards homeliness, such as posters on the walls and two plastic plants, but the room remained, at best, like a school canteen, at worst, when the day was grey and the smell was bad, a miserable basement room, always warm.

Warmth drew Derek here, away from the loneliness of his own room, which always smelled vaguely of bodily fluid — sperm, sweat, blood and urine — masked with disinfectant and deodorant, as did all upper three corridors of the hostel for otherwise homeless men, some *en route* between prison and the real world. The smell of sperm came first, like the wafted emissions from a factory making glue. The scent of fifteen loveless men was undisguisable, even when they showered, dressed and stole each other's toiletries. It was an unreal rite of passage to the real world.

"Hey up, George. How've you been?"

"All right, thanks. And you?"

"Oh, fine. I won the lottery again, did I tell you?"

George was a freak: he shone with cleanliness in poor clothes, he kept his room anonymous and he did not cry in the night. Derek, a resident for six months now, had adored him. George did unheard-of things; he ran a self-serviced car, often up on bricks (someone must have given him that car: Serena had given him that car); he had somewhere to go every day, from where he returned, refreshed and fulfilled; he fried mushrooms which he collected himself because he knew how; and last week he made a pie, for nothing, out of blackberries. That made him rich and, in the hinterland of people with nothing to lose and no idea of what they stood to gain, enormously enviable. George had a secret. George was happy. That was something that had to be fixed. People liked George: that would have to be fixed, too. Derek, small and sweet, skinny little runt with a handsome face, everybody's gofer, with just enough sense not to turn tricks in public loos in a small town like this, admired the stockiness of George and the muscles on his arms, fancied himself in love. All George wanted was to keep his bum clean, but he had been flattered and loved the easy flow of words and jokes. Derek had made him laugh.

"There was a bit of a fight in here, dinner time," said the man who had greeted him and watched, hungrily, as he peeled potatoes.

"Oh dear," said George, not inviting further particulars. There were often squabbles. It was dangerous to be a one-eyed man in the country of the blind, perilous to be in possession of his own particular source of peace. He knew he had to watch it.

He should never have talked to Derek. Have let Derek take him to the old furniture place to sell stuff, as if he was a fellow thief. Have let Derek find out, from his own, unguarded, tongue, what there was to envy.

"We've lost the letters," Serena said next morning.

"George took them," said Isabel for the tenth time.

"I want them back."

"You can't have them back. Never mind, you've written some more."

Which she had. Two, three letters a day. Or pieces of paper stuck into envelopes that bore addresses Isabel could not read and doubted if any postman could, either. Isabel was not going to point this out. Letters were therapy and Serena was entitled to whatever secret life she wished to lead behind those scratched glasses.

"I want to go to town *now*."

"Come on, then."

"I'm driving, aren't I?"

"No, Mummy, you know you can't. Be a good girl."

It horrified Isabel the way she had so quickly got into the habit of talking to her mother as if her mother were a child. It seemed to rob them both of dignity. Mother was a petulant child this morning. Isabel had been craving a child of her own for the last few years, her body had been crying out for such a burden, but not a child like this.

Isabel's car, which Serena loved and envied, to the extent that Isabel locked it out of sight in the ramshackle garage, was the vital link between town and home. There had been three or four fairly successful forays to the shops: today they would try the market. Isabel had grown accustomed to the rutted track, knew how to avoid the worst of the holes without dipping over into the fields, even enjoyed the challenge. There was nothing between this small, powerful bullet of movement and the sky, nothing at the end of the track but the church and the grave-yard, the farm and the cottage and then five miles more to civil-ization. A party, Isabel thought again, suddenly longing for company. She shivered slightly. However many times she had visited her mother here, she had never done more than nod at the neighbours. Makers of hay and tillers of the earth, nothing in common with either of her parents. She shivered again. How exclusive they had been.

"Are you warm enough, Mum?"

"What?"

Of course she was warm enough. Serena wore an ancient fur coat, a hat suitable for a wedding, with a scarf tied beneath it, huge earrings, shiny black boots. She needed no help with washing and dressing, although the end result was alarming. Her eyebrows were painted black; the remainder of her face pale with thick powder. She was docile in the car as long as music was played.

They both watched with pleasure and curiosity as countryside gave way to the outskirts of town, the sight of people inspiring Serena to point and squawk as if she had never seen people before, while the presence of populace made Isabel homesick. The pointing and gesturing was fine inside the privacy of the car, less so when she guided Serena into the marketplace. Years before there had been some pleasure in shopping with her mother. Isabel looked forward to it, failed to comprehend how different it could be now.

"I want lots of things!" Serena yelled.

"Shh, not so loud. What sorts of things? We need soap and tights and fruit. . . ."

"Things!" Serena yelled again, waving her arms about, hitting a man in the chest. He staggered to one side and swore. She darted to a stall, where autumn apples lay in polished splendour next to glowing oranges and bright bananas. The day was grey: the colour of the fruit, artfully assembled in serried rows, beckoned invitingly. Mother wanted the grapefruit at the back, scrabbled at the display, clawed and pawed until the careful symmetry was destroyed and oranges bounced on the cobbled floor of the market square, apples fell in dull successive thumps, plums softer in their quiet bruising. The woman behind the stall was shouting before Isabel pulled Serena away, amazed at the strength she needed to shift her from this orgy of desecration. The shouting made Serena pause; the restraint made her wild until she stopped as suddenly as she had begun. She stood back, looked at the plump owner of the spilled fruit, pointed at the double chins and cawed with laughter. It was a loud, abrasive sound, cutting into the silence.

"Fat!" Serena screamed between her laughter. "Fat, fat! Oh yes, very fat!"

There was no right reaction. A child can be slapped for bad behaviour. Slapped and made to cry in public, but not a seventy-five-year-old woman. Isabel placed herself between her gesturing mother and the stall, blushing with shame, murmuring apologies, picking up the fruit. A plum squashed beneath her heel: money changed hands as the woman, too, realized that she could not shriek at senior citizens, or at least not for long.

Behind her daughter Serena clicked her tongue and stamped her feet impatiently, as if she were cold and there was nothing more important. "Hurry up, hurry up," she was chanting. "Hurry up. Got to get things."

The stallholder watched, fury transformed into contemptuous pity. The outburst had a calming effect on Serena. Fear, Isabel told herself, seeking an explanation to suppress her own anger. Surely that was all it was when Mother was faced with crowds of people, colour and choice becoming mingled into one mad abstract canvas, violent in impact. The aggression of frustration.

"What was all that about, Mum?" Her voice cooed. She hated her voice for having to make that cooing sound: she loathed the stallholder for the final benediction of her pity. Mother was marching on, carving a path for herself. She was gazing into the faces of shoppers, smiling widely at each with startled recognition, as if they were long-lost acquaintances, greeted with delight. People avoided her gaze as Mrs Burley sailed down the central aisle of stalls, giving away smiles like presents, Isabel following like a bag carrier, suffused with misery, catching up without wanting to catch up.

"Why did you do that to that stall, Mum?" It was a pointless question for a piece of petulance already forgotten.

Serena stopped. She took her hands out of the pockets of

her coat, looked at them slowly. Made fists of them, then let the fingers uncurl, one by one, counting under her breath.

"One, two, three . . . I wanted five thingies, Issy. Only I don't know what they are."

"You wrote them down, darling."

Serena looked puzzled, then definite, shook her head. "No, I didn't."

"Yes, you did. In your pocket?"

"No, I didn't. I don't do that."

Was that what all that fury was about? A forgotten list in her cramped script? Was that all?

Isabel cooed like a pigeon. "Don't worry, I can remember what it was you wanted."

Serena looked at her with the same pity she had herself received from the stallholder, the glance given to a lunatic.

"Of course you don't know what I want. You can't possibly have any idea. I want to go home, is what I want. I want George. Now."

The voice had risen a pitch. Serena rubbed her eyes, smeared the blackened eyebrows, making her look like a clown.

So they set off towards the multi-storey car park, Serena giggling and pointing again, forgetting the imperative of haste. A ludicrous progress, akin to a pair of drunks, Serena clutching then pulling away, as the mood struck, Isabel embarrassed to restrain her. At one point Serena darted away to stroke the blond hair of a teenage boy: he reacted as if she had slapped him. Isabel hated him, too. Then Serena homed in on a posse of women, engaged them in earnest conversation until they fled in various directions. Then she sabotaged a group of children: she stood by the exit of Tesco, pulling faces, crossing her eyes, putting her fingers in her ears. The youngest child did not object, the eldest giggled with shifty embarrassment. By the time they were back at the car, Isabel had learned to keep a firm hold on her mother's arm and maintain an adamant, insincere flow of loud chat. Serena refused to get into the car, claiming it was not hers, hers was bigger. Persuaded, finally, she slumped into a sulk in the passenger seat until Isabel remembered the music. Pausing to pay at the booth, Isabel aware, for the fiftieth time, of the now familiar glance of pity from the attendant.

"When are we going to have this party?" Serena asked, suddenly sane again.

"Never. Not ever."

There was a pain throbbing at Isabel's temples: she wanted either to weep or to sleep. It was wrong to feel thus, the opposite of virtuous or forgiving. Wrong to feel this dreadful shame.

They were turning into the homeward stretch at the beginning of the fields by the church, Mother twitching and humming and finally unearthing from her pocket the shopping list which she greeted with a crow of pleasure. She wanted to go back, she announced.

"Back where?"

"Shops."

"No."

"Shops. Yes! I know what I want. I want to go back."

"No. Absolutely not." No cooing in the voice, merely desperation.

"I want to drive the car!"

Serena had refused the seat-belt and Isabel had failed to insist. She had no preparation for the lunge towards the steering wheel, Serena's ringed hand catching her face, the temporary blindness of her hat in front of her eyes, the screams emerging from her own mouth as the car rocked, bucked, slewed from side to side on the track, romped off the road and into the field. They stalled to a juddering halt. Serena's head hit the windscreen with a gentle crack. In the breathy, sobbing silence that followed, Isabel could feel the soft flesh of her chest pinioning her mother's hard knuckle to the wheel. Beneath her left breast, the fingers began to move like tentacles.

Serena began to whimper.

They were out. They were out and Andrew was pleased; there was an enormous release from his own sense of not quite looking forward to this. There was an old car outside by the stable yard, back door unlocked, but no one in. Good. Andrew was tentative, but unashamed, of trespassing. The house remained as he remembered it, the outside obdurate, but a house which drew in strangers like a sponge drew water. He went into the kitchen. Same old stove, same old quarry tiles on the floor that which sloped into the corridor that led through the centre of the house towards the relative grandeur of the black-and-white tiles spread back from the front door. He moved to his left, into the living room, remembered with startling clarity the fact that this was the first place he had kissed Isabel Burley, when she was twenty. How they had managed to make contact in the vastness of this room puzzled him for a whole minute. Maybe such things were best forgotten, as was the infrequency with which he had kissed women since. He shook himself, remembered he was here to look at furniture, not reminisce.

He sat on the vast sofa with the broken springs. It was so deep, the springs could be avoided: it was for sprawling and snoozing, arguing and making up, this beast. He was a sentimental man: he saw the surface of the cover was not entirely clean, a feature he was almost ashamed to notice in this pale, distinguished place as he rested in it. Lay back against the pommel of the arm, cradling the left side of his face against the right palm of his hand. He moved his fingers over his face, testing the position of his eyes and bones as if he were his own lover exploring his features. She had felt him thus, examining the parameters of his face with the palms of her hands warming his cheekbones. Andrew drew his knees to his chest and opened his eyes. The skin of his palms and his face was suddenly soft. This was indeed a beautiful room, full of beautiful things.

Windows on two sides washed the whole place with light. Three hundred square feet, he reckoned, mostly covered with Indian carpet, whitish, greenish, with some faint design, fringed, frayed, faded, valuable and friendly. Sunlight bleached fabric, warm with age, the Knole sofa, covered with damask, similarly worn and soft. To the left, Serena's rolltop desk, a perfect, well-used piece, like this sofa, glorious wood never-the-less. On the other side, a fantastic rosewood credenza, a bureau, a chest, an assemblage of gossiping chairs by the west-facing window, each different, as if designed for an individual occupant. The chatelaine loved chairs, he remembered. One squat chair with a scrolled back, one gorgeous piece of curved tapestry which belonged in a lady's bedroom, one low-slung bergère armchair. They were married into a group by their sense of expectancy and the plump cushions that invited guests. Old tapestry covers, like the kind found in church, he noticed, not uniform but united by colour. Where had Serena found them? There were curtains which were never drawn, but which drew the eye, a fireplace and, even with the chill on the room, with such comfort implicit in it, he wanted to remain. Carpet worth one thousand, chairs two, bureau three, and so on. He wished it was not so automatic to place a monetary value on things at the same time as admiring them.

Splendid rooms, surely. These were the rooms that gave the house a reputation for beauty, he thought, crossly. While all the time it remained essentially an ugly house designed on a grand scale without much sense of proportion.

He swung himself to his feet and moved across the hall to the dining room. Sat on a carver chair that had seen better days, as had the scratched and glowing walnut of the oval table. This room had the feeling of disuse; it needed flames in the hearth to encourage the latent warmth, a fire and a crowd, candles down the length of the table adorned at the moment with nothing more than two superb silver candlesticks and a vast grape ivy plant with dusty leaves. Andrew looked at his watch. Table worth at least a thousand, matching set of eight dining chairs considerably more. There were fingerprints and smear marks on the table, as if someone had stroked it.

He could venture this far, he decided, but he felt he could not go upstairs without someone to take him. Bedrooms were private places: people kept their secrets there rather than in desks. He could invade only the public domain, and even that was beginning to feel intrusive.

"Excuse me, but what the hell do you think you're doing?"

He turned to find himself looking at a small, faintly familiar and very belligerent red-headed man carrying a stick in one hand, resting the knob in the other palm, flanked by a dog. The voice of inquiry was challenging but polite, although the position of the stick and the square-legged stance of the man left Andrew fairly sure that the benefit of doubt he was being granted was only temporary. The stick was not for decoration.

Beside the man, the dog looked redundant. Petal did not bark in the afternoon.

"I'm sorry," Andrew said pleasantly. "I came to see Mrs Burley or her daughter. Perhaps I should have waited outside, but the door was unlocked."

George clicked his tongue. "They've gone to the shops. What was it you wanted?" He still held the stick, reluctant to relinquish authority.

Andrew shrugged. "Nothing that can't wait. Only Mrs Burley's son asked us to look at the furniture, check the insurance. After that fire, you know" He produced a card.

"Oh." George was disarmed, also curious. "She's got some nice things, Mrs Burley."

"Yes. Yes, she has. Valuable things."

"They're all old things," said George, dismissively. "Worth a bob or two, I expect, but not much. And she won't be having any more fires. Not with me around."

George decided he did not dislike this harmless-looking man with thin legs under the suit: there was none of the air of understated threat with which George was so familiar, but still he wanted him out of the room.

"I can fix you a cup of tea if you come into the kitchen. No one eats in here any more."

"And who are you?" Andrew asked meekly, following him.

"I'm George. I walk the dog and look after Serena. Mrs Burley." George said this with a note of defensive pride.

"Who does the cleaning?"

"Nobody much at the moment. Oh, Miss Burley moves things around, but Mrs Burley did most of it herself. She's not mad, you know."

The back door stood open, so they heard the car above the

sound of the boiling kettle. Music blared as the doors opened, then ceased abruptly. There was the sound of one weary voice, one angry one. Serena was framed in the doorway, crushing her hat. There was a lump on her forehead; her mascara extended past it into her hairline; she staggered slightly. George leapt to her side, clucking anxiety. She gave him the full force of her smile.

"Hello, my lovely. I hit my head, didn't I?"

Andrew did not know the format of this household, nor its hierarchy. He could only interpret the look George gave Serena as one of tender affection and the glance thrown in Isabel's direction as one of murder, which Isabel, three steps behind and clearly struggling for self-control, failed to notice. Her face was blotched: she looked like someone suddenly familiar with defeat. And she was still beautiful. Andrew forgot to notice the complexities and palpable tension of this trio as he stared at Isabel, last seen, how long ago would it be, a dozen years or more, the memory largely ignored in the interim, as if it could ever go away. The long brown hair with the oriental sheen, tied at the nape of her elegant neck, the perfect, slender figure over which she had agonized even then, and the huge, deep-set eyes which defined her face. A house is only as good as what you put in it: Andrew's father said that to customers. Isabel would give credit and dimension to the most unpromising of rooms. She could be hired to lean against furniture, like a model posed against an impossibly expensive car. Good bones: she would always look like an uncertain girl. The nose was a shade too long, he told himself; the mouth too wide. It would devalue her price at auction, but why was it that bidders did not stare after her in the street, and why had she ever let herself be touched by lesser persons than princes? Andrew could not fathom. She was edibly gorgeous, yet removed. Never looking at herself without anxiety. Never looking round and saying, What power I have.

At the same time, he could not believe how he could have been so hurt by something as insubstantial as a letter. He was one person for whom the demise of the letter-writing habit in modern life was not a source of grief.

The resurgence of fascination intrigued him. Isabel Burley had been nothing more than a promiscuous bitch who had wounded him and others. Gone through half the promising men in town and chucked them away. He had thought he would no longer mind in the least about that, and had arrived prepared to treat her with the distant courtesy of the professional he had become. He would have suffered no pain at all if he had not dwelt in those empty rooms first and she did not look first so impressive and then so . . . diminished. While Serena, bruised but plump and glowing, looked as if she was already guzzling on her daughter's vitality.

"What did you do to her?" George was asking, his voice dangerous.

Isabel did not look at him. "I didn't do anything, George. She did. She tried to grab the wheel and took the car off the road. I managed to get it back. No harm done."

Then she noticed Andrew. I am always the last to be noticed, Andrew thought.

"This chap says he's come to look at the furniture," George muttered, dismissing him as Isabel's responsibility.

"How lovely," Serena trilled, assuming the role of grand hostess. "You must come to our party." She was extending her hand and Andrew wondered if he was supposed to kiss it. "Do sit down, won't you? I think it's time for tea."

"I think it's time for brandy," said Isabel. "Hallo, Andrew. You haven't changed a bit. You remember Andrew Cornell, Mother, don't you?"

It was a pointless question, but Andrew remembered Serena as a gracious, welcoming mother, smiling the extra-wide smile he saw now and which Isabel was coming to recognize as reserved purely for men. They were all smiling at each other. Except George.

"What's all this about furniture?" Isabel asked, breaking up the tableau. George shuffled. He took a clean handkerchief out of his pocket, wandered to the sink, ran it under cold water and took it back to where Serena had retreated to a chair. He placed it lovingly against the lump on her forehead, pressing the cool handkerchief to her skin, keeping her head steady by a gentle touch on the back of her neck. The action was practical, a reminder to those present of their priorities. It was also curiously intimate. It made Andrew shiver. Serena moaned. Isabel sighed. Andrew realized he had not yet opened his mouth to either of them.

"Your brother Robert," he began. "Worried about the insurance. I can come back another time."

"Trust Robert," Isabel said. "Full of long-distance ideas. Come into the living room. We all spend far too much time in this kitchen."

You need help, he told himself, following the graceful curve of her back down the dark corridor towards the fading light of the living room. You need help in the way I have needed help. You have lost your pride. Somehow that reflection neutralized everything and made him calm again.

"George does the fires," she was saying chattily, rallying herself into some pretence of an ordinary social animal, albeit one who would never have her mother's grace. The fire was laid with old-fashioned skill, he noticed. Newspapers, kindling wood, firelighters, arranged in order with coal on top. He now observed with horror that the marble surround of the fireplace had been painted white. The paper crackled in the hearth at the touch of a match. He wanted to laugh at the sight, wondered if she remembered other times in this room by the light of the dying fire, with everyone else in bed.

"So what have you done for the last few years?" he asked, over-heartily.

"Oh, don't ask. This and that." Spending that inheritance of hers, he thought with a shade of jealousy. He leant forward, curiosity overcoming shyness.

"And why are you doing this now?"

"Because someone must. She needs me. I need her. I mustn't give up. I've never done anything else worthwhile, you see. So I mustn't fail either. I'm sure I can make her better. Anyway, what does that brother of mine want?"

"He probably wants to make sure that the furniture remains intact, or at least properly recorded and insured. Photographed, perhaps. Your mother won't be able to stay here for ever," Andrew said carefully. What did she mean she needed her mother? How the hell could something as stunning as this still need her mother?

Isabel looked round and frowned, suddenly determined. "I don't see why not. It's her home. Moving her would be incredibly cruel and besides, how can it be done? She would never see the necessity. As for the furniture, Robert's welcome to it in the end, but it has to stay put for now. She finds her way around because of the furniture. Like a series of signposts, you see. The furniture orientates her in time and space, somehow. Do you know, I've never really noticed it?"

Ah, he thought, relieved, we are still poles apart. Not notice furniture? Remain immune to things chosen with loving taste in the days when they were affordable? She was what he had half hoped she would be, a silly woman.

"Tell me about it," she said suddenly, leaning forward towards the light of the fire, depersonalizing the conversation, one ear cocked towards the kitchen. "You know about these things. What makes all this old wood so special?"

"Age," he said pompously. "Age makes everything special."

She looked at him, amused by his intensity. "I'll show you upstairs," she said.

Later he was in his own small house, mercifully free of envy, taking refuge in the things he liked to touch, making an inventory of his friends. Visualizing mother and daughter sitting by that fire, the beautiful and the damned. You cannot be a good daughter, Isabel. You are not the stuff of which good daughters are made. You cannot be a good daughter because you cannot make your mother better.

He remembered how his father's dependence had distorted everything, and he hoped that mother and daughter would be happier.

The kitchen was a cocoon; the house in a time warp; and Isabel was not happy. What had she done to earn such disapproval? Food spat out at supper, the façade of manners gone. Isabel had done nothing to deserve this. Yes, she had left George with Mother, which pleased them both, raced back to the dismal supermarket on the outskirts of town, loaded a poor selection of supplies into the smart car with the crumpled fender, raced home, careful over the fields. Telling herself, I must make this work, I must forget about everything else in order to make this work. Why did Andrew Cornell, and everyone else, drop me so abruptly all those years ago? Too busy to wonder if it still hurt, quickly deciding it did not. Andrew, and James Reilly, and John Eliot. One after another. Damn them all.

Stopping at the gates of the house, Isabel tried to see it the way George might see it, visualizing instead the picture of her mother, rocked in his burly arms. Trying to perceive the elegance of the carefully collected contents of this house in the way Andrew might see them, failing there too. Doubting everyone, herself most of all. Feeling alien, stupid, weepy, even before Mother spat out the food. Then there was a phone call from Robert. Mother answered, with that articulacy of hers which came with evening. No one could see the harridan of the market stalls. Isabel did not want people to see that. She did not really want anyone to know what her mother could be like. She listened to her mother complaining to Robert about the bump on her head, poor darling. Found herself too listless to respond to his scolding: how could she be so careless? Come and see, she told him with her new mildness; come and see for yourself. Was she such a failure that she had grown to this age purely to be so comprehensively blamed?

Bedtime. Peace for the wicked. Go first, Mother. Please go first and leave me alone. Shouting at her, none of this cooing nonsense for a nasty, naughty, wilful little girl, the brat that she was.

"Go away, you silly old woman! Go to bed!"

Simply orders. And then the final act in the day's drama. Going upstairs past her mother's door, with no desire to kiss and make friends, hearing the sound of hopeless sobbing. It rose and fell, this muffled sound of grief, a cadence of sublime misery like the cat at half throttle stuck somewhere inside a cupboard, screaming for release. The sound paused, coughed into silence, continued quavering and helpless.

The heavy door of her mother's room was shut, yielded to a shove. The tester bed which Andrew Cornell had valued with his eyes and admired with well-disguised soul, stood rumpled and unoccupied. Serena resented any interference with her room: she kept it clean herself. The draught slammed the door behind her daughter: the sound continued, deafening to the conscience, in reality subdued. There was a row of dolls and teddy bears over the bed, which Isabel would swear she had never seen before until she recognized some of them as her own.

Serena stood by the open window, plump, forlorn, clad in her embroidered nightdress, curlers in her hair, sobbing as if the world had ended. Her body beneath Isabel's spontaneous embrace glowed like a furnace; only the extremities were cold.

The words were blurred at first, then clear. "I want to die, Issy. I want to die. I don't want to be like this. I want to die. I want to die and set everyone free."

"Of course you don't. Shhh. You'll get cold."

"Cold, dead. What does it matter? I should be dead."

"I never left you, Mumsy. I shan't leave you now. Don't fret. Come to bed."

"I'm sorry, love. I'm sorry. I can't help what I do. I go crazy when I'm frightened. So frightened . . ."

"I know, I know."

She did not know, but she understood grief. Serena succumbed, put her thumb in her mouth and allowed herself to be rocked to sleep. The lump on her forehead was pale and shiny. Her size seemed unutterably pathetic: so did the curlers in her hair. Her face was still slack with tears: her daughter's, puffed with love.

My mother loves me. Everything is worthwhile. She keeps my old teddy bears in her room. We truly love each other.

Isabel went downstairs again, carrying the cat dragged from under the bed. You go outside, cat, she told it, feeling slightly cheerful in an odd kind of way. She had made her mother better: there was no anger any more, only sorrow; there was nothing to forgive, simply love in buckets. She shook the cat. I thought you were out already, I put the milk out for you, I remember now. Isabel was feeling capable, fiercely protective, wise, even peaceful. There was no such thing as perfect peace. Peace was for the brave. Neither she nor the cat had done enough to deserve an easy life. They had to reconcile themselves to difficulties.

She could not tell at first what the thing outside the door was. It was russet in colour, lighter than her own hair and she saw it through the opaque glass of the back door, lapping at the saucer of milk she had left. Isabel did not begrudge the milk, nor was she all that partial to the cat which littered the kitchen almost daily with signs of savagery, but she was suddenly enraged at the impertinence of the alien usurper, all sinuous arrogance blurred by the glass in the frosted pane before she opened the door and shouted at it. Shouted into the dark emptiness of the middle of the night.

"Go away!" Then, less self-consciously, "Piss *off*!"

How long had it taken her to realize that shouting was permissible here, even encouraged by the fact there was no one to be disturbed? Two weeks? Time was already immaterial.

She was too much a townswoman to know the difference between stoat and ferret, or to know the nature of either. If she had, she would not have startled it into such spitting and hissing, its low snarl at odds with its sinister beauty, little white teeth bared, eyes huge. The ferret advanced towards her: she slammed the door shut, watching through the glass as it shook itself delicately and then returned to the milk.

"Coward!" Isabel said loudly, addressing herself. If she left it the victor this fastidious thing would return every night. Seizing the broom she opened the door again, shoved it towards the milk saucer, hitting the thief with energy, wanting to watch it run, yelling at it until, with spitting fury and a snarl, the creature launched itself at the bristles, biting and scratching in a whirl of teeth and fur. Isabel crashed the door closed again, stood trembling on the safe side of the glass, unable to move. The creature hurled itself at the door, then settled back to wash.

There was a sensation of acute loneliness in watching that elegant little beast preen with such nonchalance. Isabel could feel teeth snapping at her face. She was unscathed and unscarred, simply feeling foolish, but if that creature had leapt towards her eyes or fastened on her wrist, no one would have heard the screams. She was the one with the fear, it had none, while upstairs there slept a human being who would never provide help in an emergency.

This was the way she had committed herself to live, for as long as it took. The protector, never the protected. She was numbingly, blindingly, tired.

She was going to be brave. Resolute, indispensable. She was loved.

Chapter Four

"SHE'S BEEN THERE A MONTH. What do they do all day?" John Cornell asked his son. "I mean, what does a lovely young lady do every day with only an old woman for company?"

"I don't know. How should I know? What does anyone do all day? What did we do all day when I was locked in with you?"

"You had a job of work, that's the difference. Somewhere else to go. What does it take to look after one old granny? They don't eat much."

"I think it's more like looking after a child."

"Was I like a child?" Father was teasing. Andrew looked at him and saw a grin of monkey cunning. He had a long memory.

"Just like a child," Andrew said smoothly. "But you also had a working brain and you couldn't move half the time. That had distinct advantages."

"Good old days, son. You should have left me to it."

The auction room was ready to go. People filtered through the porch, paid for the catalogues Andrew had copied that afternoon, wandered between the rows of beds, chairs, tables, speaking to each other in hushed tones, as if this place were still a church. Ah, the reverence of buyers without the refuge of shops. Andrew tried to count how many of them would buy because they loved an object, or because they thought it was a bargain which might turn into an investment, or because it was useful, and how many simply adored the business of poking around among dead people's things. He was never ashamed of his own propensity to do just that: it was only sensible where objects endured beyond lives. He respected auction-house customers: even the collectors, looking for one cup or figurine, crowing with delight over a teapot without a lid; he did not mind the weirdos who simply came in from the cold; he liked young couples with optimistic faces, tentative buyers, to whom bidding would mean a pounding of the heart and terrible suspense. Lesser in his affections were the dealers who waited for the best and squabbled with one another. How much his father might have aided and abetted these foxy men Andrew did not know. His father was too bent to stand up in the pulpit. Andrew was the auctioneer. And he was exceptionally good at it.

"Right. Let's get going. Six o'clock. Where's Derek?"

"Just come in, little bugger. He likes to cut it fine."

Andrew felt he could smell Derek. Derek, waif and stray of the parish, was the kind of general helper his father would always find in his limping travels round bar counters. He could spot the man in need of cash payment, who would lift furniture, obey orders and not ask questions. Bright, personable and sly; that was Derek, a foil for the other porter, big, thick, reliable Harry. Andrew felt a twinge of guilt. Harry's cousin Bob had been laid off with a bad back. Soon Harry would have a bad back, too.

Two hundred and three lots: Andrew, rising to full height, all shyness, all painful awkwardness, gone, speaking with a voice some called handsome, clear and authoritative. Shy Andrew Cornell, who could not have told a joke to a girl at a party, even when she wasn't listening, told them easily to an audience of dozens.

". . . Lot number five, ladies and gentlemen. A large framed print of a woman with blue skin in an ornate plastic frame, provenance, Boots, 1956. The telephone bids have been rolling in from Japan . . . Who'll start me at one pound?"

Isabel sidled in at the back. She did not know what she wanted, company perhaps. There had also been the reluctant thought that maybe she ought to persuade her mother to use a commode. Perish the thought of such a prospect, but the weather grew colder while the distance between bedroom and bathroom remained just as long. She hated the creaking of floorboards in the night, imagined an old-fashioned commode made of mahogany, so that it could sit at ease in her mother's room, like any other chair, looking as good as a seat with a potty inside it could look. A poo chair. Isabel's long hair hung down her back, glistening with rain. A commode seemed to be a disgraceful thing to buy so publicly: she was beginning to change her mind about the whole thing.

The figure of Andrew on the rostrum, his lean frame enhanced with the elegance of authority, caught her attention and filled her with amazement. He had never been a talker, but a man who yearned to talk. The audience laughed with him: she laughed too at his comic descriptions, and found her own laughter an unfamiliar sound. Maybe she could wait until the end, ask him about better commodes. No, maybe she would not wait. Not even to listen to that pleasant, persuasive voice. Minimum of sixty lots per hour, the man on the door had told her; bidding open for lot thirty, now. More than an hour to go and the place so swollen, so gummed with people and things, so quiet between the laughter and the sound of the gavel, she did not want to explore. There were people here who might have known her from a long time ago, school friends with babies, people like that. An hour was the maximum to be away from Mother and, with Robert and his family coming tomorrow, she had her tasks. Preparing herself for the question he would ask and she had taken to asking herself, never getting an answer: what did she do all day?

Andrew watched her arrive and watched her go. He registered every face in this room, caught each imperceptible nod, remembered each name: that was his skill, and there was room in between to feel grateful that she had at least seen him, once, at his best. What would he bid for Isabel Burley?

She went home distracted by food for a family. Little Isabel, Serena had mocked, busy as a bee. Solid food, homemade pork pie, a joint of ham, a dish of potatoes sliced and baked with onions and cheese. Isabel trying to show her contemptuous brother how well she could do when she did not take her mother shopping and encouraged her to sleep in the afternoon. It was all laid out in the larder, more in the fridge, except the trifle and the cream, which were in the cellar for lack of other cool space.

Alone, Serena gazed at the display. She had locked the cat into the cellar to serve it right for being so frightened and so plaintive about going outdoors. She broke off pieces of the pork pie and enjoyed the sticky sensation of pastry crumbling between her fingers; saw the gelatine uncovered and went "Ughh!" There was a dim memory of eating the best food in the world and never liking wholesome fare like this: she was doing someone a favour by trying it first and finding it lacking. She hacked at the glazed joint of ham with the new breadknife Isabel had bought to replace those that went missing in the weeding expeditions Serena made in the garden. She tasted a clove and removed it carefully from her tongue, dug it into the surface of the spuds. She knew they were spuds: spuds had a lovely sound.

The larder was so spick and span, unrecognizably clean and reorganized, that Serena could not imagine what it had been, only that it was logical to suppose that anything edible in here was for herself, since Isabel was always telling her to eat. Eat, eat, nag, nag. Isabel did not make food, she made mountains: she would make some poor man a good wife. There were lights from the car. Serena opened the cellar door, scooped the fleeing cat into her arms and scuttled down the corridor into the living room. She had a vague sense of being righteous, but also of being naughty. The cat curled on the sofa and began to wash, assiduously. Serena resumed the writing of letters, equally concentrated.

Food. It was the first time George could bring himself to admit even the most grudging respect for Isabel Burley. If anyone had asked, which no one would, he would have said in his abrupt fashion that they did not get on, although he minded his manners and did not think she noticed the way he winked at Serena and she winked back at him to signal their conspiracy against this silly little girl who kept on changing round things that were perfectly all right as they were. But when it came to cooking, there she was, all afternoon, creating the same sort of things as his own dead mother, making his mouth water. He was fascinated by the sight of another person cooking. He sneaked a look at cooking programmes on the telly: he liked to see food taking shape from lumps into edible things. Oh, she was extravagant: she bought apples, for God Almighty's sake, when there were apples for the picking, though admittedly past their best. She had to look at a book to do half of what she did, but she was doing fine. Then he remembered he could not afford to like Isabel or court any improvement in the atmosphere.

George had been able to manage Janice, who kept her hours and went home without ever entering into Serena's affections, but Isabel was different. There was less loud music, fewer furious questions, and the end of that closeness he shared with Mrs Burley and no one else knew about. Such as sitting on her bed in the morning, telling her what to wear today, coming back in the evening sometimes, after Janice had gone, sitting by the fire so that he could postpone going home. Since the advent of Isabel, he had pottered in the kitchen and garden, taken Petal for longer and longer walks, kept his distance. Isabel had poured him coffee when he came back today to witness the cooking. Different coffee, he noticed, disliking the bitter taste of it.

"I think she's so much better, don't you? I hope my brother thinks she's better."

"Your mother? Oh, yes." He had thought for a moment Isabel was talking about the dog. He did not think Serena was better. She was having a quiet spell, that was all. There was nothing wrong with her in the first place: she was fine as she was.

"George, you've done so much for her, I don't know what we'd do without you. She says you won't take any money for all the time you spend here. Can't we put it on an hourly rate? It wouldn't be much. Cash, though."

George thought of the things Serena had pressed upon him. The vase, the teapot, the ornaments, all sold under Derek's direction. No great profit; enough for the purpose he had in mind, which was a good purpose, but not good enough to stop him half knowing it was, in some way, corrupt: the extra money was not for himself.

"I never did want paying," he said, hideously embarrassed. "I've got a place to live, unemployment. If I get any money, that'll stop and I'll be worse off."

He could not have begun to explain to her why he did not want the money. He had no real use for the stuff: money got him into trouble, had him hanging round women, made him feel he could drink. He felt safe when he was here: he had enough to keep the old car going and that was all he needed. Besides, payment for his presence would inexorably alter the whole status of it, and he supposed that was what Isabel wanted. Serena always made him feel a dear and exclusive friend who could arrive when he wanted and stay as long as he wanted. Money would change him into the hired help.

"Something towards the running of the car?" she suggested tactfully. He was tempted, but he shook his head.

"Well, think about it. Perhaps we could settle on what time you get here and what time you leave?"

Bile rose in his throat. He had made his own routine: now she wanted him tied down to hours. She'd soon have him clocking on and off, like in a factory.

"Can't do that," he said. "I've got other commitments, see?"

Like now, hiding. Shivering with remembered guilt.

Derek had come into his room about eight o'clock. Flourished those letters about which he had almost forgotten, a shade pissed, the way Derek usually was when someone, somewhere, had given him cash and he wanted company. He sat on the bed and looked at George owlishly.

"Hallo, gorgeous. Why aren't you talking to me these past weeks? I've got something of yours. Picked 'em up by mistake. Sorry about that. Are you coming for a drink?"

"Not tonight, Derek, I'm tired. Another time."

"Another time? You're always saying that." He sighed like a beauty queen deprived of the prize. "Come out for a drink, George. Meet people, have fun. I want to talk to you."

"What about?"

An evil grin appeared on Derek's dark features. He looked like a wizened jockey, magnificent eyelashes flattering the lined face of a man much older than his thirty years. Something ate Derek from within. George did not think it was disease, merely a hungry tapeworm thrashing around in constant discontent. In the days when George had given half his food to Derek, the lad could have eaten a horse.

"I want to talk about the place you go every day, where you won't take me. It's not fair, George. You told me about a beautiful woman, a princess, you said, and you never let me see her."

"You've not got a lot of use for women, Derek. Never did have."

"Not like you, George. Six years of rape. You must have liked it once. I don't know what makes you so fussy now. You're over fifty."

Age was everything. It was supposed to bring a scintilla of wisdom. Why had he departed from the habits of half a lifetime and opened his mouth to this boy? George smiled, one man to another, waiting for worse.

Derek waved the crumpled letters. They were all disorganized: they could not have told anyone a story. Especially Serena's, which consisted of lists of words, like a child's vocabulary book. Hope flared and then died in George's slow imagination.

"I'm telling you, George, there's one here with a lot of really hot stuff. I bet it's your princess, writing to a bloke. She's telling him she loves him and she's sorry she bit! That's what they do, women. Bite people. You're better off without them. But it turned me on, it did."

George lunged for the letters. Derek was only on the cusp

of drunkenness and drew back in time, playfully. The letters disappeared into the top pocket of his bomber jacket. He smiled coyly, fluttering the magnificent lashes.

"Naughty," he admonished. "Very naughty. Come out for a drink, George. I got money. I miss you."

George had gone for the drink he did not want, in the hope of getting back his letters. Two halves of bitter to Derek's three Carlsberg Specials made his head spin and left his senses raw, sending up thanks for the food he had eaten and Derek had not. He tried to be polite to Derek's other friends, Bob and Dick, but he did not like them either and it showed. Big, silent men who kept themselves apart. Dick smelled of sweat and his eyes moved incessantly, his gaze lingering on the women at the bar. This much George had understood by the time he took the letters from Derek's jacket pocket when the others went to the lavatory. Derek had made the connection between his own daily destination and the address on the letter which begged for a reply: the one about biting someone and being sorry about it. George cursed Isabel, not for whatever she had done, or the contents of the letter which clearly gave Derek such unholy glee, but for the clarity of her writing when she wrote her home address. Where is it, George? Where is it, this big house full of old things and the princess you told me about? Where is it? Derek now knew where it was. He would not need the letters to refresh his memory.

George bought the fourth round, resenting the money. There was a disturbance by the door. Bob, touching up a woman who screamed abuse at him; the beginnings of a fight. Under cover of the noise, Derek leant forward and kissed him. George could feel blood ready to explode from the pores of his forehead. He wanted to hit the man, the way he had once wanted to hit a woman. If he could have borne the proximity, he would have undone Derek's dirty, tight jeans, seized his prick, twisted it, torn it off and thrown it away. That was what queers made him feel like. Even if he had once been convicted of rape, they were worse, coming on strong like this. Derek went back to the bar, the kiss unreciprocated, the thirst unslaked and the cash still sufficient. George fled.

Nowhere to go and no way to cope. He could not go back to his room with the useless warden off-duty and Derek knowing exactly where he was. Nor could he get in his car at a time of night when the police were busy enough to notice the rust on the side and the smell on his breath. Wait in the dark, until sleep overtook them all? He opted for that.

End of October: mist beginning to settle on the so-called old end of town. One mile walk from the suburban end, where the hostel nestled in anonymous ugliness among the rest, next to the brand new Methodist church. Now he was crouched against the wall of the alleyway between a row of shops and the old chapel furniture exchange where he had sold Serena's things. His feet had crunched on rubbish and there was no light. Wariness of Derek and his friends had grown into a terror of revulsion. They wanted something and Derek wanted most.

The alleys of the old town stretched either side. George was shivering cold, dressed in clothes that were fit only for the warm room he had left. The warmest things about him were the letters scrunched up to his heart beneath his sweatshirt and the desire to dance in the dark with Serena Burley, whom he knew he had already betrayed. Someone else now knew where she was, in possession of all those old, damaged things which someone would want. It was not the immediate prospect that troubled him now, but living long enough to cope with it, what with the voice of Derek in the near distance, wandering the streets in the fog, shouting. He could not face Derek: he would strike him.

"Come out, George. I know where you are: I'll find you, promise."

George closed his mouth, willed his shivering limbs to stay still. He crossed his arms over his chest and squeezed his eyes closed, bracing himself against the wall.

"Come out, George. I loves ya, George."

He stuck his thumbs inside his ears; he placed his little fingers into his eyes and, ignoring the dirt where he crouched, he rolled himself into a ball with his back facing the glow of the street lamp.

"I loves ya, George. Where are you?"

The voice began to falter; then it faded. "I love ya, George" died away into the night. The effort needed to take his hands out of his ears was enormous: the energy required to move his limbs from curled to straight seemed greater. He writhed in an agony of cramp, of unsound mind unhinged by confrontation. He would stay there for ever to avoid a fight.

He thought of December, when he might freeze as he lay, parcelled up for the dramatic discovery of rubbish men in January. Serena would miss him. She needed him. At two in the morning he unscrewed his arms and walked back to a silent dwelling.

Robert Burley was teased about his name because it matched his physique. Big, tending to fat because of a liking for solid food — cake, real ale and potatoes. He was the kind of solicitor who studiously avoided making real money on account of his principles: knowledge should be placed at the disposal of the community. Conspicuous wealth brought out the Trotsky in him. All property was theft, unless it had a huge mortgage on it, like his terraced house in Manchester. His moral crusades, which were born out of an inability to compete, were never quite as sincerely felt as he imagined. He simply wanted to be worthy. The end result was a wretched practice and a life of endless complication. Envy ate at him like a worm, without making him thin. Only in his own house was he a king.

"Joan! You ready yet, woman?"

"Nope. Take the baby. Look, Robbie, are you sure we have to stay the night? So much easier if we just go there and back."

I've said we'd stay, so we're staying. C'mon, love, give me that girl."

A soft, enormously fat fifteen-month-old lump of baby, made in his own image and liking. He could not have ordered up anything better: his daughter, his one and only. The four-year-old son, a thin child of quietly precocious habits, was beaten into second place by his sister and did not seem to mind. He had the undiluted love of his mother: he preferred women.

"Don't hold her so tight, Robbie. She'll suffocate."

"No, she won't. She's all right, aren't you, Cathie?" The child grinned and squirmed. Robert put his finger in her mouth and let her suck. Joan accused him of spoiling her. He strapped the baby in the front seat beside him, even though it was supposed to be safer in the back, a fact he ignored because he wanted to go on sneaking glances at her and because he believed implicitly that his own superior skill as a driver was all it took to avoid accidents.

"My God, this car's like a travelling circus," Joan complained. "Why do we have to take so much?"

"Because we aren't going to a place equipped for kids, as you well know."

Joan sighed. "I wish we didn't have to go at all."

Joan was a placid wife, but a shrewd one. They made a duty visit to his mother every few weeks, purely to satisfy conscience. This time they were going because Robert had received a valuation on his mother's goods and he also wanted to make sure Isabel was not colluding with the help. He wasn't worried about the house. There were only a few years left on the lease, which made it worth little to any inheritor. The only hope of getting anything out of Mother was keeping the contents intact and keeping her in it. So much for principles. The prospect of a third child was eroding them fast.

Oh, be fair to him Joan told herself, handing the boy a carton of orange juice with instructions not to spill it. He does care for his mother: he cares for everyone. He's beaten himself to death caring.

"Is she asleep?"

"Not yet."

You could not spoil a child by adoration alone, he told himself. Surely not. It took love of a particular kind to do that. Like the love his father had had for Isabel, who could do no wrong, Father's little piece of perfection. He could remember rushing towards his father on Father's return from a foreign trip and being literally pushed to one side, to stand with his arms outstretched and nothing to hold, because Isabel had been behind him. He might as well have been invisible: so might his mother. It made him burn with humiliation, even now. It was one thing to prefer one child to another, he reflected with the wisdom of parenthood, but you had to pretend to be even-handed. Father had not dissembled. And it was not just Father who preferred Isabel so outrageously: there was also Aunt Mab, who signalled it by leaving her everything. One way and another, Robert Burley felt his sister owed him a lot. He owed her nothing.

The afternoon was pleasant, the drive in the past-its-sell-by-date Ford Sierra uneventful. The boy in the back expressed no curiosity whatever about their destination. When they arrived he got out carefully and ran indoors.

They went to the back door, as family should. The front door was for the parties Robert remembered before his father died. Gross over-consumption, where Dad danced with his daughter and Mother flirted with the men. Men who were mostly dead now, he supposed. Perhaps Serena's sexy partiality for men might explain the dearth of women friends now. Widows have long memories. Robert doubted if Isabel had thought of that. He contemplated his own life with satisfaction. A serious man was better off with a plain wife.

"Hallo, Isabel. You look terrific."

His voice boomed over the garden. Out of the corner of his eye he saw that odd little man, George, sidling away in the direction of the fields. If Robert was startled, not to say faintly satisfied by the change in the sister he had last seen three months before, he did not show it. The slenderness of her was even more extreme: it was pinched. She was breathless and anxious to please. Serena was magnificent. In his bitterness, Robert always chose to forget whose favourite he had been.

"Darlings, wonderful!"

A flurry of warm, scented kisses, smothering him, arms round him like steel, face nuzzling his hair, her mouth finding his ears and his nose, like a puppy. She would never have shoved him aside.

Sun streamed through the dining-room windows reflecting in the table, which Robert was relieved to see had not been chopped up for firewood. More than a thousand pounds, the valuer had said. They went straight in to eat, Joan telling Isabel she should not have bothered: they could have gone out and, anyway, they'd bought sandwiches. It was a strange meal: cooked ham in a kind of casserole that tasted of tinned soup, a bit gluey, baked potatoes. Serena fed hers to the dog. The boy, Jack, attached himself to Isabel like a limpet, refusing to eat anything unless she gave her approval to each mouthful. It was almost normal.

Isabel watched her mother, who seemed transfixed by Robert's face. Serena smiled and nodded, apparently following every word: the sight made Isabel choke with sadness. She knew by now that words reached Serena through a fog. She was merely mistress of a splendid, deceptive social façade which knew the value of keeping silent, fooling most of the people, most of the time.

"What do you do all day?" Robert boomed. Serena laughed, imagining he had said something funny.

"Nothing," Isabel said.

What a stupid, unobservant man he was, to produce this brilliant little son, the possession of whom Isabel craved with a passion of need. She had seen the boy as a baby, twice a year since, and each time the sight of his little bird bones melted her own. He knew it, rewarded it with his unblinking stare.

"You know what you do?" Isabel said to him as they wandered in the orchard, taking in the last of the light, giggling as they mashed dead apples underfoot. "You make me broody. Broody as an old hen."

"You look like a hen," he volunteered. The maggots in the apples fascinated him. He looked at everything gravely. "Are we staying here tonight?"

"Yes, I hope so."

"I'll come in bed with you, then."

"Only if your mother says."

Suddenly she liked the idea of her family. Blood was thicker than water. Robert and she would become friends. They would work out something for Mother. They would have civilized conversations about it, beginning now, this evening, when she would tell them Mother was mad, worsening fast, should not be living thus. She would ask Jack to stay. She would tell Robert what Mother had done to the food. It was simple: she would demand help and receive it. Not cover up any more.

"Have you got a daddy, Bella?"

"A daddy or a sugar daddy?" she teased.

He spread his thin arms. There was a blue vein on one wrist she always wanted to stroke. "A big man," he said, as if that explained everything.

"No, I haven't." She thought of Joe whom she loved with such passion and who had not replied to her letters, and thought, no, he is a little man. So are they all, little men.

The orchard was a satisfying distance from the house. No sound reached it until Joan came out to join them. There was about her a smug, conspiratorial air that boded trouble. But Isabel decided she did not dislike her sister-in-law. There was not enough there: doors open, lights on, no one definite at home. A big "Halloo!" yelled into the peaceful air made her squirm but caused no reaction whatever in Jack. He was collecting maggots into a matchbox.

"I say, Issy, there's a rather nice man, Andrew he said it was, called to see you. Brought some flowers for your mother. Said I'd come and find you. What have you got there, Jack, darling? Put them down."

"Andrew? Oh, yes."

Joan propelled them back towards the house. It was dusk and the sandstone walls had taken on a life of their own, glowing like a soft beacon. Isabel faltered in her step, arrested by a shock of affection and appreciation, punctured when Joan took her arm like a jolly school friend on the way back from hockey, a gesture of the camaraderie Isabel had never found in the days when her mother wrote to her and Joan was captain of netball somewhere else.

"He seems awfully keen, Isabel dear. He might have brought the flowers for you, but Serena took them, so I suppose they're hers, now."

It seemed somehow obscene to explain in front of the boy that his granny had lost her love of plants and wanted her blooms to be *replicas*, unable to distinguish between the two except for the fact that one sort needed water and were a nuisance. Equally useless to explain to Robert that Granny would have limited interest in his baby; she preferred the durability of dolls. Joan squeezed Isabel's elbow.

"Is this an old flame or a new one, Issy dear? Robbie says you had a lot of chaps around before you left home. I mean, this one looks a bit old for you, I would have said, but very respectable."

A lot of old flames, Isabel thought, even after I left with my inheritance. They all doused themselves, even the ones I brought home afterwards. First they were there, then they were gone. Have you got a big man, Issy? No, they all disappeared like smoke: I lived on my own. The sweet smell of rot in the orchard and the unwanted touch on her arm made memory part of a cycle. One in the dying phase, while fecund Joan was longing to impart the news of rebirth. The elbow was squeezed again, roguishly. The grin given with the squeeze was supposed to say, Come on, sister, you can tell me, while the school-prefect voice went on.

"Well done, Issy, I say. Must be a bit lonely for you out here on your own. Glad you've got yourself sorted out so quickly. Got to get a man on board. Never at a loss in that direction are you?"

Issy, Bella. Each vision of her shortened name made her smaller, unless it was done with permission and affection. Patience in the face of unintended insult was something she was learning fast, so she kept her voice mild, mindful of the boy who was holding her hand.

"That'll be Andrew Cornell. He's a valuer. I'm sure he's come to see Robert."

Joan giggled girlishly. "I don't believe you," she said.

They had traversed the lawn at the front quickly in response to the onset of darkness over dusk, no one noticing how weedy it was. Jack had his matchbox safely in his pocket. He sniffed the air like a dog.

"Nice," he announced. "Ever so nice here. Mum, why is Cathie screaming?"

"What?"

"Cathie. Screaming like that."

Joan broke into a run.

When George came back with the dog the kitchen was a nightmare of suppressed screams, the adults frozen in terror. There were dirty dishes in the sink and the overhead light illuminated a series of harsh faces. For a moment he could have been back in his hostel, waiting for a fight to happen. Only Serena's expression was blessed with contentment as she crooned to the baby in her arms, rocking it with rhythmic violence, squeezing it hard. Peripheral to this embrace was Robert, who was trying to unhinge her arms from round the baby's chest while Cathie bawled for redemption. They were the screams of distress from a child beyond pique and discomfort and well into the realms of hysteria, face flushed, choking on tears.

"Let go!" Robert yelled at his mother. She grinned, squeezed harder, raising bruises, hummed louder and moved her burden in the direction of the corridor. He had visions of the child's ribs popping out through her ample flesh, her cries dying away into a series of gurgles, then silence. Two doll-like arms beat at Serena's face; the thick, frail neck wobbled dangerously; the china-blue eyes formed slits and the two fat legs hung out of the bundle like helpless sausages with feet. The little boy laughed to see such fun: Jack was beside himself, yelping. Robert was desperate. Tears had formed in his eyes. He balled his right hand into a fist.

"Dance for your daddy. . . ." Serena crooned.

"Put her down! I'll kill you!" Joan's voice was hoarse with threat.

Serena took no notice. The baby's screams descended to a steady howl of pain.

Andrew appeared from nowhere, the last visible person, pushed Robert to one side.

"You look lovely today, Mrs Burley. Where did you get that hat? Isn't it noisy? Shall I carry this for you? It is very, very heavy, isn't it?" He spoke loudly and firmly, kissed her on the left wrist, held out his arms beneath the child.

Jack's laughter fell into silence as his mother slapped him. The fridge hummed. They all watched. Mrs Burley smiled more widely than ever. Her arms opened with such abruptness that Andrew's thin back bowed under the weight of Robert Burley's daughter. George was behind him. Andrew passed on the bundle of flesh, bones and shawls with practised tenderness. George hoisted Cathie over his shoulder, holding her under the nappy, letting her fingers claw at his eyes, bending back so she lay on a curve, free as a bird. Murmuring, My aren't you a beauty? Aren't you just a little beauty? The crying descended into a series of hiccups. The women recovered from paralysis. Robert moved.

"I should let her stop here a minute if I were you," George said amiably. "She's just filled her nappy. That's what all that fuss was about. What a treasure. Is she yours? What's her name?"

They packed the Ford Sierra and had left within the hour. George had gone before them. Robert said he was not staying in a house where his child was not safe; he would not believe that his mother had simply forgotten how to hold a baby. Enough was enough. Serena was Isabel's responsibility. He would be consultant.

Serena had no idea what she had done. How silly people were. She cried when Robert left, but he could not bear to touch her. She turned on Isabel a face of puzzled desolation.

"Why doesn't he love me?" she asked.

"He does, Mum. He does, of course he does. We all do."

Later, when all the dishes were done and the place restored to tidiness, Isabel saw the ferret, waiting outside the door.

"IT IS NICE AND WARM TONIGHT," *Serena wrote in block capitals. Writing in capitals took up so much time she began to scribble. "Someone stole my doll. Someone stole my man. I can't remember which was worse." Sitting on the big carver chair watching the moon from the window reminded her how these clearer spells were becoming briefer, since she had obviously been en route to another place entirely in order to do something different and useful. She sat upright and considered the problem.*

She had been looking for snow to fall, snow being an easier option than a knife, but it was too early for that. Or she might have been looking for a book to read. Or, more likely, she had realized that Isabel had heard her tiptoeing downstairs, and that was enough to suspend all movement. It was awful to be followed, terrible to be captive in her own house, and purgatory to have some other woman dancing attendance. Any female with sense, Serena announced with her breath reaching the table, hates the dominance of her mother, but not nearly as much as the other way round.

There was fucking dust on this buggering table, which was nicer than paper, and the light of the moon was preferable to bursting lightbulbs, which blew up in her face out of sheer spite. She watched her own finger waver, hesitant to commit. Something was important. Nothing she could remember. Serena got up and made her regular parade of touching things, as if she loved them. She had never had much time for things, only people. Edward, her husband, had loved things like trophies. She had loved him first as long as he loved her first; she had loved other men second. There was about as much time left for women as there was for God. Neither had ever saved her from anything.

She looked at her fingers. Still five of them. What a relief.

Nothing really changed, then. She did not change. Bits of her died was all, like gangrenous toes on bodies in frost. All those lovely manners, which had covered her like a coat. It was not the same as being mad, Serena told the table: she could still dance, still march to a different tune. As for being good, she was not good, never had been.

She added an extra 's' to the word in the dust, so that the sound of it would end in a hiss. Lonelinessssss was a fact of life sometimes cured by illusion, mitigated by the love of a man. For some women, she wrote, being alone on the planet is cured by the love they have for their children. She had loved hers, but never to death and never as a replacement. Mab had loved them as if they were her own.

Serena stopped, shaking her head until her eyes rattled like marbles. Why should it be so difficult for children to accept they were not the centre of the world? Why on earth impose such expectation? Serena put her mind to the task of communication. A game of noughts and crosses which must not be wiped away in the morning. In case somebody won.

She was playing a game with Isabel. First she kept winning when Isabel was small, but then when Is grew into a girl, she wiped the board, stole her father's heart and got row after row of kisses until her mother had nothing left. Not that Edward ever did anything: he hadn't the faintest idea, but that was not the point. The point was the row of Xs. The memory of being insanely jealous. And now this same child was demanding love. "Give us a break," Serena scrawled. She could not remember what she had done the day before. Something bad. Her eyes widened.

Look at that! The cat was on the table, smearing the writing. All because she had opened the window on account of hating anything to be locked. The bastard cat had brought her a mouse without a head. That was what lack of inhibition was all about.

Balls.

Chapter Five

ANDREW WAS DREAMING.

"Hush," someone told him. "Hush. Whisper who dares. Christopher Robin has fallen downstairs."

He and Isabel were sitting at either end of that big Knole sofa (worth a few hundred, bad condition), avoiding the springs and talking to each other. They were both a little drunk, which eased the talk and made it slip and slide between things that mattered a lot and things that had no importance whatever.

Listen to me. Listen. It is no person's duty to look after a parent. I should know.

My mother loves me.

Yes. Like a fungus loves its culture.

No. I want to be like her.

At that point Serena crashed through the door, wearing nothing but curlers and demanding a car.

Tell me, Miss Burley, were you in love with what she was? Why did you leave me? Why did you write me that filthy letter?

When Andrew woke, he was on his own bed, fully dressed, with everything crumpled and uncomfortable. He could feel the weight of a baby in his arms.

Dr Reilly puffed towards the back door. For country calls he wore boots, which gave a certain edge to the challenge of controlling the pedals of the Volvo. At midday the air was fresh with rain, the temperature mild with only a hint of winter warning. Bonfire night: he could smell the smoke in advance, knew he would need his energy and his sobriety for later alarms.

He took off his boots at the door, revealing fisherman's socks of odd colours. Those made Isabel trust him, although she knew he was a wily old bird: Aunt Mab had said so, and what Mab said was always right, although none of her observations meant that the Doc was anything less than an excellent practitioner. He seemed to be the same age now as he had always been, which was old enough to treat as a reliable uncle.

"Anything in particular wrong, m'dear? You said on the phone you wanted me to take a look at your mother. I'd been popping out every week to see her, y'know. George would have called me if there was anything wrong. Anyway, after you took charge I've waited to be asked."

Looking at the girl he wondered which of the two female occupants needed treatment. She was a funny grey colour: those great deep eyes of hers seemed to take up as much of her head as a bush baby's, but her smile still went straight from ear to ear. A mouth like Brigitte Bardot; no wonder his son had suffered such a bad dose of calf love once. In his eyes Isabel had improved with age: most women did. His son had two daughters of his own now: the photographs were in the doctor's pocket, ready to be shown.

"It's just a check-up. I don't know. Just to give me some idea of how she really is."

"Surely," he said kindly. "Does she still smoke?"

"Yes. Not very often. She seems to forget how to hold it."

"Well, there's a mercy. No need to come with me. I know the way if she's still in bed. And then we'll have a chat."

Half an hour later, on her way to the bathroom, Isabel heard the sound of laughter from Mother's room and felt a spurt of envy for Doc Reilly. She had never had it in herself to make her mother laugh, she wanted to snap at him when he sat himself down so solidly at the kitchen table in front of a cup of coffee, but then he smiled and patted her shoulder.

"You've chosen a lonely path to furrow, miss. Don't worry about your mum chortling. Your mother never did mind being examined. She says it makes her tickle. The stethoscope, I mean. She likes it."

Isabel felt ashamed. "Can I tell you something?"

"Course. Anything."

She hesitated. "Sometimes I want to hit her. My fingers itch to hit her."

"I don't blame you. I'm amazed more people don't succumb. I don't even know why it's considered worse to hit an old child than a child." He laughed. It was not the laugh she had heard from the bedroom: that had been Serena's.

Isabel placed her palms flat down on the table. He noticed the prominent bones at the wrists. Then she clasped her hands between her knees, as if wanting to hide the evidence of temptation.

"I could do with some help, I suppose," she added, lamely.

He frowned. "Well, to be honest, there's not much of that to be had unless you hire it and I doubt they'd come out this far. You've got two options. You can carry on, or you can abandon ship and leave her to it."

He gulped the coffee as if his mouth had forgotten the difference between cold and hot.

"Once there's another fire, or the place gets infested, but not before, the Social Services will step in. They'll pretend they have a budget for so-called care in the community, people coming in every day for an hour, you know, but it wouldn't work. They can't afford people staying overnight. It would stagger on for a bit, and then, provided you kept your distance, they'd take her away. There's a nice home in —"

"No," said Isabel. "I couldn't consign her to that. She'd lose whatever it is she has left."

"She won't go any other way than in a straitjacket," he said roughly. "And she'll be what they call difficult to place. I don't want to point out to you that there would be a lot more help available if you simply didn't exist. Didn't she tell you about the home helps she sent away? No, she wouldn't, would she? Janice was the only one she could stand, perhaps because she paid Janice herself. You could perhaps get her back."

"She won't."

The Doc shook a grizzly head. He hated this kind of problem, couldn't believe the contrast between fact and expectation. Nor could he believe any planner could have imagined care in the community was any kind of cheap option. Speaking for himself, he had no plans to quit drinking or smoking. Once he retired, he would look for other, carcinogenic things to do.

"The only thing I can tell you, if you don't already know, is that Social Services have a legal duty to your mother. They have. You do not. Odd though that may seem. But they won't do a single thing about that duty as long as someone else is exercising it, see? You *do* have a choice."

She nodded.

The Doc drained his cup and rose. "Shout for me any time you want," he said. "Good coffee. Get out and about more, I would. Now, will you do me a favour? Show me that living room of yours. I used to love that room, had some good times in there. They were great party-givers, your mum and dad."

"Would she be able to cope if we had a party now?"

Doc Reilly broke his stride across the kitchen floor. "I doubt it."

He did not add that he knew of no one who would come voluntarily, and that you couldn't dragoon people to a party. Not even his sainted wife, who had visited longer than most and whom Serena had called a pig, would come. You had to have a big heart to let an old lady get her rocks off by insulting you.

He strode to the west-facing window, looked into the rain-streaked garden, wanting to get his hands on it. Shrubs needed pruning, lawn was like a shrinking hayfield. A movement caught his eye: two sets of twinkling training shoes disappearing round the side of the house. In the distance he heard a door bang shut.

"Do you get many kids coming up here?" he asked sharply.

"Yes, sometimes, asking for water, apples, that kind of thing."

The doctor moved swiftly. Back in the kitchen Isabel's handbag was open on the table, undisturbed. Outside the door of his car stood open.

"They don't want water," he snorted. "They want cash."

All his loose change, in the glove compartment for parking, was gone. No sign of them down the road. Too cunning by far to let themselves be framed in the lights of the Volvo over the field; too swift for someone who had to pull on his boots. The Doc turned on to the road at the end of the track, purple with irritation. Could have been Serena's purse they robbed, had probably done already, sodding little truants. He could hear them now, explaining it all: "We didn't take it, Mister. She gave it to us, honest." He would take a bet that Serena Burley's house was not as well stocked with small objects as it had been a year ago. These were sparrows, gathering to lead in the birds of prey.

There was a white van parked in the place by the graveyard, with windows slightly steamed up and two men inside, drinking their lunchtime tea. The Doc did not notice them. Thought instead of buzzards, hovering in a bleak sky and the way Serena's body had moved in the days when they had danced.

George manoeuvred his old car between the holes in the water-logged track, spirits lifting in direct proportion to his distance from the town. Beginning as it did at rock bottom today, his mood had a long way to go before it reached buoyancy. He called at Sal's house, just to say hallo, received from her a piece of cake and the day's letters. The mere sight of letters made George squirm: he had never again acted as postman for the Burley household's outgoing letters: let Isabel take those. But the postman still left the incoming post with the neighbours. Nice, willing people they were, but the letters which he dropped on the sideboard at the house as if they were so much nuclear waste, burned a hole in his pocket. Letters should be for ever outside his remit. He was never going to write one.

"Tell that girl to pop in and see us when she's passing," Sal had urged him several times. "I don't know why she doesn't, really I don't."

George had never relayed the message. He had hinted to Isabel that the neighbours were private people who had never forgiven the débâcle of their wrecked car. Frankly, Sal was someone else he did not particularly want to share: George was anxious to keep his acquaintances in different pockets, in case they got together, pooled information and found out where he came from.

He heaved a sigh of relief when he got to the gates of the house. A trail of smoke emerged from a chimney. Back at the hostel, Derek had gone quiet, possibly ashamed. No repercussions for last week's rejection. What a fuss over nothing.

Not quite nothing. Trying to avoid the shameful memory of fear, George could see what Derek meant about the unposted letter from Isabel Burley to her lover. "I'm sorry if I drew blood," she had written. "Sometimes I want you so much it makes me claw at you . . ." The sentence had been reread dozens of times and made him hot. They were all like that, however they disguised it, bitches in heat. George could not catch Isabel's eye, but after the business with the brother, when she had been so helpless, and after his slow absorbing of a letter containing more nonsense than sense, he found he did not mind her quite as much. It was a dull, sullen dislike he carried now; no longer acute. His mind would not stay still but skittered around like the dog when shown her lead: he wanted to chastise it.

Two skinny boys who should have been at school skulked by the gates and scattered as he drove through. Little kids, more down at heel than he had ever been and even less safe. He pitied them for having nowhere to go. George trusted small children and people far older. It was the swathe of humanity in between which made problems.

Everything was as he liked it. Quiet. He put down the letters (two bills, one personal) with care. Serena was dressed and waiting for the kiss to be given behind her daughter's back. It seemed a long time since he had been free to intrude in her bedroom. Sit on the bed and listen to her telling stories, before he told his own. He still had the silver teapot in his car, but he already had enough. Nearer Christmas he would buy the princess her present. Something to help with the problem of words.

Darling Issy,

Yeah, I did get your second letter, also no. 3, but no, not the first, I'm afraid. Please don't send any more to the office . . . even if you mark them private, they can get read. I'm not the managing director!!! As for apologies, well I don't know if I deserve any of those. I probably deserved what you did. Even when I had to pass it off as a kind of mugging!!! One thing you do, Issy, is make a man think and you have made me think a bit. I've got to sort myself out, haven't I? I hope you've got used to country life and I hope you come home soon, 'cos I miss you.

Can't stop. Must catch post!!

Joe

In the privacy of her room Isabel read this missive with something like distaste, trying to embrace the idea that it was wrong to judge a person by the style of letters he wrote, especially if letter-writing had never been part of the arrangement. A letter from Joe, although yearned for, had a strange effect. It was a revelation of limitations, rather like a very large and handsome man opening his mouth to speak and a high treble coming out. Isabel knew that she was not very bright, but even with the awkwardness imposed on them by her violence and sudden departure she knew she had written far better, more honest, letters than this.

Passed off a bite as a mugging, did he? How odd to be able to tell lies with such inventive ease, when she herself was congenitally incapable of telling them at all. And how passionless his prose. She had a funny sense of superiority, born of her personal, illogical and deep-rooted loathing for exclamation marks. They were like someone coming up behind you and making you jump for no reason.

Nor could she understand how she had acquired this aversion. There were so many books in this house, carried from the other houses. Books Mab had made her read and then describe to make sure she had understood. The habit of reading had not persisted into adulthood, although there had been book-worm phases, usually at times when all else failed. And the height of literary thrills in the remoteness of school had been Ma's letters, which always flowed and told stories without ever resorting to using punctuation like cudgels.

Perhaps she would read aloud to her mother. The idea had a quaint, spinsterish charm: Isabel enjoyed thinking of herself as the kind of lady's companion / governess found in the Jane Austen she had once adored. Readings by the fire. How genteel. If Joe could see her now.

There were books lining the walls up the stairs. Books in shelves in the spare rooms, on the old presumption that a guest might need to read. Books in the dining room, floor to ceiling, flanking the fire. Books simply hanging around, acquired on a weekly basis by Serena until only twelve months before. Books she still claimed to read in bed and at her desk. Books Isabel tidied away, noticing without a great deal of interest how the reading had never actually progressed beyond a favourite page, chosen by number; Serena was stuck at page twenty-five of anything.

"George is just off, darling. Don't you think you should say goodbye?" said Serena.

It was one of those uncanny days. Sanity and mildness ruled the house. Water dripped through the bathroom ceiling upstairs and it did not matter. George had taken Serena out in his car to the horrible supermarket and peace had reigned.

"No, there's no need to say goodbye. Goodbye never meant anything, did it?" Serena was yawning. "I shouldn't look in there, if I were you," she added. "I really, really wouldn't."

Isabel was selecting books from those middle shelves in the dining room which were the easiest to reach, without stretching or bending. Book after book, hardbacked, softbacked, stored at random, fell to the floor with pages torn.

"Coffee time," said Serena. "Or is it tea?"

"Did you do this, Mother?" Isabel held aloft a book from which the torn middle pages waved as she shook it.

Serena nodded vaguely. She seemed to be struggling with the temptation to lie.

"Yes, I did. They . . ." She struggled for expression. "Insulted me, I suppose." She went on in a sudden articulate rush, so rare now that Isabel thought wildly that the Doc must have given her a magic pill from his old bag. "You won't know. You dust tables, you don't read. I couldn't read, you see. All of a sudden, I could not read. It broke my heart. Put them back, dear. It was a bad thing to do."

Isabel gazed at her. Honesty made a person so endearing. So did the absence of exclamation marks. The times when she wanted to hit her mother were equal to those when she wanted to enfold her. Say, Yes, I do not read, but if I were told I could not do so again, if the books would not do what I wanted, I would scratch the pages in the way I would want to scratch a face. She bent to pick up fragments of paper containing all those elusive, tormenting words. Pages fluttered to the floor.

"Silly old books, Mum. Time for tea."

What did they do all day?

When Andrew left the town, past the park, straight through the roundabout, he saw the municipal bonfire, built to discourage the amateur from constructing some dangerous inferno in his own backyard. He passed his father's house in the old part, near the church on the one-way system, where his car always wanted to stop, and stalled if he did not, from the transference of guilt from his head to the clutch cable. There was a white van on his tail as he hung left on to the road that led to the hamlet that led to Isabel, the lights of it in his eyes until he slowed down. The van dropped back and he turned up the track, so carelessly that rain from the puddles hit the screen in a great, muddy splash. He felt as if this were the middle of the night and he the bearer of contraband. Fireworks. The rain had stopped. If you wanted to court the daughter, which he did, court the mother first.

Bonfire parties had been favourite occasions in his adolescence. They were a convenient cover of darkness for uncertain fumblings. First put your arms round the girl's waist, light the blue touch paper and wait for protest. That was the way he had been in his romantic, irresponsible years. All the girls, excluding Isabel, had said no. Not in so many words, but with plenty of shuffling excuses: I've got to go somewhere; wash my hair; meet a friend — and find someone better than you. Except Isabel, who did not say no, simply said where? Andrew did not envisage a repeat performance of Isabel's uncomplicated acceptance of sexual overture, but after all this time, he saw a kindness in her generous obliging of a gauche young man which was quite inconsistent with her later unkindness. He had only to look at Isabel now to see that she was incapable of spite and always had been. And what had he done about it? Visited, briefly and awkwardly in the last month, brought flowers, and thought about her all the time.

This spontaneity and determination to beat down his own shyness came at the end of a dreadful day. Moving furniture in and out of the auction room, three valuations with garrulous housewives — two of whom considered their disgusting imitation Welsh dressers to be worth a fortune — and all that with the additional hazard of young Derek in tow, because his father had decided "the lad had a brain which deserved encouragement." Derek was ignorant, but he got inside cupboards, shone a silly little pencil torch on things and made loud remarks. His own native dislike apart, Andrew had to confess that Derek was good company. His incessant questions about the value of things, his apparent fascination with their texture, made Andrew wax lyrical and lengthy in reply. Explaining, with his own residual excitement, how it was one piece of wood was worth money, another not; how some pieces of furniture would achieve value in a future generation because they had style, others not. Things did not need to be a hundred years old to acquire status: they only had to be good, built on pure lines and made with pride.

Neither of the Welsh dressers had been made with pride, unless there was any sense of achievement in knocking out a copy of a piece of furniture for shipment to a country you had never seen. Derek liked that. His own remarks on Mrs Brown, with her bouffant hair and best dress to greet the valuer of her goods, as if she was for sale herself, had been funny, but for all his enjoyment of a keen and caustic companion, Andrew did not feel easy introducing the man into the trusting heart of so many homes. Derek had eyes on springs: they seemed to leap out from his head and touch things, leaving a drop of moisture.

Wide eyes greeted Andrew now in the kitchen. When Serena smiled in that fashion, it made him think of Prospero's daughter opening lovely virginal eyes to her first view of young mankind, and it made him feel a prince. Most males, in his experience, did not deserve the accolade of poetry.

"I bought fireworks," he said. "In case you didn't have any." Serena understood: the smile grew wider.

Isabel's smile was graver, equally warm. "That was kind of you, Andrew. She used to love them. I didn't dare . . ."

He understood: he would not have relished sole charge of Serena around a box of explosives, doubted if she was safe with matches.

"Shall we?" he asked.

"Oh yes, yes, yes."

They began with sparklers. Andrew planted three of them into a raw potato and put it in the middle of the table; then he encouraged Serena to hold one in her fist, waving it wildly to make ribbons of yellow. She was unafraid of the sparks which stung her wrist, but awkward at first, then fluent, brandishing the sparkler like a conductor's baton.

"I can write in the air! Look! Read it!"

The dog whimpered and shivered: the air was fuggy. They progressed to the damp outdoors, where Andrew's long-distant and loathed boy-scout training came to the fore. He pinned Catherine wheels to a broken fence, stood the rockets up-right in empty bottles, moved quickly to keep the display almost continuous. The first Catherine wheel was a blinding, whirring, furious thing, turning madly as if wanting to escape or kill in the process. The third one would not move at all, only spat at them.

"Will someone worry that we're on fire again?" Isabel asked.

"No. Too much distraction." He pointed. The sky in the direction of the town seemed to glow pink and black.

"More," Serena begged. "More."

Rockets, the biggest and best he could find, while wondering at the time if the expense was ludicrous, then failing to care. Andrew was a careful man only on his own behalf; for others, there was no limit. He steadied the rockets, lit the first. It rose heavenwards with a magnificent rush, like Concorde, he thought proudly. There was a second's pause while it hung in the firmament, and Serena cried out in disappointment. Then a pop; a cascade of blue and purple stars; three more explosions as soft as polite burping; a shower of emeralds, rubies and pearls; then slow, red, hot, plummeting to earth. He lit the next and the next, all three of them breathing *aahh* as the rockets popped, a longer, more lingering *aaaahhhh* as they descended. There was magic in the sighing, pure magic.

Serena actually danced with joy. The lumbering body swayed in an ecstasy of delight. She put her hands over her ears, made little whoops of amazement at the roman candles, whirled her arms and laughed. The laughter and the happiness were as clean as rain; looking at her face, innocent in such intense enjoyment, Andrew could see the point of caring for her. Witnessing such complete absorption made him glad to be alive. If that was Isabel's reward for her labours, he could suddenly understand the sacrifice.

"Soup? Sausages?" Practical Isabel, captivated but, unlike Serena, still rooted to earth. One of us has to be, he supposed. Serena protested sadly, then accepted the show was over. Back inside Andrew persuaded the trembling dog out of her basket and fussed her into calmness.

In the harsh electric light which made them all blink Serena's face turned a sudden and ghastly pale. "I wanted to dance," she gasped and was sick into her handbag. All very tidily done, as if she was in practice.

Isabel swept into action like a seasoned nurse.

"Too much soap," she said cheerfully, increasing Andrew's shock.

"Soap," Isabel repeated. "My wretched sister-in-law brought her a present of pretty soap, shaped like apples and pears, highly coloured. I put it away but she was nibbling it this afternoon. Don't know why. I can never persuade her to eat the real thing."

Serena tottered to her feet, colour returning, looking for her handbag.

"I'll keep that safe, Ma. Are you going to bed?"

A slow, unsmiling nod for her daughter and an enormous wan grin for Andrew. Nausea made the old lady bewildered and tired.

"It's not fair," Isabel said fiercely. "Being sick is so confusing for her because she never knows why." She blew her nose on a piece of kitchen roll. "Will you follow her, Andrew? Make sure she gets to the top of the stairs, but don't interfere. She wouldn't like that, even from you."

Andrew walked softly down the corridor, watching Serena's progress. Into the dining room, touching each chair one by one, trailing her fingers along the surface of the table. Moving slightly faster into the living room, opening her desk, looking inside it, closing it again, giving her armchair a pat, as if reassuring a friend. Nodding to the sofa and the piano, moving at a fixed rate between them all, so that even stumbling over the edge of the Indian carpet seemed part of a ritual. Up the stairs, waving good-night to the pictures on the uneven walls. She did not hear his footfall behind her, moved like a ghost, retreating with gratitude and grace into her own world.

"I should like," Isabel announced when Andrew returned to the kitchen to find her sorting items from the handbag, some already washed, some amazingly dry, "to get extremely drunk."

Andrew stood next to her, reaching for the paper towel and automatically wiping dry a powder compact, a lipstick case and a plastic purse. His eye fell on a medley of stained envelopes, covered in neat writing, next to a chequebook.

"Are those yours or hers?" he asked.

"Hers. We write in the same way, almost exactly. I can forge her signature, which is proving useful when it comes to paying the bills. I tried to copy her writing when I was at school. I wanted mine to be just the same."

The lining of the handbag hung into the sink, saturated, old, worn and torn. Isabel washed her hands as thoroughly as a surgeon, far longer than necessary, in water so hot it made Andrew wince.

"Do you suppose that means I shall be like her one day? Like she is now? With half a mind? Incapable of forming my own words? Waiting in vain for everyone else to translate?"

He turned her from the water and put his arms round her. Holding her wet hands free, she wept into his shoulder.

"I wanted to be like her," she mumbled. "Not like Mab."

He did not know what she meant. There was no romance in this embrace, he concluded miserably. There were things he wanted to say, questions he wanted to ask, but he could not find the words.

Chapter Six

ISABEL HAD WANTED TO TELL ANDREW why she did not want to be like Aunt Mab, but she did not because she could not. "Those with power," Mab explained, "cannot bear to lose it. Face it, child, life's a bitch. It's easier for mere observers like me to relinquish hold. I was the war artist, you see, painting camouflage, hiding behind it. Never a front-line hero. So I don't want a hero's farewell."

Bonfires and Christmas, the occasions of colour which made memory eclipse into clarity. Good old Mab had died in grey November. She had been gifted in the giving of solace: receiving it was never her style.

"Heroine, Mab. The female of hero is heroine. You ought to get it right."

"Don't be pedantic. Heroines are entirely different animals. They have trembling chins. I'm dying: indulge me."

Her big, spatulate hands were clawing at the blankets in order to make them tidy, while Isabel looked on. As Mab pointed out in plain words not then understood, life at twenty-one and death at seventy did not suit. Mr Burley and his sister-in-law died within months of one another: cancer for her, industrial accident for him. He therefore remained handsome until the end, losing nothing with age, gaining a certain asceticism to his features. She remained as plain as ever; even her terminal gauntness quite anonymous. Mab was Mab, like a slab of rock.

"How are you, dear? How kind of you to come and see me. Tell me news."

Always these manners, this ability to welcome, make the visitor feel special. Fascinated by the hideous conundrum of what it must be like to have no future, Isabel could not discuss the present. Or believe Mab's interest in her own, youthful life.

Mab smiled comfortingly. "Look, poor child, you've got plenty to endure and I don't want fuss at nearly three score years and ten, do I?" she stated from her tidy bed. "I've had enough of the commas. This is just a full stop. I don't want any of your exclamation marks."

So that was where the aversion originated. Isabel shot up in bed. Lay down again, aching for the selfless common sense of Mab. Three in the morning, thinking of all those suppressed dreams that were not really dreams but episodes. Listening in the meantime to the creaking of floorboards as someone passed the door on tiptoe. Ghosts. Not Aunt Mab's ghost, far too silent, and besides, Mab's ghost belonged in another house.

When Mab had walked, she rattled. She carried about her person innumerable bits and pieces. She was a spinster, the keeper of other people's keys, carrier of enormous handbags and more secrets than a handbag could ever contain. Sublime in her kindness, embarrassing in her excess. Pulsating with unheard wisdom, booming with her big voice. Don't cry, said Mab, please don't cry. Big girls don't.

Isabel woke into a morning of sweet light, hazy with mist, the kind of day when she could imagine she was on the edge of the sea. There was a fireplace in each of the bedrooms, chimneys long since blocked off, leaving the mantelpieces for decoration. For a moment she thought she was back in Mab's cottage, expected to see the rows of Mab's ornaments. Cups, figurines, bottles and shells, things gleaned from beaches and junk shops for pence, ugly things, curios and objects of beauty all mixed in together. Mab liked Bristol blue: there were vases and jugs in that pure colour all over her house, the only things which Serena did not scorn. They had come to Serena when Mab died, but Isabel could not remember where they were or if they still existed. It was a minor puzzle for a fine and silent morning, something to be attended to later. In the distance, carried on the stillness, there was the rare sound of church bells, tolling for life with doleful joy.

Sundays had little significance, but Isabel had a sudden sentimental longing for the sort of church Mab had favoured along with a token belief in Christian doctrine as a sort of insurance policy. "You never know, my dear. . . it *might* be true. Even if it does make good people better and bad people worse. Try it: you can always spit it out later." Mab's true belief had been of the pantheistic kind; ashes to ashes, she said, with the laughing rider that when she died she might become what she had never been in life, a flower.

Downstairs Isabel passed the telephone that never rang, and the dining room, where the window had been flung open. She pulled on a jacket and stepped out into the milk of morning, disorientated by the diffuse light which made her vow to clean the windows. How far she had come to accept this solitude, even while fearing it and filling it with tasks. Halfway down the track towards church, she began humming. Hymn tunes remain stuck inside the head like a virus in the body, Mab maintained; always ready to reinfect with enthusiasm. Towards the end of the track Isabel thought of Mab's grave, detoured into the cemetery out of curiosity rather than guilt. Years since she had been here; so many she could hardly remember where it was; years since Serena had mentioned either her sister or her husband, buried next door to each other for no other reason than the existence of a space.

Was that all? Isabel wondered. Father and sister-in-law were firm friends. Or did her handsome father merely owe Mab a debt of gratitude for all the care she had taken of his children while he and Serena swanned abroad and Mab scooped up little Isabel and stout Robert from their various school gates at the end of term, embarrassing them in the process because her car was always so old and her voice so loud? What a snobby little bitch I must have been, Isabel thought, but I learned a certain lack of inhibition from Mab. She was the one who told me sex was not that important, only what it produced. Get on with it, if I were you, Mab advised, proffering contraceptive prescriptions: get rid of the mystery.

Edward Burley's grave was pristine, the plinth filled with weeded gravel and the headstone free of mud. There was a miniature shrub at each end and the whole thing looked as if it had been dusted. Mab's grave was a mess by contrast, a flat piece of dew-damp hayfield with the parameters of the grave itself scarcely defined, and some shocking dandelions crowding the stonemason's record of when she had lived and died. The disparity between the graves made Isabel feel Mab had been insulted.

Cleaning things had become automatic in her life. Becoming a housekeeper made Isabel mop and polish with a certain relish, as one of few activities which gave her any sense of achievement, gave framework to the day. It was natural to kneel and tackle Mab's grave with bare, cold hands, scratching at the weeds like a hen, pulling up the grass, patting the soil until at last the thing looked gravelike, identifiable as a small and decent monument. The church bells had ceased while Isabel worked, immune to the sound of cars which heralded the arrival of the congregation and the silence that followed as the church swallowed them up. Finally Isabel regarded the grave critically. She doubted if unsentimental Mab would have ever demanded this task of her. She would have touched her niece on the shoulder and reminded her that the spirit had fled.

Mabel, mentor, teacher and useful person, long dead, would have wanted her to go to church instead of wasting time, simply because it was more helpful to belong to a community than not, and because, once in a while, it was perfectly splendid to belt out a hymn without having to worry about the fact you really couldn't sing at all. Mab would have marched in there while Isabel, approaching the kind of edifice she had always taken for granted as offering something to others, felt a certain shyness. It was not the presence of God that deterred her, only the presence of people.

The porch was warm sandstone with a stone seat set into the walls on either side. The door was heavy oak, with a round, iron handle, cold to the touch and clumsy to work. The ring operated a noisy latch which rose and fell with a resounding clatter, announcing the latecomer like a pistol shot. Isabel stumbled towards the smell of humanity. The congregation were at the stage of prayer, bent forward with knees on tapestry footstools made by people like Mab, all of them following the invitation of the vicar to examine their consciences before the next hymn. They were open to distraction. Two dozen heads, some with hats, swivelled in her direction and in one second she saw herself as she imagined they would see her. Stuck in a shaft of sunlight, wearing jeans, boots, black jacket streaked with dirt like her face and hands. At best, a dreamer, at worst, the madwoman's daughter. Half of the faces turned back: the other half continued to stare in shuffling silence. Someone coughed, a prayer book was dropped, then silence resumed. Isabel ran.

They reminded her of something, these eyes staring out of darkness: resurrected the most abiding of all adolescent memories, which had nothing to do with church, and everything to do with rejection. The association was only warmth, dim light and all those eyes. She could see herself, those years before, frequenting the disco she had held semi-sacred in her teens, far more sacred than church had ever been. Rolling into town, feeling blue because Andrew Cornell never phoned back and he was the last of an impressive succession of boys and men who seemed to dump her. Well, three at least in the last year alone. What did it take to hold on to one? Brains? A better job than her unambitious role of secretary? Should she have been what Mab called a blue-stocking? She had not known. Mother was distant, Mab on her downward spiral, the house in mourning and all she had to cling to was her own selfish energy and what she had assumed was considerable popularity. A gaggle of local friends, daughters and sons from the better end of town, home from university, drifting as she drifted, liking her, greeting her with whoops of welcome in the normal run of events, but not on that day. The disco was somewhere to go for the unemancipated young. Isabel, dressed up in defiance of gloom, the way Mab encouraged, standing at the door in clothes that sparkled, meeting first the darkness and then the hostile silence, seen by them all, unable to see herself.

Until Doc Reilly's son swaggered to the front and the music stopped. "Get lost, Isabel Burley. We don't want you here."

He was childish, pompous, and his words stung. Girlfriends, busy with drinks, hiding their expressions with curtains of hair; other faces either pitying or enjoying scorn. Isabel grinning, sticking one hip forward, striking a pose in her tight skirt, making a joke of it.

"What's the matter? I got the plague, or something?"

"Fuck off, Isabel. Just fuck off."

No one had ever given a reason for this banishment. The defection of friends had been more hurtful than the death of near relatives, more corrosive to adolescent vanity. People dying was not her fault, but the public loathing of her contemporaries was the petty indictment which sent her out into the wider world soon after, with Serena's fervent blessing and Mab's money. And she still did not know why.

So what? A long time ago. Perhaps one of her boyfriends had been jealous; she was free with favours. Perhaps one of the girls had spread rumours with all the moral outrage of the young. From the distance of a dozen years, she could see how old-fashioned and parochial they had been, how insignificant her own offence might have been, although the wound felt mortal at the time and still ached when she probed it. Too late to wonder now. The road leading to the house was dry underfoot: lonely in a friendly way, receptive to her own voice repeating, I must not be silly, I must not be silly, although it was far from silly to be wary of the scrutiny of crowds. People and piranha fish have much in common, said Mab.

A white van approached her from the direction of the house, moving slowly to avoid the potholes, as if the van were brand new instead of old, dented and dirty. She stood back into the field to let it pass, unalarmed by its presence. Walkers with dogs used this road, people took wrong turnings. The man behind the wheel acknowledged her presence with a slight ducking of a grey head, a smile and a wave. They bowed to one another with Sunday-morning courtesy, which Isabel, fresh from an abortive visit to church, felt she deserved as an alternative form of blessing.

"Tea?" Serena suggested in a voice like a stage butler, a voice straining above the sound of music from her radio. "Coffee? Whisky? Brandy?" She beamed with self-approval. There were a dozen cups and saucers on the kitchen table, a trail of crumbs from the biscuit tin. Serena looked thoroughly stimulated by the morning's events. Best china from the dining room. Two cups broken. There was a smell of cigarette smoke.

"Been entertaining?" Isabel asked. "Who was here, sweetheart? Children?"

She was alarmed, but not dismayed, thought of the courtesy of the man in the van. Serena smirked. She was oddly dressed, a regular phenomenon which seemed especially strange in a woman once so particular about clothes, but, like the preference for plastic flowers, not without a logic. Clothing in layers, as if she intended to cope with any eventuality the day might offer by shedding and re-arranging an array of garments that could take her from Arctic to fireside. Lace-up shoes with little heels over thick, turquoise stockings, a petticoat hanging slightly below a russet corduroy skirt, a T-shirt evident below a black silk blouse, a scarf round her head, a maroon blazer and the whole ensemble finished by a light cape slung round her shoulders. Isabel had grown used to it in the same way she had grown used to a number of habits, learning as she went along to discern the difference between what was important and what was not. Clothes were not; love was.

"Who was here?" she repeated, wondering who would want to be here. Andrew perhaps. Wondering at the same time if her complete acclimatization to solitude and half conversation meant she would become unfit for anything else. Serena's skittering across the floor in a pretence of being busy exaggerated a certain shifty demeanour.

"Very nice men," she volunteered, distinctly. "They were lost. I showed them round. Made coffee. Couldn't find the brandy."

"What men? What did they want?"

A saucer crashed to the floor. Isabel gazed at it without interest. Little shivers of blue, red, gold leaf, ready to be crunched on the cold floor. What had happened to Mab's Bristol blue? Robert would roar with outrage to see any form of destruction, even the careless kind, and the thought was not unpleasant. Two weeks and not a word: she could phone him this evening and tell him Mother was playing hoopla with antique crockery, tearing up first editions, playing Houdini with the silver . . . but then, what silver? Kings silver laid out in rows in a dining-room drawer once. Not any more. Who cared? She didn't, much, except about Mab's Bristol blue.

"Were they nice men, Mummy?"

She bent to pick up the saucer as if indeed it did not matter. What else was missing?

"None of your business," Serena growled. "They were friends of mine. Friends of George."

"George doesn't have any friends."

"Oh, yes he does. They've got a van." Serena's face took on a wistful look.

"Such nice, big men," she said. "They danced with me."

"Mother!" Isabel shouted over the din of music. "Mother!

What did you do with all those blue things that Mab gave you?"

"What things? What, what, what?" Then she leaned forward, bent over the table until her pale eyes, lit with concern, wavered within inches of Isabel's own. She raised a hand as if to stroke, let it fall, shook her head.

"Why are you so silly, darling? So silly."

There was no such thing as absolution.

Do you love me, Mother? Mab did. And I often thought she was silly too.

"God rest ye, merry gentlemen . . ." His fingers drummed out the tune on the steering wheel.

"Aw, shut up, Dick, will you? It's nowhere near Christmas."

"Look at them all. Cunts. Don't fancy any of them."

Dick was the driver of the van. They sat three abreast, with Derek squashed in the middle and Bob on the passenger side, each looking through the dirty windscreen while they waited for the cars blocking the end of the drive to disperse. The congregation was slow to move.

"I never could fancy anything wearing a hat," Bob grumbled. He was grateful that Derek blocked him from proximity to Dick, because Dick smelled slightly. Bodily fluids shown insufficient water: dead meat. "And all those mothers are the same shape."

So they were, like tulip bulbs in coats, chatting by car doors in cheerful voices, full of virtue. A good congregation for the day, drawn by the age of the church building. The service had more meaning if they had to make a special expedition to reach it: the modern churches in town, with their lack of adornment and tradition, were less popular despite access from so many more doorsteps. The vicar here had a nice way of reminding his parishioners that God was still on their side whatever the evils of their society. The church had style and a noisy choir. Also the prettiest graveyard where all the agnostics wanted to be buried and the vicar did not mind that either.

"Do you suppose he gets a bonus for every person he pulls inside on Sundays?" Dick queried, looking at a portly figure in a cassock scurrying towards a Ford Fiesta. "Like Dan does at the bingo place?" Dan was another itinerant from the hostel, not party to this enterprise.

"I doubt it," said Dick. "His wife looks like a baked potato." Then he began to giggle. The giggle smothered itself into a series of snorts as Dick put the van into gear and moved off sharply, making all three bump back against the hard seats. Bob winced.

"Didn't we do well, though?" Derek crowed through his laughter. "I can't believe it. She invites us in, shows us round, turns on the music. Makes tea in the best china . . ."

"China's not worth much," Bob grunted, "unless it's really special and you get a whole set of it."

"Gives us the guided tour! All you have to do is play with her."

"Whose car is in the garage, is what I want to know," said Bob. "And who was that girl in the drive?"

"George never mentioned anyone else. Only his old princess."

"Look, Derek, we've seen other people going up there. She ain't all alone all the time."

"No one permanent. Stands to reason the old dear has some help, doesn't it?"

"Of course. So she should."

There was muttered agreement, as if it were abhorrent she should not. Moral outrage at the thought of her being on her own. Disgraceful. Derek lied with fluent ease, not wanting to put them off. He had been persuading them into this for weeks.

"Nothing we can't cope with. So? When?"

Silence. A grunting of gears as the van whined uphill, protesting an unhealthy engine. Dick it was with the cash-paying job of driving vans for the abattoir. He had access by night to bigger, better wagons than this.

"What's it all worth then, Bob?"

Bob, with his bent back and uncertain future, knew values better than anyone after years in the trade hanging around John Cornell. Derek was learning fast.

"Depends on where we take it. Coupla blokes in Leicester would give us twelve thou."

"It's worth much more than that!" Derek yelped.

" 'Course it is. But you have to sell cheap." The contempt in his voice was apparent. What a pair of wankers. Bob had done this kind of thing before often enough, and had never been less sure of his companions. Derek giggled again: he was a petty thief and a queer, despicable on both counts. Dick had plenty of muscle, access to vehicles and those were his only virtues, Bob thought uneasily.

This was a rum way to augment dole payments, but then John Cornell wasn't going to give him a pension and would not pay him when he was sick, although his son had been round with money out of his own pocket, called each week. That made Bob uncomfortable, but the discomfort was like the pain in his lumbar region, intermittent, variable, better than it had been the day before. Dulled by contempt for his companions, who acted like cinematic villains planning a farcical murder. Pain also dulled the planning stage. It could not compete with the fact that the contents of the living rooms of that house would fetch three times what he had quoted, although two-thirds of that would belong to middlemen. Four thousand each if they were lucky, not a fortune but already organized and relatively risk free. Bit of a scam, taking stuff from someone who would never be able to describe you. If they did not rob her someone worse would, and the gypsy in him did not distinguish between a lot and a little. The big time was for others.

"Why did you tell her we were George's friends?"

"There's no harm getting George in trouble. I wonder what she sees in him? His body, I expect. She made us extra welcome, didn't she?"

"She might remember what you said," Dick said.

"No, she won't. She won't remember fuck all. She talks jumbo. Get a move on, Dick: he passes this way about now. Got eyes in the back of his head, Derek says."

"You've got a big mouth. Don't know how you feed it."

Dick put the van into high gear. Bob shook his head. The way they went on, you would think they were bank robbers planning a heist, not a bunch of men down on their luck. Such a palaver, and far too much chat.

"Soon," he said. "Before the competition arrives."

Which it would. He could scent houses like that, marked for plunder.

George had always considered that men talked too much, as if there was anything worth saying. He adored the sensation of silence so profound it became a buzzing in the ears, filling out the vacuum of the skull until becoming deliciously oppressive. He did not use silence to dream or fantasize: he simply dwelt in it and could not remember afterwards what he had thought in his soundless cave with nothing but the hum, or why he had enjoyed the interlude. Silence of that kind was rare: churches with open doors and dim interiors, offering this kind of reward, were rarer still. George had found the church at the bottom of Serena's track on his earlier wanderings. The door had been shut.

He compromised. The countryside was not as quiet as the grave; there was a motorway at the bottom of the valley, things moving in the undergrowth, the panting of the dog and the rasp of his breath in his own ears, eugh, eugh, as he marched uphill with his arms swinging so as not to break step and slow down into a stroll, which did nothing for his muscle tone at all. Sometimes the glory of the day was such he accelerated into a run, but he ran without grace and it was better to march. Enjoy the semi-silence, knowing that this contentment was the plateau from which he could be propelled, once in a while, into a thirty-second moment of being happy. He coughed. His chest hurt.

George kept his own timetable. Which they, meaning the rest of the hostel, knew about vaguely in the restless fashion of a place where people talked and shouted and screamed and whispered and conspired all the time, as if making up for the noise in the outside world from which they were alienated. We are not wicked men, he had once told Derek, simply lost.

He stepped inside the kitchen, awkwardly aware that he did so at more or less the same time every day, although refusing to admit it, his face glowing with perspiration. Today, silence had been evasive. Too many other people out walking with a cacophony of dogs and greetings. Serena welcomed him when he collected Petal by screaming at him about fireworks and where had he been, he should have been there. George had felt supplanted. Four p.m., as usual, and he hated his own predictability, his readiness to tend the fires, mop the quarry-tiled floor if it were not already done, sit and chatter to Serena if Isabel was not around. Which she was. Sorting out the top cupboards in the kitchen — the ones that almost met the high ceiling and could not be reached without standing on a chair — reorganizing, cleaning, what she did every day to make her useless improvements, irritating and pointless. Looking at her stretched on tiptoe, George felt a pang of envy which was oddly like desire. She had no bum on her: the black-clad legs went on for ever and he realized for the first time why men would find this almost childlike womanhood compelling. He told himself he was admiring the strength of those legs and the way she could twist and bend while his own solid trunk could never manage such a variety of movement. He had endurance: his body could move mountains, while hers could twist like a snake.

"George, can you grab these before I drop them?"

She could turn right round on herself, so her feet pointed one way and her head another, handing down to him a red vase and an old condiment set covered in dust, the sort of thing cupboards tended to contain. Items too good to discard but without current use, hidden from view and ready to be retrieved in a spring clean, exclaimed over and finally put back into obscurity. A little like some of the items Serena had given him and he had sold. Derek had guided his hand and knew about those things. George refused to think about that.

"Thanks."

The kitchen table was half covered with similar detritus. Isabel jumped lightly off the chair and brushed her hands down her legs. George decided he quite liked women to look like this, slightly dirty and dishevelled and doing something useful:

dressed in their best was another matter. His own determined reaction against liking Isabel was becoming definitely rearguard, until she opened her mouth.

"Some men who said they were friends of yours called on Ma this morning. Or so she says. Do you know who they were?"

His heart plummeted like a stone into water, ripples of ice-cold alarm extending to the fingertips that clutched the vase and then put it down with exaggerated care. He turned his back on her question, unable for once to sustain a split-second silence, moving away and turning on both taps at the sink to wash his hands aggressively.

"Oh, I don't think so, Miss."

The sound of Serena's radio came from somewhere, echoing. George looked into the garden, longing for interruption.

"Well, that's what she said they said. Where do you live, George?"

"In town," he babbled. "Got a bedsit. Used to look after my mother, see? Used to work at the factory, got laid off. Don't know many people, don't want to. I like my own company, see?"

"Have you got a phone number there, George? Just in case?"

"No, I haven't. Just in case of what?"

"In case your friends come back."

"They weren't friends of mine, I told you."

There was not a word of a lie in that. She was looking at him curiously, debating how far to push. Serena could not live without George. They needed George. She could not afford to irritate him.

"I saw them on the track. Three men in a white van," she added conversationally. "Very dirty. I could have written my name on it."

George laughed. It came out like a yelp. The dog nuzzled

his hip and he wondered if she had bothered to bark at the strangers. Probably not.

"I certainly don't know anyone with a dirty van," he stated more clearly. "I wonder what they wanted?"

"They were lost."

"Oh. Well, you can't leave her alone for long, I suppose. She'll always let people in, you know, always did. Comes from being so friendly. There's no telling her; I've tried that many times I can't count. Tell them to come back at four, when I'm here, I've said to her, but she won't. She's cunning, you know."

He could hardly believe his own words. Here he was, on the brink of criticizing his princess, entering into a kind of conspiracy with Isabel and all because he could not say these men are not friends of mine, but they may well be your enemies and I have led them here. Could not say, look, there's a simple explanation: I live alongside cons in a hostel for ex-cons, being a con myself, and you would banish me from this place if you had any inkling.

Isabel sighed and smiled. He almost smiled back.

"Don't I know she's cunning? Did she tell you she ate the soap?"

The sound of Serena's radio, swinging from her hand, moved nearer the kitchen and George knew the meaning of reprieve. He forced back into being all the former detestation for Isabel Burley. Nothing had been quite right since she arrived. He had not let intruders in here, she had. Her letters. Her presence. Her bloody stupid kindness. And all those surplus words.

Here we are again, Serena Burley said to the frayed and frantic patterns on her drawing-room sofa. *Wouldn't I just respect God if only he would concede he was an idiot. Like I am.*

She was in love with those firework flames. Things, spitting into the air with all that sound and fury, raining down blessings and hidden messages. She had loved them to pieces, willed them to go on and on delighting her. And she knew that the witching hours grew briefer and less sure, because only an old mad fool would stand here in the dark and cold, craning her neck upwards in the hope that the fires would all start again, or leave a permanent imprint of themselves on the sky. They had blinded her. She wanted them back, missed them and hated them for what they did to her. Reminded her of what it was like to feel transfixed with wonder, taken her eye away from the main chance. Made her want to live. She should have swallowed one of those rockets and have done with it. Eating soap did not work.

Serena hit her shin and recognized the possibility of a bruise. The kitchen was a detestable place and she resented the fact that she seemed destined to spend so much time in here. Mab was the person for kitchens, making jam and other disgusting concoctions. Madame Burley, sometimes known as memsahib, preferred to be a lily of the field: they sowed not, neither did they spin, and they never fucking cooked.

Serena made her words in the stainless-steel draining board, presently filmed with cleaning fluid. *I have changed my mind about Isabel,* she wrote. *She is secretive and devious. Without quite knowing the whys and wherefores of what she does, she has sanitized this place. That's what she does all day, removing implements like knives and scissors to the nether regions of shelves where I cannot reach.*

Serena could not work out if Isabel behaved thus on account of reading all her own messages about wanting to die. She doubted it. The clearest of messages left on windows and tables and paper were cleaned away with daily savagery. Serena stamped her foot. She could not kill herself with a fork; she had not got the strength. She would never die of normal cold. She was far too hardy.

She put her head under the cold tap and found it a nasty experience. The darling daughter lacked insight. She was supposed to give purpose, not take it away. She had the means. Once or twice the child had flown at her father, flown at Mab and knocked a tooth out. Mab was patient, gloating about what the child had in her. Isabel flies at people and impales herself on them, Serena told the dog. Like a moth with a light.

The draining board was splashed and the words were gone again. Supposing darling Isabel could be made to detest her mother as much as her mother loathed herself? There was always the chance she would indulge in a sort of lethal lashing-out. Then she would have to go, leaving Serena with darling George and a wider range of choices, unless Serena was dead already. This was all too complicated for mere words. Serena decided she preferred the idea of being able to orchestrate her own demise.

There were grazes on her knees from where she had fallen over in worship of the Catherine wheels. Time to go back to bed with a saucer of milk and a nice strong man. Fading away like the wallpaper.

Moving slowly, swearing softly, kissing the unloved things goodbye.

Chapter Seven

SEVEN WEEKS. Home, sweet home and no one watching.

"Dear Joe," Isabel wrote in a letter that would not contain a single exclamation mark, covering a few sheets of paper she would probably never send. The fire spluttered safely behind a guard. Serena liked to sit close in the evening, crowding it, resentfully, otherwise quiet and preoccupied. The television in the corner muttered, creating a kind of absent conversation. A man ran across the screen waving a gun, his mouth yelling an order.

"I think this was my vision of home," Isabel continued. "A fireside in winter and the thought of not having to leave it and go out in the cold. Sitting by the side of someone comfortable. She's being very good . . ." Isabel paused. Joe would not want to know this. His notion of home would be warm bed, food, and bugger the fires. Never mind what he might want to know: she was uncomfortably aware that he would have no curiosity about her life at all. She wrote to put things into words, making a letter out of the words was merely an excuse for writing them and it seemed timely to write. To make something of the time.

"We are strange here, Joe, and yes, sometimes comfortable, but not often. I can hear people asking, what do they do all day, the way I used to wonder what mothers did when their babies slept all the time. They don't, Joe, not old babies either, and you can't have conversations with them or expect reasonable conduct . . . You can't even tell them about the dangers they face. (I wish she was not so secretive about the post, hiding the bills.) And the difference with an old baby is that you can't shout or slap, either. I learned the basic rules about don't run in the road from my Aunty Mab, because I was afraid of her. I can't make my mother afraid; I should hate it. And I wasn't ever afraid of her; it was more complicated than that. I was so proud of her. She made everyone else's mother look so drab and fat while she was exotic, did exotic things, lived in exotic places, married an exotic kind of man . . . which may be why I'm almost content to hole up with her like this, because I don't quite like the idea of anyone else seeing her in a state which is neither proud nor anything like the way she was. Does that make sense?"

Serena coughed loudly, a stagey kind of cough, not exactly a plea for attention, but a preliminary. Isabel had the vision, coming from nowhere, of Mother removing the fireguard and sitting on the coal, squatting on the flames without any sensation of pleasure or pain. Serena's glasses remained dirty, despite a daily wash. She preferred them that way.

"I only say strange," Isabel scribbled, "because it is strange to be around someone all the time and not really talk in anything but a kind of baby language. It alters my vision on everything. Did I tell you about taking her to the pub? She wanted chips again, but when she got them, she put half in the top pocket of the man at the next table and smeared him with gravy. Affection, of course, but we won't be welcome back. But I won't let go, Joe, because she loves me, and I need to be loved."

That sounded pathetic, so she crossed it out. There was another cough. Serena was transfixed by the TV. She raised her hand, pointed two level fingers at the man still running across the urban landscape with his gun and wide open mouth, and shot him, twice.

"Then there's George, who comes and goes. I don't know who he is, where he comes from, I don't know anything except for the fact he turns up. We've never questioned George, you know: not even Robert demanded his credentials, because he is so useful. Too late now. Even though Robert does nothing, I'm afraid to ask. Two reasons, I suppose. I want to make her better all by myself, with no one else getting the credit. I want to be able to endure it, and be proud of what I've done. And I don't want people seeing in the windows. Looking at her like something from the zoo."

Serena sat back in her chair, obviously satisfied. She knitted her fingers together and nodded at the screen. The dirty spectacles dropped to the end of her nose.

"He's dead," she yelled. "That one there. Dead. Shot himself. What a good thing."

Doc Reilly had given Isabel sleeping pills. He had not specified who should take them.

"As long as she loves me," Isabel wrote, "as long as she loves me, I can do this. Only I'm beginning to see things which are not here. Perhaps they never were. Perhaps I need glasses."

Robert Burley was not without conscience. That was the way he would have stated his ambivalent state of mind apropos his mother, although no one asked him to state anything except a case. Part of the relative ease of his conscience came first from the fact that his mother had tried to crush his daughter, and although he did not believe this was anything other than clumsiness, the lack of malice aforethought did not quite mitigate the crime. Second was the fact that Isabel deserved the burden of looking after her mother because she had led such a feckless life to date. The third factor was that he knew, by comparison with some of his clients, how lucky Serena Burley really was. She had a house to live in, didn't she? A pension and a modicum of health, which was a damn sight more than a lot of other little old ladies.

At the same time he could not quite leave things as they were. He blustered by phone to social workers, without realizing that this long-distance intervention, not discussed with Isabel, created an animus against her for instigating a nuisance and against himself for hectoring. Discussions were not helped by the fact that Robert no longer really knew what he wanted for his mother. An element of control without effort, a salve to his conscience, one social worker surmised. They quite understood why his mother could not stay with him, nor he with his mother. Indeed they were astonished that he should go to such lengths to explain it when no explanation had been requested. Alzheimer's and the distance between parents and children were both diseases of contemporary life, unlikely to go away. The psychiatric social worker could call upon Mrs Burley and assess the situation, certainly: so could the consultant psychiatrist: indeed, one had done so, at his behest, both before the fire and immediately afterwards, did he not remember? Verdict: she suffered from an affliction of the mind, but could still maintain an independent life with existing support. Now there was a voluntary daughter in residence, there was even less reason to act and besides, what could they do?

"Mental health orders are for extreme cases of danger. Is she still able to pay her bills? Does she eat and wash? Is she incontinent?"

"Yes, with help. Yes, yes and no, I don't think so."

"You could try and persuade her to come and live in a home nearer yourself . . ."

"Get her off your patch, you mean!" he yelled, furious at the dulcet patience of the tones.

"Mr Burley, I've got a call coming through on the other line."

Activity was better than inactivity, so Robert was standing in the foyer of a residential home three miles from where he lived, unaccountably nervous. It was all very well to fear death, that was as logical as a dread of pain, but fear of old age had never occurred to him before. Insofar as he considered his own, which was not often, he had envisaged himself as a senior states-man with pipe and slippers, adviser to the neighbourhood, heeded by the young and accorded respect for his wisdom, dying conveniently, as his father had done, before serious infir-mity began, his death the object of grief and obeisance to his memory. Indignity did not feature in any of these visions.

"And this is the lounge, Mr Burley. We have bingo on Wednesdays, the chiropodist once a week, a hairdresser Tues-days and karaoke on Saturdays. Plenty to do."

He wanted to say he could not foresee the day when the biggest dose of memory loss would make his mother enjoy bingo or the company of the other women who sat in their chairs lining the walls of the lounge like so many puppets pay-ing disinterested homage to the huge television in the corner. These were images familiar enough to save him from showing his shock, but the view was still dispiriting. These were the sentient beings who watched the screen in the way his baby would watch a moving, glistening object. The thought of kara-oke was appalling.

"And these are the rooms. Some people like to share..."

Dens with single beds and the overpowering presence of the floral. Rose-flavoured air-freshener, chintz bedspreads, everything Serena had despised. Just as she would the antiseptic corridors of polished linoleum, the open doors to bathrooms with pulleys, lavatories with handles set into the walls and, in the distance, the sound of someone howling.

The mentally infirm, the lady told him, live at the back.

She had a face shining with kindness, free of hypocrisy. The proximity of a good heart made him realize that he had not got one.

The overpowering presence of wickedness in the world was not what oppressed him on his way home, but the existence of such reservoirs of kindness with which he could not compete. Saints were so much more irritating than sinners. Especially when they informed him that as long as his mother's wounds were bloodless, the state would bleed her dry. Parents of his mother's generation owed it to their inheritors to die young. And who would look after him when he was old?

The sight of Aunt Mab's Bristol blue glassware, safe inside the cabinet which housed it along with Serena's silverware and her pieces of porcelain which he did not really like, hardly filled him with satisfaction, but not with guilt either. Isabel had not noticed, which was her own fault. Pragmatism had dictated the removal of various items on past visits. One day he would give to his daughter those objects Serena no longer knew she possessed, and the love of daughter for parent was surely more enduring than that of son. After more introspection, self-justification and righteous anger, Robert decided to leave things as they were.

"You were very kind to bring the fireworks," Isabel said. "Very kind. I haven't seen her so happy in ages."

Andrew had a good telephone voice, echoing the authority of the auctioneer, deep, calm, reassuring. She had liked the smell of his tweedy shoulder when she had cried into it, even though she had withdrawn, wiped her eyes, become a hostess. Whatever it was her mother had told her, with varying degrees of emphasis, about never being a nuisance to men, the dictate had remained as solid as an undeniable memory, like the imprint of men's bodies. They existed to be pleased, but in Isabel's present role the necessity of being pleasant all the time had faded away and she did not have either the energy or the inclination to flatter Andrew Cornell. She owed him nothing. He was not her kind of man, since Isabel's kind of men were rarely so undemanding, and he was not a priority. Besides, after weeks of isolation with her mother and taciturn George, she felt she had lost her knack with men, whatever the knack had been.

"I thought you might like to go out for a meal," he was suggesting. The sound of the phone was so unfamiliar during the day, it had startled her. Serena hovered near, alive with curiosity.

"Where is there to go?" Isabel realized she sounded ungracious.

He chuckled. "You're out of date with local sophistications. Chinese, Italian, you name it, we do it."

"I'm not sure about leaving Mother." The longing must have sounded in her voice, replete with memory of Serena's capacity for sabotage. Broken crockery. Cat's pawmarks in the trifle. Soap down the gullet. Torn books and frantic letters. That was what she did all day: she repaired wreckage and found it impossible to explain.

He hesitated. "Batten down the hatches. She'll be all right.

Promise her next time we'll take her too. You've got to get out, Isabel."

"Yes I have."

"Where would you like to go? What would you like to do?"

Deferential questions of this kind always irritated her. If a man issues an invitation, he should also make the plan.

"Wherever you like. I don't know. Somewhere nice." Nice: another word despised by Mab. Pleasant then, a break, a change.

Andrew put down the phone in the auction-room office feeling slightly deflated. He weaved his way across to where his father sat with Doc Reilly, occupying adjacent corners of a large table of scrubbed pine, each nursing a cup of coffee in front of a shared ashtray.

"Anyway," Doc Reilly was saying. "I've told the police it's only a matter of time before she gets burgled, so would they take the patrol out there at night? He says resources are stretched, old son, what with Christmas round the corner. Anyway, most of the young lads, including his own, don't even know where that house is. Safety in obscurity. There ought to be a Latin phrase for it."

"Who?" said Andrew.

"Old mother Burley. The same old sweetheart you were asking after earlier on. There's been kids up there, pinching things. Kids have grown-up brothers with bigger eyes. That dog of hers is as much use as a wet blanket. Scarcely wags its tail without wondering if it's still attached."

John Cornell nodded sagely, plucked a cigarette out of a packet and held it to the light, as if looking for a hallmark to prove that this one, at least, was good for his health.

"There's a man up there half the day, though. What's he called? George?"

"For what that's worth. Mustn't judge a man by his history."

"What's that supposed to mean?" Andrew asked sharply.

Doc turned a cunning eye on him. Andrew could detect the guarded glance of cynical compassion.

"It means he was in my surgery two weeks ago. Being brave about what looked to me like bronchitis. Gives the address of the hostel on the estate. You know it. Oh no, you probably don't, they won't be asking you in to value furniture, miserable dump. Sort of closet institution, where they put ex-convicts. To rehabilitate. What a joke. No wonder he likes going up to Mrs Burley's. Does all of us good to get out of the house, but it surely applies to some more than others."

"Where is this bloody place?" John Cornell lit the health-giving cigarette, shifted in his seat. The doctor recited an address. John Cornell nodded slowly, scratched his rump. Doc Reilly wagged his finger at Andrew.

"Don't you let on I told you that, will you? George loves dogs, so he must be all right. And the old lady loves George, even if society hasn't much time for him. Whatever else there is about him is none of our business, is it?"

"Unless he was a burglar himself."

Doc Reilly patted Andrew's shoulder with heavy-handed condescension. "Not as far as I know."

"You going courting, Andrew?" his father asked, still absorbed in his cigarette. "The fair Isabel again?"

"Chance would be a fine thing," Andrew smiled. He had learned never to rise to the bait with his father. Or keep secrets that could be held in evidence against himself later. "Thought I'd get her out of the house. Good for us all, like the Doc said. You should know."

"She's a nice young woman, that," said the doctor, watching

Andrew walking away whistling, trailing his fingers over the dusty furniture. "But what was she thinking of when she was eighteen, nineteen and twenty, John? Men. Nothing but men. We aren't worth it. They give us what we want and we call them tarts. Did you ever hear about those letters her aunty sent to her boyfriends? Or maybe it was her mother. I've never been sure."

John Cornell scratched his rump again, an irritating habit.

"Hostel for ex-cons on Acacia Drive? Do you know, I think when young Derek comes in this afternoon I might just tell him we don't need him any more. I don't believe in rehabilitation. Or leopards changing spots."

"Now, that isn't fair, John."

"Nothing's fair, Eamon. Look at it outside. Night already. That isn't fair, either."

The gang came across the fields about ten o'clock at night in a big three-ton truck, which Dick informed them, too late, he had never driven before. He was really the butcher's boy in disguise, used to delivering small parcels. He was also as high as a kite, nerves, grass or what, Bob neither knew or cared, as long as he did not let go of the wheel when smiling as constantly as he did. The sniggering unnerved Bob, but there was no smell of alcohol and the back of the lorry was clean, hosed down every day, Dick said. Bob had supplied a mattress from his back shed, which made the others laugh in unison from the moment they pulled away. What was so funny about a mattress? His other contributions were ropes, old sheets of the kind his incurious wife despised, blankets and other forms of protection for what they were about to steal. May the Lord have mercy on it, the way Dick drove and Derek, with his wicked little elbows extended like chicken wings, digging into their ribs, snorting with laughter although there was no joke except a wagon that behaved like a bucking mule resentful of the saddle. This was all going to go wrong: Bob knew it in his bones, jolted by the van, jarred by the company. He felt like a bride *en route* for a wedding ceremony she already regretted; all dressed up and nowhere to go. The back of this thing, still sweatily damp on account of the lack of warmth needed to make it dry, resembled a shambolic travelling bordello, equipped for a cheap sex maniac. It was only later he realized what had made the others laugh. The mattress was already stained; the bars against the side were designed for the safe carriage of meat. All it lacked was confetti for the takeaway bride of Dracula.

Halfway up the track from the church to the house, coming through a puddle of water, the engine stalled. That was the second time they should have turned back, but they did not. Within half an hour, the engine had dried out and on they went, still exactly like a wedding procession: slow, sure, late.

A clear night with a kindly moon and the promise of frost. There was another chance to turn by the gates of the house and leave. The near side of the van hit the lefthand pillar with a noise as loud as a scream. Dick reversed away, turned off the engine, waited. All conversation died. Then they went on.

I could get six years for a few hundred pounds, Bob muttered to himself: it don't compute. They coasted slowly down the slight incline to the back door, stopping far short of it. The house glared at them. The passenger door opened with a creak that felt like an injection straight into his spine, making him choke back a groan. They could have been a team of clowns waiting in the wings to perform to an audience already inclined to jeer. They moved towards the back door, one sniffing loudly, the other one hands in pockets, each hanging back, Dick swinging a hammer from the end of his torn sleeve. Then Derek, taller than usual in the cuban-heeled boots that gave him an extra inch height, overtook the other two and reached the door, tripped over something, swore softly, moved to the window on his right. They could see the mist of his breath against the glass in the light of his silly little pencil torch. Two things happened in quick succession. The outside light above the kitchen door sparked into life, as if it had been waiting for something to jolt a loose connection. It illuminated a ferret astride a bowl half filled with milk; the ferret turned and hissed. Next to it, spread over the step, lay a ginger cat, limbs extended in a parody of sinuous fireside stretching, frozen for all time. Definitely dead: you could tell from its peculiar immobility, the angle of the throat and the awful spread of the jaws.

Then the other lights, inside the house, came on. Derek at the window, standing lower than room height in a flower bed, found himself chest level with a naked woman. She had an arm outstretched, doing something with the curtain, which she yanked so it half covered her form and also made her impatient. One large bosom, as big as a melon, exaggerated by proximity and condensation, waggled with the effort. A half-drawn blind behind the curtain obscured her face. The pen torch dropped behind a clump of ragged dahlias. Derek staggered back, hypnotized by flesh so close he could have pressed his nose into her belly-button. When he turned, he saw Bob and Dick moving back towards the van. They were retreating uncertainly, away from the cat. The ferret followed, spitting. In terror Dick grunted and farted, flinging the hammer. It hit the ribs of the ferret with a tiny thud; there was a shriek of pain.

Derek threw himself against the bonnet, pushed like fury.

The wagon was moving as he clambered through the open door, remembering, foolishly, not to slam it, as if the noise of the engine were not already loud as they coasted back through the gates with accidental ease and a whining noise. Halfway across the road the brute stopped again and again Dick kicked it into life. The travelling bordello accelerated back in the same direction from which it had arrived, all of them shamed into silence as they lurched over holes in the track until they reached the main road. Turned left past the church; you could swear the dead in the churchyard winked, stuck two fingers out of their fucking gravestones, but that was what Bob said later. For the moment he was speechless.

Dick spoke first. "Who was it? Her with the curtain?"

"I dunno. Must've been someone."

"You're fucking right, someone. Old or young?" Bob had found his voice.

Derek faltered. "I dunno. Big on top. Big. She had a fork . . ."

The giggling began again, relieving them. Great snorts of giggles, hands between knees, nearly wetting themselves, so infectious the sound that Derek joined in.

"In her hand," he added. They were hysterical by now, utterly helpless. Dick, hugging the central white line, swerved to avoid a saloon car coming up fast on the deserted road. He had got the hang of the wagon, even felt grateful to it. Everything was outrageously funny. Bob roared, Derek giggled, Dick insisted they stop for a pee. In this camaraderie, against the backdrop of failure, suddenly brave again, they pretended that this had been the dummy run and planned the second attempt.

Maybe this was a second attempt. Maybe Andrew was treating her as man does woman, flirting without being obvious. Maybe he was simply as kind an individual as he seemed and was being nice to her. Whatever the reason for his actions, Isabel forgot to question, and since there was no reason to impress, failed to try, found herself relaxing. She was also starving for the kind of food she no longer saw: tagliatelle, green salad, the sort of meal it was a balm to eat, a million miles away from Mother's favourite fish and chips. Serena liked the food she had liked as a child; porridge, bread and butter, jelly and custard. Isabel tried to tell Andrew this, joking and gesturing between mouthfuls, gulping wine. He listened in a way men rarely listened, teased her about the sheer amount she consumed. It wasn't flirting, she decided; it was talking, about something and nothing, while on the other side of the small table his smile grew more attractive, his eyes browner and the grin she had remembered more endearing. On top of that, as well as zabaglione, she could see him persuading Serena to release her baby grandchild and watch fireworks. OK, he was a nice, unpretentious man with the dress sense of a grandad.

He saw something else. A beautiful, insecure woman with a comic propensity to pull faces and mimic voices. One who defied her intelligence, pushed it down like rubbish in a sack. Acted as she was expected to act until no one was watching, unsure of her authority or talent to amuse. Ready to trip over her feet and let someone ride roughshod over her too-thin body and too-unsatisfying life. All because of the chasm within. He did not know if his observations were right, but since he had done more observing of women than touching of them, watching them dance attendance on furniture, husbands, himself, he hoped his perceptions were accurate and despised himself for the sense of distance that encouraged him to make them. Before grace, after grace, eating food, digesting it, driving along in his car, he was always looking at people like a mild, uncritical voyeur. As if passion were something he had eradicated with the help of an inoculation. He ordered more coffee. Half a bottle out of two shared hardly counted in the drink-driving stakes: and she was steady as a rock as she moved through the place on the way to and from the ladies' loo, not a tremor. He was ashamed of observing that, too. He had a head for the stuff as good as this girl sitting opposite, laughing one minute, then looking at her watch.

"Cinderella time," she said. "Gotta go. My mother will turn me into a pumpkin."

"You give life, you take it away," he murmured, finding her coat.

She paused in the act of shrugging into it. "What do you mean?"

"That's what your mother will have done. If this goes on and on, that's exactly what she will have done. Taken your life in exchange for the preservation of hers."

"It doesn't matter." She was agitated, to the extent of pressing one arm into the wrong sleeve. Cold outside, winter, instead of autumn. She did not want to go home. Thought of breath on windows, a house where heating demanded labour and preparation, like all the tasks from slow dawn to early dusk. The constant watching, of her mother and herself. The hard-won patience, the constant reiteration to herself of how much, at last, her mother loved her.

"As long as you know," he said cheerfully. "I looked after Dad for years. I wish I'd done more with the time, that's all."

"Does he love you?"

Andrew considered the question with some surprise. "Yes, I suppose he does, after his fashion. Doesn't like me, though."

They had reached the car, clambered inside quickly because of the sudden cold and sat, waiting for the heater to melt the pattern of a delicate frost on the windscreen.

"Seems a pity to ruin it," Isabel said, watching moisture form out of crazy flowers. "Do you like me?"

"Yes, very much."

"Which is more important?" she demanded. "Liking or loving?" The car engine was quiet as the ice trickled away.

"Liking, in the long run. It means respect. Love doesn't always mean that."

"Oh."

The silence was not uncomfortable as they cruised away from the lights of the centre, through a suburb and then on to a road lit only by their headlights. He did not play music as they drove, for which Isabel was grateful. Serena's constant music had begun to eat at her nerves.

"I wonder if I've ever been liked, in that case," Isabel said thoughtfully. She thought in this warm car of Joe, and his heated demands, and his habit of never listening to a word she said.

"You may not have noticed being liked," Andrew suggested. "It isn't always easy to detect."

She had never counted the miles from town; six or seven; ten, fifteen minutes, longer with Mother, but always a journey from one extreme to another, a passage between alien lives. Joe would probably have refused to drive his fancy car up this track and be careless of damage the way Andrew was. Yes, she liked Andrew, even though she disliked making comparisons.

"I don't suppose I was very likeable at twenty, was I?"

He laughed, uncomfortably. "Does it matter? You were, as a matter of fact, and also entirely lovable. Until you took to writing obscene letters."

"What?"

They had turned through the gates, stopped by the back door.

"*What?*" she repeated. "Me?" There was less outrage in her voice than puzzlement, but she no longer wanted to sit beside him. She fumbled with the seat belt and slammed the door behind her. He followed, cursing himself.

Drawn curtains in the kitchen, porch light winking over the corpse of the ginger cat. Isabel thought it was sleeping. Even while knowing that no cat slept thus, still she bent to pick it up, then recoiled. There was a wound in the throat, spots of blood on the paving of the yard, a hammer lying a few feet away. She backed away, colliding with Andrew. He put his hand on the nape of her neck, where the hackles rose. She avoided his touch, sidestepped the cat with a shudder, put her own hand on the kitchen doorknob, turned it, watched the door yield.

"I locked the cat out," Isabel whispered, her face stricken with guilt. "And I locked Mother in."

Chapter Eight

*Y*OU DO NOT, SHOULD NOT, lock your mother indoors so that you can go out and play. Upstairs, listening for the stroke of midnight from the grandfather clock, Serena sat in the armchair in her room, conducting the orchestra in the overture to *My Fair Lady*. Her slippers were an unmatched pair: she extended one slim ankle and admired it. The bundle of post, which she carried around like a talisman, waiting for the miracle that would make it meaningful instead of merely important, sat at her feet, free from Isabel's interference. She made one foot join the other, turned both inwards so the toes met, and gazed at them with considerable satisfaction.

There was someone knocking at something somewhere. The music rose to a climax announcing the imminence of Act One.

Such a nice young man, standing in the doorway, dressed so unnecessarily in a winter coat. The music had reminded her obscurely of another form of dress, which bore no resemblance to his. He seemed to be looking for something; eyes everywhere, speaking pleasantly, half of him there and half of him not. A spasm of disappointment crossed her features since the man was not George, but he was still, quite definitely, male, so she smiled.

"Hallo, Mrs Burley. Remember me? I've come to see if you're all right."

His was a face she had seen before, although not one of those villainous ones with gun in hand which she shot with such regularity on the TV screen downstairs; this one was one of the nice guys she had applauded. A sort of prince, apart from his dull clothes. Far too many clothes on his frail frame. What a waste, when he needed no embellishment other than his boyish grin.

"Fireworks?" Andrew suggested, thinking she might remember him if given a reminder.

"Not at the moment," she said, wondering what it was he wanted. Her back felt stiff. All that reaching up over the kitchen curtain pole, where Isabel left the spare keys (what a silly place to leave anything), hoiking them out with the aid of a fork, getting down off the chair to open the door, had been activities that reminded her body of the existence of ribs. But it was imperative to resist being locked in, however kindly that had been done. The instinct to remedy such an unpardonable situation had occurred halfway through preparations for a bath. Windows and doors had no business being barred: no one could walk through walls, although this man had. He smiled as she smiled back.

"Mind if I look around?"

That, too, reminded her of a familiar phrase from somewhere else, and, in response to almost any set of words framed in familiar patterns and delivered quietly, Serena could usually dredge up some formulaic response. Her replies were often way off beam and, equally often, uncannily correct. She had what Doc Reilly called an excellent social armour. She could pass for a wise and articulate old crow, capable of appreciation, even while half of what she said was inspired guesswork.

She inclined her head graciously; winked. "You're welcome. Go ahead, son, why doncha?"

He opened her wardrobe door, appeared to admire the contents, looked behind the curtains. Looking for a stiff, she told herself. Stiff or stuff; Raymond Chandler on the page or a drugs raid on TV, same difference, same response.

"Are you looking for Stinker?" Serena asked.

"Stinker?"

"The rat." She laughed gaily. "He sometimes hides under the bed. He's a very naughty rat."

"I didn't know you had rats, Mrs Burley."

" 'Course not. Stinker eats them." Nice, this young man, but slow on the uptake. She was enjoying herself.

Andrew looked under the bed. There were signs of spasmodic dusting from each edge in, not quite reaching the centre space. Something was hanging down below the headboard at the pillow end. He shifted the whole mattress while she watched him in the way she might have watched a maid sent into a hotel room to arrange a complimentary bowl of flowers, giving him her full and indulgent attention. When he raised one end of the thing on her bed, she indulged that too, as an activity which seemed without purpose but nevertheless was conducted by someone who knew what he was doing. Even if she did not.

"Quite a collection of hardware, Mrs Burley. What's all this doing here?"

All this? All what? Her spectacles were in another place: she felt around for them. Two carving knives, a small saw and a twelve-inch length of barbed wire were displayed on the end of the bed. Serena's smile wavered.

"Mine," she said, falteringly. "I think."

Of course the bed was hers: why did he doubt it? She had no recollection of the things he held aloft, only a sense of sorrow that he might take them away.

He bent over by her chair, bringing his face level with her forehead, and took her hand inside his own calloused palm, a sensation she liked so much she tried to imprint it on her memory, along with other dreams of being touched and held by someone who was not waiting to let go, even though this man's hands were colder than hers. Fresh-air hands, whereas hers were ready for bed, made of paper and full of fragile warmth from sitting in the chair in nightie, slippers and winter coat while the bath water in the bath, long since forgotten, cooled. There was strong, wiry hair on the backs of his hands; he was more like a dog than a cat.

"Puss, puss," said Serena, stroking. "Where is the Stinker?"

"Did anyone else come in and see you this evening?"

She looked at him, eyebrows raised, as if the question were impertinent. Pausing in this fashion was guaranteed to make people repeat what they had said several times in quick succession, for as long as the inquisitory look demanded. Sometimes it triggered understanding; not always. Andrew followed the cue.

"Any more visitors, Mrs Burley?" he said, louder, and then repeated himself.

"People? You mean people?"

"Yes, people."

"No." She leaned forward, about to impart a secret. "They can't. People can't get in. Isabel. My girl Isabel. She scares them away. She won't even let me have my cat. She locks it out." Nodding wisely now. "She locks everything out." Her voice descended into a whisper. "I should look out if I were you. Isabel eats people."

For a moment Andrew wondered if that were true. The conversation, such as it was, had begun to exhaust him. It was similar to the effect of talking over a din, shouting to make oneself heard, receiving a coded response which demanded he shout louder. Perhaps Isabel was in the habit of scaring people away, for whatever purpose. The motives of others were ever mysterious, even if usually reducible to greed or fear. Or perhaps the erstwhile friends of this grand dame simply no longer had the stamina for little chats such as these. He was surprised to find he minded not being recognized as the provider of fireworks.

"I'll let you get to bed. Thanks for asking me in." She beamed in benediction, maintaining hold of his hand.

"Don't leave me with her," she said with sudden distinctness. "Kiss me good-night?"

He bestowed a kiss on her cheek, felt the hand that relinquished his own move round his neck, drawing him down, murmuring in his ear with sounds he associated with someone enjoying food: yummyummyum. Then, without quite believing the sensation at first, imagining some ghost, he felt her other hand creep between his legs, touching his corduroy-clad thigh, lightly at first, as if feeling the cloth. Then kneading and patting it, in a manner less suggestive of sexual invitation than of someone tickling and pulling the ears of a dog, which, in his case, had no idea how to respond. He stood upright, slowly, detached her hand with a smile and put it back into her lap. The music from her tape deck swelled into the First Act, and the plaintive voice of a street singer.

"Bollocks," she said, still smiling with wide-eyed innocence. "Fucking bollocks, is that it?"

He had finally released himself. Close, like that, she had smelled both sweet and sour and on his way downstairs, he wondered if the smell lingered on his coat.

The grandfather clock on the upstairs landing struck a gentle midnight, sweetly and hurriedly, as if getting through the duty while making apologies at the same time. Norwich-made, eighteenth-century, fairly valuable, Andrew noted on the way down. The knives and the saw were tucked under one arm, the barbed wire carried gingerly between finger and thumb. He wondered where she had found it. There was something particularly cruel about barbed wire: it had no value; it existed for nothing but the potential to harm.

When he and Isabel had come into the kitchen, they had known the non-existence of intruders from the sheer quality of the silence. The clock ticking with no need to turn its face to the wall, the dog lazy and docile, the drip of the tap, all clues to the lack of trespass and the sensation that the danger lay within. He and Isabel had looked through the downstairs rooms before he, at his own insistence, went alone to the upper landings. There was no real bravery in a search that could serve no purpose other than the confirmation of innocence. Isabel had resented him for it. By the time he came back, the cat lay outside where Isabel had left it for burial in the morning, with the respectful addition of a shroud fashioned from a tablecloth.

"Nothing," Andrew said, "but these."

She gazed, stupidly, at Serena's armoury, laid out next to the hammer. Then she glanced at Andrew's face. A sense of guilt made her skin glow pink. Serena purloined things all the time — scissors, forks, screwdrivers — they turned up on window ledges, in the fridge, in the bathroom, and in due course Isabel returned them to their own corners, pretending they had never gone. But she had never imagined there was a theme to this harmless kleptomania, other than a simple feature of her mother, busying herself ineffectually and then forgetting whatever it was she had been going to do. Sew a button on something; change a plug; everyday tasks with everyday reminders and no memory to achieve them. In better days Mother's contempt of domestic chores had not excluded pride in a level of self-sufficiency. She had needed to do everything for herself.

"Do you think she could have hurt the cat?"

Isabel thought of the ferret with the white teeth, then the hammer, shook her head. There was not enough coordination between hand and eye in her mother's slow movements to do such frightful damage, although there was still plenty of strength.

"Might she want to hurt herself?" Andrew asked, inexorably. Isabel felt the undertone of accusation in his voice, hinting at her own inefficiency; it made her clam up in defensive fury.

"I don't think so. But then I rarely know what she thinks. Do you want some coffee?" Without waiting for an answer, she began moving about the business of preparation, like a child sent out of a classroom, walking like a marionette. Andrew came close to her, touched her shoulder lightly.

"Stop it, Isabel. I'm not blaming you."

"Yes, you are."

"I wouldn't know how. Look, do you want me to stay? I think I should, even if it was a false alarm. Nobody's been in here, I'm sure of it. She must have found the keys to open the back door. Why she threw a hammer in the backyard, God only knows. Perhaps she's contemplating a new career in joinery and found the thing surplus to requirements?"

Isabel laughed. She looked a little like her mother when she laughed. Any sexual frisson between them engendered by the evening had disappeared. He could still feel Serena's hand, patting the warmth of his thigh, killing desire more effectively than any dead cat or full stomach. Andrew yawned, half naturally, half contrived.

"Get me some blankets for the sofa, would you? I'll freeze in there otherwise."

That was neatly done, she thought later. A considerate man. The kind who was gone before breakfast and so diplomatic he could assess the furniture of your soul and not show he found it lacking, the kind who could dispel fear with pragmatism and who always seemed to know better. Which did not mean that he could begin to understand the pressures and realities of her kind of existence: you had to live it to know it. Before Isabel had started this chapter of her life, she had been sick of other people always knowing better. She still was.

She brought him a duvet, glad of his presence in the house but not wanting him closer. Thanked him with grave politeness not designed to wound, and having exactly that effect.

"Oh, by the way," she said at the door. "Mother might wander during the night. She does, a bit. I never try to stop her."

Such a beautiful room. Estate agent's dream for the family with everything, including money. A house, which should have rumbled with laughter, rows, warmth and the presence of children, settled into silence so complete it made Andrew listen to the sound of his own breathing. An hour passed in sleepless contemplation that owed less to the effect of weak coffee than to the slow ebb of adrenalin. Words paraded through his mind like soldiers marching on display, up and down, down and up. Surely there was more than madness in this house: there was jealousy and hatred.

When he heard the echo of the grandfather clock announcing the second hour after midnight he got up and turned on lights for the sake of sanity, beat his arms across his chest for warmth, and sat at Serena's desk, which he opened without a tremor of guilt and no anticipation but to indulge his own curiosity.

It was tidy inside, pigeonholes stuffed with paper in apparent order, leaving a clear surface. "Dear Andrew," he recited in his mind. "Don't you know that Isabel Burley has sucked more cocks than you have had hot dinners, as well as doing it with her father? If you go on doing it with her you'll catch something nasty. Your balls will drop off into her mouth and she likes holding them, doesn't she?" Two paragraphs of this puerile prose had made him recoil in horror a dozen years before, as much for the recognition of Isabel's own fair hand in the construction of the writing as for the content. She had never been particularly clever with words: the letter had been a boast of achievements. You and who else, it said. John Reilly, Rick Murray, David Mason, Jim Partridge, a whole fucking football team. It might have been a child writing in the third person. It was as if she were not writing about herself, sticking in the rude words for effect, but it was more than enough to insult his own manhood, even though the description bore no real reflection of the somewhat shy nature of their own coupling. The shyness and inhibition were more his own than Isabel's, he had to admit, and that alone lent some veracity to the written word. Isabel had become, in his imagination, the writer of poison-pen letters, an unstable and unstoppable sexual fantasist who was not even articulate beyond four-letter words, a neurotic motivated by malice. He had never wanted to see her again.

The desk was commodious, containing correspondence that Andrew supposed predated his own birth, let alone adolescence. The pigeonholes to the right were full of scraps of paper less yellowed by age, folded neatly in halves and then in quarters, reminding him of childish games played with paper, aeroplanes constructed on winter afternoons. Serena's pages were densely covered with words. Bollocks, he read, fucking bollocks. Life is a bitch and God is a cunt. Outpourings of frustration on to the pages, rude words plastered on to the backs of envelopes, poison-pen messages to self. All in the small but legible hand her daughter had tried to emulate.

Andrew replaced the papers. He considered whether he would ever be able to tell Isabel what her mother had done to that particular fledgeling affair of her younger life, wondered if her Mama had done the same to every hopeful young man Isabel had ever brought home. Written them the kind of letters that would insult vanity, destroy affection and make the recipient either despise her daughter or laugh at her.

He nodded to sleep, debating without much logic the character of a mother motivated by the desire either to destroy or to protect, moved by either jealousy or the kind of love he could not comprehend, glad on the whole that his own mother had died in his own infancy. He thought at the same time how eavesdroppers hear no good of themselves, and how his discovery tonight reflected badly on the self-centred youth he had been. And should he tell Isabel; deciding not. If Isabel lost the illusion that her mother loved her, her life would be untenable.

And then he would lose her too.

He slept through the sound of slow, uncertain footsteps on the stairs and the changing of dark into the beginning of day. Woke to the rumble of the dustbin van, removing two sacks of rubbish and a dead cat before reversing back down the drive in a hurry, covering with their own the marks on the grass left by the big white van.

George had a bedroom window that faced west, dark in the

mornings and light in the afternoons. Dark as all hell whenever he was in it. It was a blurred room, featureless. Once inside he felt and behaved like a mouse, nesting tidily inside his own stretch of skirting board, never requiring the prompting of light or noise to wake him. In the last hour of sleep he descended into a deep, dark pit out of which he sailed with the ease of a cork on water.

Into that darkness came a voice, carried on a thick breath.

"Georgie boy, wake up. Wake up, fuck you."

Stale, sweet smell of alcohol decomposing; sweat crystallized on a cold body, giggle in the voice. George felt his hair being pulled, his ear tweaked, his shoulder shaken, all in a parody of affection. He never locked his bedroom door. The locks were no great deterrent to a shoulder: better to have nothing worth the taking.

"Give us a cuddle, George. Naa, all right then, forget it."

George had formed his body into a ball, hands over head, knees to chest. In the manner of a baby waiting to be born and a man who knows what to do when faced with a kicking, it was a pose he adopted by instinct.

"Talk to me, George. That's all, talk to me. Why won't you talk to me?"

The bantamweight of Derek, sitting on the edge of the single mattress, made the bed tilt slightly. George kicked him on the hip, and in one movement sprang upright, hurled the duvet over Derek's head and leapt out of bed. Threw himself at the duvet-covered lump and hit it. Derek yelped; George hit him again, lightly, tightened the duvet over his face and then let go.

Derek lay halfway up the bed, face pink, breathing deeply, legs straddled over the end. He still carried the bottle of double-strength lager, held it to his chest like a religious symbol.

George turned on the light, reached for the threadbare sweater on the chair, pulled it on over his pyjamas and stood over Derek with one fist raised.

Derek began to cough.

"S'all right," he said, raising the bottle feebly. "Wannad a thingy to take off the thingy. So's I can drink it, see?" He raised himself on one shoulder.

"Sorry about that cat," he said distinctly.

In an odd kind of way, drunken talk resembled Serena Burley talk. Without any rationale, George knew instinctively where Derek had been. He had known it would happen. Come to think of it, Derek looked like Serena Burley's cat. Big eyes, pink nose, ginger fur poking out where his shirt rode up over his pink belly. George clawed his own hair. He did not look like that. He had dark red hair and was sallow, a different creature entirely.

"What cat?" He asked quietly. He had told Derek about the cat, and the dog which did not bark. A million years ago. Derek rubbed his eyes, sat up slowly, still clutching the bottle. The big eyes disappeared into slits as he laughed. An unhealthy wheeze that turned into spasmodic coughing that went on and on until Derek's skin turned from pink to purple. Angry though he was, wishing Derek dead as he did, George was alarmed, banged him on the back and watched with concern until the din ceased. When it did Derek sat and shivered. The stupid boy never spent money on a decent sweater for winter, nor on food, and the cloying warmth of the rooms seemed unable to penetrate his bones. George put a jacket round his shoulders, resentful of his own solicitude.

"What have you been up to, you daft bugger?"

The boy was in that state of drunkenness where further

inebriation was impossible, although fervently desired to dull the feelings of depression, nausea and general seediness. It was in these maudlin states that Derek came closest to the desire to tell the truth, simply for the sake of it, or simply to pass the time by shocking himself.

"We went to call on your princess. A social visit."

He wanted to mock and to boast, but the words stuck in his throat. George looked frightening. Ridiculous in sweater and pyjamas, but the big fists bunched by his sides resembled a pair of monkey wrenches. The mist cleared. Derek began to think very clearly indeed.

"And I've been sent to say, why didn't you come with us?" He articulated the words slowly, careful to stress the regret.

George sat down on the bed next to him, keeping his distance, his fists still clenched. Derek sensed an immediate danger had passed, cursed himself for a fool and longed, suddenly, for breakfast. He put a tentative hand on George's arm. George let it remain.

"You could have done, you know," Derek suggested.

"What? Go and rob an old lady on her own?"

"Is she on her own, George?"

George gave up. The room had the stench of fear. "No, she's not. You know damn fine she's not. There's this girl . . ." Derek nodded, dropped the bottle and fumbled in his trousers for a fag. "Yes Georgie Porgie, I do know. And I'm surprised at you, thinking we were calling up there to rob an old dear. What's she got worth having? A lot of old furniture? No market for that, this side of Christmas. No, it's just Bob being curious. He likes girls, does Bob. Dick likes 'em even more."

"Get out, Derek. Leave me alone. I'm on my way round to the police, tell them all about it. Soon as I'm dressed."

151

Derek stood, his groin level with George's face as he tucked his flapping shirt-tail into his trousers.

"Naa, you won't do that, George. 'Cos we didn't do any harm and we decided we wouldn't go back unless you came with us. Think about it, George. Think about it, is all I ask. Bob just wants to take that girl for a ride in his car. . ."

"Get out," said George.

By the time he got to town it had begun to snow. Flakes twirled like manic dancers, melting on the pavements. Snow without conviction; not the genuine kind which tipped itself out of the sky like a blanket off a rooftop, hushing all protest, but snow designed for the mere creation of misery and nuisance, cold feet and muddy footsteps trailing in shallow brown puddles that had the appearance of gravy. Two weeks into November and the first signs of seasonal paraphernalia marked the beginning of the only time of year when George could properly equate himself with men of violence, on account of a desire to kick out at Christmas decorations and bellow above the saccharine sound of carols. Early days yet: it would only get worse.

He sat in the hideous lights of Littlewoods' cafeteria, watched the early-morning assembly into trays of hot lunches that would congeal before they were eaten, stirring a cup of milky coffee. When he picked it up, he left fingerprints around the rim, the way he must have left fingerprints all over Serena's house. If Bob and Co. did go back to that place, he would probably end up being blamed anyway. He had left traces there, like a spoor. Derek would say he had set it up: Derek had already made him a conspirator. All he could do was stand back and hope. Derek said they wouldn't go back. Derek might be telling the truth, although Derek rarely did except by accident. Derek might be right in saying that all Bob wanted was the girl. He clutched at that thought; knew it to be a false hope and allowed himself to massage it into a real one. Let them frighten Isabel Burley half to death, then; just let them. She might take the hint and go home and . . .

George wandered round the shops with the aimlessness of a stranger unsure of the way and too embarrassed to ask. Something for Serena, a single item lurked among all these goods with the sole purpose of helping her with the words and making her happy.

He found the tape recorder he had long since decided to buy. Gazed at it, full of wonder, his heart contracting with love. He could talk to her on this; she could talk back. In the nether regions of the night they could leave messages for one another. Not a lot to say. I miss you, I miss you, I miss you, put coal on my fire and let me be. Love me like your plastic flowers.

If Isabel was chased away, George would get a gun and guard the princess with his life. He stood holding the dicta-phone until a stern sales assistant asked if she could help.

She frightened him. He put the display model down and walked away.

Chapter Nine

"SHALL WE GET A NEW CAT, MOTHER? A nice little kitten? What do you think, George?"

"I dunno, don't ask me."

Isabel turned in appeal to Doc Reilly, who sat at the kitchen table as if he had been born there, feet enclosed in his favourite thick socks of an indeterminate blue. He was known to joke that the state of a man's socks said much about the state of his marriage.

"What do you think?" Isabel asked. "She's been going round hunting for that cat for two days. Even accused me of killing it, haven't you, Mother?" She spoke in the direction of Serena, who sat smiling at George as George fed the dog. Toying with a mouthful of cereal, Serena seemed able to eat only if he so instructed.

"Eat up, Mrs Burley, there's a dear," he murmured. She ate, obediently. Doc Reilly watched her surreptitiously. She turned her smile on him, and waved the spoon.

Doc Reilly thought with a touch of horror of Serena's large hands clutching a kitten. He shook his head.

"You'd be better off getting another dog," he volunteered. "One that barks." The retriever, food finished inside thirty seconds, ambled across to him and put a large sticky muzzle on his lap. "No, Petal," he said. "Not instead of you. Alongside you. So, what happened to the cat?"

"George thinks a ferret got it. Don't you, George? I think so too."

The doctor nodded. "You'd have to keep a kitten indoors then, wouldn't you? No point raising animals to feed ferrets, is there?"

George echoed his laughter politely. So did Serena, who laughed when it seemed apposite to do so. Isabel did not. The Doc turned to George.

"Well, it's lucky something's guarding this house. Even if it is only a ferret, for God's sake. Do you ever think of stopping over the night, George?"

"No," said Isabel quickly. "George has his own home and he does far too much for us already."

Oh, dear, a bit of an atmosphere. Doc Reilly got the clear impression he was treading on toes, curled his own under his chair and sipped his coffee. No love lost here, he could tell, and he should have kept his mouth shut.

"Anyway," Isabel continued, "Mother and I refuse to be scared by silly talk of burglars. Mother's never been burgled yet. Why should it happen now?"

Pride, the Doc could see it. The sort which might come before a fall and would tolerate no interference. He admired it. Ah well, the nights had fully drawn in: burglars needed daylight and they despised the cold. Isabel was probably right. It was long summer evenings and school holidays like the half-term break, which was when he had last seen the kids; those times were the worst threat. In the meantime he had two dozen patients making strenuous efforts to die and he lumbered to his feet in anticipation of poorer houses than this.

"Look after that cough, George, won't you? There's a lot of it about."

"Aren't you well, George?" Isabel asked with genuine concern. "I thought you looked a bit pale."

He winced under her scrutiny, shrugged his shoulders. Sympathy from Isabel was not something he solicited; receiving it sent an arrow into his conscience.

"He's very fine, aren't you, George?" Serena volunteered, nodding in his direction. It might have been a comment on his health or his physique, difficult to tell. Isabel followed Doc Reilly out to his Volvo.

He stood by the door of the car, reluctant to leave. She wanted to ask him something and he wasn't sure he wanted to answer.

"Thanks for coming out," she began.

"She's doing well," he said robustly. "Getting worse, of course, but still much better than most."

She held the door. "Doc, you've been around for ever. Longer than me. You listen to things — people, gossip, I mean. You have to. Can you tell me what it was that made me so unpopular before I left? Can you remember that far back?"

Twelve years was nothing; a mere fifth of his sixty. Out of the blue like that, the question took him by surprise. He had thought she was going to ask something equally awkward, but rooted in the present, like the true prognosis of her mother's illness. He decided on a version of the truth, delivered rapidly.

"Nothing, really. You were just the prettiest girl around, and for a couple of years the most precocious. Your Aunt Mab told me she thought you were a bit wild, you know. Someone circulated rumours that you'd given a couple of the young men the clap. Anybody's for a halfpenny."

She nodded. "So I heard. Written rumours? Only Andrew mentioned something about letters."

"Yes. Childishly vulgar. I saw only the one, mind. My son James, remember him? He got one. He was a stuck up little brute then. He's better now, I promise . . ."

"Who wrote them, Doc? Who would do that?"

"I don't know, love. Somebody jealous. Long forgotten now."

"Somebody must have hated me," said Isabel. "And no, things like that are never quite forgotten, are they?"

"Sure they are," he said reassuringly, although, even to his own ears, his voice was a trifle hypocritical.

Oh God, whatever did you do with human beings except patch them up and send them on their way? She was right. Sometimes he felt he was good for nothing more than tranquillizer prescriptions and sick notes. He could visualize the scene inside the kitchen he had left. Serena, touching George, the way she yearned to touch all men, both of them springing back as soon as the daughter came in, and she herself ignoring the evidence. Evidence of what? Forbidden affection? The occasional malevolence, as well as the occasional clarity and love in her mother's eyes?

Ignorance was a good idea. There were plenty of things it was better not to know.

"Have some lunch, George? A sandwich, at least?"

Isabel had taken to feeding him, whether he would or not. A ploy, George thought, or preferred to think it, against the other conclusion, disinterested kindness and gratitude for his unpaid labours, something to compensate for their mutual aversion. As long as he could imagine that Isabel gave him food, even of the bread-and-cheese variety, as a means to make Serena copy him in the act of eating, or as a bribe to make him stay longer in order to preserve the peace while she shopped, tidied and did whatever she did all day, he could tolerate the generosity. If it was simply a gift from her to him, he could not.

George was particularly useful less for the heavy tasks, such as getting in coal, and more for the ostensibly light ones, such as persuading Mother to eat cereal and bread in the early afternoon without the deafening sound of the radio she carried with her everywhere, apparently as a means of blotting out other sound, particularly that of her daughter's voice.

George cleared his throat.

"I could come back and sort of babysit in the evenings," he suggested. "If you wanted to go out, I mean."

Serena drew breath audibly. Understanding of the words seemed to come and go like a lighthouse beam. Isabel had long since concluded this had much to do with what Serena wanted to understand, and knew that to be a harsh judgement.

"That's very kind of you, George. I'll think about it. Was there any post today?"

"Nope."

"I can't get her to give me the bills," Isabel went on, distracted by the prospect of a dozen minor tasks and Doc Reilly's words. "She's been hiding them. Do you think you could give any letters straight to me in the future? And I ought to call on the neighbours, thank them for taking in the post, should have done that weeks since . . ."

"She's not well at the moment," George said quickly. "Not keen on callers."

They ate in silence. Sitting across the table from them both, Isabel felt like a guest. She had a sudden urge, horrible in its intensity, to slap both their faces.

As long as she loves me, she told herself with the familiar flush of shame, it does not matter if she does not love me best.

Robert phoned in the evening. Was going to come and visit at the weekend, but things had got on top of him, did Isabel understand what he meant? Life was full, he hinted: the baby was sick and the boy in pain from the dentist. Another time, as soon as possible, certainly before Christmas. Had the doctor called and was everything all right?

"Is it OK to forge her signature on cheques?" Isabel asked. "Or is it a criminal offence?"

He hesitated, nicely alarmed as Isabel had hoped he would be. Envisaging his sister emptying his mother's account.

"For the electric bill," Isabel added. "I've only just found it."

"Fine, I suppose. How are you, er, off for money?"

"Fine," she echoed. "Everything's fine."

Which it was. There was a bright full moon set high in a sky full of scudding cloud. Mirrored in the windows facing the phone, Isabel could see her mother by the fire, scribbling. TV substituted for music; sound for thought.

She wished Andrew would phone, without quite wanting it. She had a longing for the sound of words formed into sentences, ached for company. A fourth glass of wine seemed a good idea.

This time they came down the track in another van, slightly more deluxe. There was no laughter. Sure they had laughed before, but that was the first time and the denouement rankled still, despite their joking about it. Derek was wondering how long he would have to keep the auction-house job after this — for the sake of appearances, couple of weeks he supposed — as he chewed a fingernail and thought about money. Bob had a dull pain in his back and thought about money. Dick's jaw was slack: his trousers were dirty and he fiddled with coins in his pocket. The equipment in the back of the van was the same as before. Derek was not wearing enough clothes and he shivered.

Three in the morning and the night dead. The sky was clear enough for snow and the track was like a grey ribbon. There was not a single light in the cottage at the end.

"What do we do if she wakes up?" Derek said, still gnawing the fingernail. Now was the time his lies might find him out.

"I told, you," Bob said, his voice thick with impatience. "How many times? You know where the phone is. Unplug it, put it somewhere else and if the old dear disturbs us, we shut her in a bedroom and get on with it. For Christ's sake . . ."

"OK, OK . . . No lights?"

"No lights."

"Gloves. Don't forget gloves."

Yellow gloves. Dick had got them from work. Very decorative.

They reversed up to the back door. Bob muttered how this was sensible, get in as close as possible, save on labour and have the thing ready in case of anything which necessitated a quick getaway. A giant in the kitchen with a machine gun, Derek suggested under his breath, stifling the whistle he needed for courage. He looked uneasily towards the window where he had seen the fleshy figure last time, turned and winked at Dick. Dick's jaw still hung open. The memory had surfaced in his brain: the flash of skin had drawn him on, it was the cat that frightened him off. Derek had lost his pencil torch and brought another identical to it. He tried the back door, expecting it to be locked, ready to fiddle with it, because it was he who was best with locks, but it was open. That worried him a little: it was almost as if they were being invited in. There was always something sinister in other people's stupid naïveté.

The moon lit the kitchen through the big windows. It lit the sitting room where he went to unplug the phone, take it back down the corridor and stick it in the van. His training shoes were soundless, he was pleased with that; the yellow gloves twinkled like fireflies. Dick followed with the blankets and, without the aid of any electric light, began a skilful packing of the contents of a credenza. Bob it was who crept upstairs, checked that the bedroom doors were all firmly shut. One was ajar: he did not look inside, but closed it softly. There was within the gentle sound of snoring.

Bob had the list written on the back of his hand; Dick had the list off by heart; Derek too could recite it like a parrot. A sort of shopping list of what was going to be moved and in which order. Get the noisier business done first, get the stuff down that awful corridor either into the kitchen or the back-yard, because of the bedrooms being at the front; load the light stuff as you go along and the heavy stuff last. They weren't such a bad team after all, Bob decided as the pain in his back subsided and he watched them work in unison. Dick carried bookcases with the ease he carried carcasses, as if he had done nothing else since he was five; he stacked the dining chairs, got them out of the house and into the van without much of a sound. Then he set about the task of dismantling the table with the aid of in- genuity and Derek's little torch. Derek was good at this too, stacked up drawers from a chest, cantered out with them, never carrying too much or too little, never taking the risk of dropping anything. Ground floor only, Bob had dictated. Pity: he didn't half like the look of the grandfather clock on the landing. Maybe... As they worked, all communication was by whisper and signals. Thank God for the moon, which seemed to inspire them. Made them sweat. After an hour they were huddled in the kitchen. They had dismantled half a house. The bloody dog had not moved a muscle and they already felt like kings.

"Fancy a cup of tea?" Derek hissed.

"Fuck off, I found the brandy." That was Dick.

"Where?"

"Back of that rolltop desk."

"Give it here, you arse."

Come to think of it, the fool had been weaving a bit, losing the knack of tidiness, spreading paper from that vast desk all over the floor. Dick must have given himself an extra turn of speed and a stagger from half a bottle of spirits, glugged from the neck. His eyes were glistening, just at that point when they needed a last burst of energy, plus precision, in order to load the heavy stuff. Bob had been cruising on confidence, ready to laugh out loud and shake his fist, but, Jesus Christ. He'd better stuff something else in Dick's mouth before he fell over. Or take something out. Dick in drink was a dangerous beast.

"Make him sick it up," he commanded Derek. "We got a long way to go yet."

They dragged him to the kitchen sink. He smiled at them until Derek held him over it, making encouraging noises and holding his neck. He snorted like a bull and shrugged them off, snarling.

"Gimme," he hissed at Bob. Bob spread his empty hands.

"Give you what?"

"Gimme!" Dick roared. Bob put a hand over his mouth, a big, meaty palm. Derek pinched his nose. He thrashed around, knocking over a chair. Just as they lowered him to the floor, footsteps sounded from the stairs. Quiet, determined, implacable, coming towards them. They froze.

The figure of an old lady appeared in the doorway. She fumbled for the light switch, bathed them all in ghastly neon which found them in a huddled trio and herself fully in command of the situation. Her hands fluttered, as if there was something she had forgotten; she beamed. Her eyes moved away to the furniture piled in the doorway. She shivered with pleasure, like a confident child on the brink of a party. Moved smartly to the drawer in the table, pulled it out, extracted three candles and handed them to Bob.

"Light these and stick them somewhere, I would. I *knew* I should have paid that bill, I knew it. Light them from this one, stick 'em on the table, it won't hurt. How *nice* to see you all again."

Candlesticks. Somewhere in this wonderful heap of goods awaiting removal there were candlesticks. Sitting in a clutch on the draining board, beautiful silver, fresh off the dining table. Bob placed the candles offered from Serena's steady fingers and, with movements less steady, struck a match from his pocket and lit them. Serena sighed, an exclamation of joy as she switched the light off again. The three men remained immobile as she marched forwards with the tape deck she had left by the door and placed it in the centre of the table with care. There was an immediate blast of sound, then the room reverberated to the music of a full-bellied waltz.

"How absolutely lovely to see you, and how good of you to come," she said, curtsying to each. "Let's dance. She keeps the booze, top cupboard, on the right. Let's all have fun!"

They were mesmerized. Obedience was automatic and seemed entirely appropriate. Bob went to the cupboard. Somehow he produced glasses as well as sherry, a bottle of whisky and one of gin. Derek stepped forward, awkward with politeness. Offered a yellow-gloved hand, which seemed to add to the sense of crazy formality. He noticed her hat, her nightdress, her coat, the little heels to her shoes, sweet. He nodded at Bob and Bob nodded back.

"We thought some of your stuff needed mending, lady. Not the best of times to move it, but . . ."

Serena paused, then took him in her arms.

"Heavens!" she trilled. "Take it all away, why don't you? Let's dance."

"Take it away, George," Derek said gravely. "Just take it away, man, take it away."

Come on. If this was going to be the worst of their problems, it was not so bad. Bob could feel laughter gurgling in his chest: the pain in his back had entirely gone. They had all the time in the world. To the tune of a waltz, then a polka, they continued the loading, while the princess, oblivious to the draught from the door, conducted her own orchestra and maintained a flow of commentary.

Isabel dreamed of being with Joe in a nightclub, surrounded by pulsing music. Glamorous darkness and spangly lights on the floor. A body pressed against her own, wanting to go home. She was waking slowly from the slurred sleep induced by wine. A reluctant awakening that did not involve opening of the eyes, but a wish for more sleep and the hope that turning her face into the pillow would send her back into oblivion. She often woke this time of night, aware of Serena's wanderings, and squeezed her eyes closed, determined not to interfere, but checking over in her mind the pitfalls downstairs. There was a sensation of having been half awake for a long time, as if her sleep had been punctuated not by dreams, but by sound.

Alien sound. Music in the distance, coming from the other side of the world, penetrating into consciousness slowly. Once she had established that it was not a dream she could feel only acute annoyance. For heaven's sake, Mother played that dreadful music all day, couldn't she leave off at night? If this was going to go on, then she, Isabel, would have to do something about the wandering, she couldn't cope, not without sleep. Mother, please do not be an inconsiderate old bitch. The phrase, fully formed, popped into her mind, anger getting her out of bed with such speed she made herself dizzy, and angered herself more. She would throw that tape deck and radio out of the house, she would, too. Start wearing earplugs, scream.

It was cold: she could not find her slippers, stood shivering in indecision. Leave it for tonight, deal with it in daylight? No. Dressing-gown, where? Here. Bare feet would do. Downstairs, past the clock with the moonlit face telling her it was four-thirty, a ridiculous, ludicrous time to be awake, damn, damn, damn. Noticing from her feet up how cold the floor was in the hall. Without rugs on the stones. Without rugs. She looked down at her feet in consternation. The cold burned. She could hear her mother in the kitchen, singing loudly. Turned the corner, saw the candlelight, thought for a moment as she ran towards it that what she had seen was flames and Mother was trapped in there, roasting and chanting.

There was a blast of air from the open back door, the kitchen a mess. Two rolled up rugs from the hall impeded progress. A large man coming in from the yard stopped and stared at her with bloodshot eyes then, slowly, smiled. A smaller man appeared at his shoulder.

"Oh, shit," said Derek.

Bob turned from the sink where he had been washing his arms free of the oil from the base of the dining table, now neatly installed inside the van. Nearly finished, all of them infected by the old lady's party spirit, full of devil-may-care, give-me-hell any day, and it did not matter any longer that Dick was dangerously drunk. Isabel flew to her mother, clutched her tight, protectively. Serena dug an elbow into her ribs, shrugged her off.

"Go away," she said crossly. "You're always spoiling things. Go away."

"Yes," said Bob softly. "Go away, girl. I would. Quickly."

"I didn't know," Derek bleated. "I didn't know."

"You haven't danced with me," Serena said, pointing at him.

"Oh yes," Dick crooned, squinting through the candlelight. "Oh yes, oh yes."

Bob moved towards her. Isabel sidestepped him, picking a bottle off the table, holding it in front of her, spilling the dregs. There was a piercing, whisky smell.

"Tutt tutttt," Serena admonished.

It was so easy to disarm her. Bob simply hit her a glancing, almost apologetic, blow on the side of the head and plucked the bottle out of her hand. She whimpered. "Look," he said to her reasonably, "if you just sit down quietly, no one gets hurt. This your mother or what?"

Isabel nodded.

"Well, she doesn't mind us, so why should you?"

"Get out," she whispered. "Leave us alone."

Dick elbowed Bob out of the way. "Oh, it can talk, can it? What's a lovely girl like you doing in a place like this, then? She is lovely, isn't she, Bob? Very lovely."

Which she was in the candlelight, all pale skin, huge eyes, breathless, a dressing-gown patterned with roses, hanging open over a low-necked nightdress that showed the curve of full bosom. Like her mother's had been. Lovely was an understatement. Ripe for the picking: he could have sunk his teeth into that flesh. Isabel felt the dressing-gown removed from her shoulders, felt the cold draught raise goosepimples on her arms, while an acrid, warm mouth grazed her neck.

"Put her down, Dick. You don't know where she's been." Bob spoke in the tones of sweet and cheerful reason that worked better with Dick than orders.

"I could put her down the cellar, but it seems a waste," Dick leered.

"Put her in that chair by the fire. Get some rope. Tie her up — loosely, mind. Just the hands. C'mon, man, we're nearly done."

To Bob's relief, Dick obeyed like a man in a daze, but not quite with implicit obedience. He manoeuvred Isabel across the floor in imitation of a dance, holding her from behind so his groin pressed into her buttocks, his hands splayed across her breasts, lowered her into the nursery chair which always stood by the stove, his hands sliding down her body, lingering. She sat, blood pounding, the sound of her own heart deafening. She would have scratched and screamed; wanted to scratch and scream, but another instinct prevailed. Be good, sweet maid, don't provoke anything: then they won't hurt Mother and they won't hurt you. Through a haze of fear she made herself smile at Serena as her own hands were tied behind the chair. Smile, to prove everything was going to be all right. The most revolting moment of all was when Serena smiled back, sketched the equivalent of a royal wave, and laughed explosively.

"Nice daughter you've got," Dick slurred at her.

"Oh yes, she likes you too, I can tell," Serena trilled.

Someone had turned down the music. Mother turned it up. Bob and Derek began to move with urgent speed, almost running in and out of the open door, laden. Dick was slower, reluctant to move from the stove. Isabel heard the sound of an engine, closed her eyes. The moments were endless; the sounds distant. Minutes passed. Emblazoned on the inside of her eyes was the image of Serena, laughing.

Dick was straddling the chair, his flies undone, holding his penis in his hand, thrusting it against her mouth. Flaccid, purple, grimy, nuzzling her cheek as she twisted her head away. He pinched her jaw in one huge, gloved hand, forcing her lips apart, stuck his penis in, his belly ballooning round her face. Vomit rose in her throat. He thrust, lazily, almost absentmindedly. Then he looked at his member in dim surprise at its lack of compliance, did not persist. The smell of him was overpowering. He grunted, zipped up his trousers furtively, looked over his shoulder as the engine revved outside. As one final action to appease his disappointment he caught hold of her cotton nightdress, ripped it to the waist, pinched one nipple between thumb and forefinger, painfully hard. She screamed.

In the background, throughout it all, there were shouted instructions, and, over the sound of the music, the noise of her mother, clapping her hands, like a child at a pantomime, her voice rising into a high shriek of utter hilarity. Saliva dribbled down Isabel's chin. The laughter continued.

A different smell now, cleaner. Bob, leaning over the chair designed for the nursing of children, fumbling with the bonds. Speaking. "Sorry about that," he was muttering.

Perhaps she fainted for a minute, perhaps oblivion mercifully arrived on demand, but it seemed to her later that she had remained where she was for a long time. Enough for the first shock to recede, the spittle to dribble on to her chest and a self-protective anger to follow in a great white-hot surge which had her screaming over that bloody music, wrenching her hands free. The kitchen swam into focus, candles still burning. Someone had trodden on her bare toes. The pain brought life. Her eyes sought out her mother.

There she was, standing by the door, one arm across her chest, the other waving goodbye into the darkness like a wistful child. As she waved, her body swayed in tune with some long-remembered dance.

Isabel's fingers and toes were as cold as snow, her head wet with perspiration. She could not coordinate her movements; nothing worked to order. Yet she limped over to where the ancient one stood, grabbed hold of the neck of her coat and slapped her face. Once, twice, four times before she lost count. The knuckle of her right index finger caught the outcrop of eyebrow: she could feel that, sensed damage being done, skin torn, and then she stopped. It was impossible to imagine that her hands had done that. Serena's face swam before hers as something hideous, requiring destruction. Isabel was not horrified for the moment, merely temporarily satisfied.

Serena staggered, fell against the door frame, then righted herself. Her hands came up to embrace her purpled face: she closed her eyes as she felt the left one, gingerly. Tears formed. Her head wobbled dangerously on her neck.

"What did I do?" she asked, clearly bewildered. "What did I do?"

The room was still blurred. Serena's ability to speak worked on Isabel's mind like one more insult, enraging her. Her own

169

tongue felt like an obstruction inside her mouth, preventing words.

"It's what you — didn't do — you filthy-minded old cow!" Isabel yelled and then found herself shaking so hard she could not speak at all. She leaned on the table to keep her balance, looked around, shaking her head unsteadily, trying to suppress the panic and find some clue as to what to do next. Something, before she shook to pieces. She wanted to lie down on the floor, but the floor, she noticed, was filthy. Someone had to tell her what to do. She could not think of it herself.

Serena turned on the light, moved uncertainly towards the candles on the table, blew them out, one by one. With enormous difficulty and greater reluctance. Three, four puffs each. Smoke idled in the air. The tape came to an end.

"They forgot these," she said sadly, gesturing to the silver candlesticks.

Isabel burst into uncontrollable laughter. Spasms of it shook her naked breasts. Loud, hysterical giggles rising to screams, descending into barks and yelps, on and on, choking her. She staggered against the stove, recoiled from the warmth, collided with the chair on which she had sat, leaped out of it and cracked her knee against the table.

"Take a deep breath, I would." Serena's disinterested instruction had an effect.

The room settled into its familiar contours, reminding Isabel of duties, obligations and the panacea of little, familiar tasks. It was imperative not to stay still. Without any conscious thought she knew that in movement she would find sanity of a kind. If she did not move, she would freeze in this attitude. She would simply freeze.

With slow steps, she went to the sink and doused her face

with water. Put on the kettle, found her dressing-gown and buttoned it, making her fingers work. While the kettle made reassuring noises she found a hot-water bottle with a fleecy cover, gave it to her mother to hold while she herself made tea. The water splashed everywhere; the finding of milk and sugar was an almost insurmountable task. There was a sense of triumph in achieving it. The cup made a loud noise against her teeth. Somewhere in the course of all this, with the deliberate steps of a puppet, she looked for the telephone: it must have gone with the van. She made Serena sip the tea and escorted her to bed with another hot-water bottle. She found witch hazel in the bathroom, soaked a pad of cotton wool and applied it to the injured face where one eye was puffed like a purple balloon. Her touch was trembling, full of revulsion. She marvelled at herself, encouraged herself, muttered under her breath; good girl, good girl.

Serena took all remarks as being addressed to herself. She was utterly cooperative, consented to the wearing of bedsocks and snuggled down sweetly.

"They danced with me," she said, over and over again. "They danced with me."

Her eyes closed.

Isabel's could not. She dressed in the dark, piling on three layers of sweaters with the same studied efficiency that had governed all her movements for the last hour. She went downstairs and lit the drawing-room fire. Her movements were steady now: they had become faster and faster. Her mind was slow; it functioned painfully. The blur of shock was preferable.

Such a lovely room, but the firelight was less kind than the moonlight. Empty, save for a single chair with a damaged seat.

They had not bothered with that and the omission, the judgement on it, was oddly offensive. Items removed from drawers and bookcases were littered against the walls to facilitate removal of the carpet. Paper from Mother's desk drifted round her feet. In desultory fashion, like a person hypnotized, Isabel began to tidy them up. She was her mother's housekeeper; housekeepers tidy up. Words hit her eyes. Letters to strangers. Fuck, cunt, damn. Mother's form of communication.

Isabel began to cry. Every ounce of her hurt, as if she had been pummelled. The words were appropriate expletives for the sense of filth and failure that paralysed all but automatic action, and the automatic movements did not quite keep realization at bay. Here was a writer of indecent missives. Here was her daughter. What had the silly daughter done?

Nothing of any merit, ever. Excelled herself. Allowed her mother's property to be removed from under her nose. Gone to sleep drunk, woken too late. Failed to stop them even then. Let herself be violated. Hit an old lady who knew no better. Had she done that too? Of course she had and of course Serena, who did know better, would remember her daughter leaving a mark which she would never want anyone else to see. Serena would remember who had done that, wouldn't she ever? She would shout it from the rooftops. Burglars are nice men in comparison to my daughter: they didn't hit me, they danced. My daughter was already filth before they started.

Isabel stopped sobbing. All the hysteria had fled, leaving a terrible and deceptive clarity.

The neighbourhood thinks you're a kind of whore, anyway. They're not going to believe in you as victim, oh no. What's the difference between a tart and someone who hits her mother? Not much. One kind of poisoned butterfly or another. She'd have to tell the police, of course, but not all of it, only some of it. Perhaps that should come first. Maybe it could wait.

She wouldn't be telling them or anyone else about the vital discovery, of how much her mother hated her. And how she would have to go on with the pair of them rattling round this great house, waiting for the men to come back and dance. Go on into the blue yonder, a happy couple who hated one another and no choice about it, because there was nothing much left in life to do right, nothing to hold dear and absolutely nowhere else to go. And it was all her fault.

She sat, dry-eyed in the emptiness of the room, willing herself to weep again. Mother had unlocked the door. Invited them in. Would have cheered them on if they had raped her daughter, one by one. Laughed herself sick.

So that now there were the two of them: one mad, one defiled.

Chapter Ten

$\mathcal{I}$T WAS SO COLD, SO VERY COLD, that her blood formed itself into crystals. The movement of a kneecap or an elbow seemed to grate. The fire in the hearth had gone out, also her own: she moved with the precision of the waking dead, tidying as she went. Picking things up, putting them down. Then the dog, that stupid, redundant old brute, came wagging towards her, paws clipping the bare wooden floor, a waddling unit of warmth wanting to be let out. She gazed into brown eyes, docile with stupidity, and at that point Isabel realized she was, still, inescapably alive.

She paused in front of a modern mirror the burglars had also left, breathed over the glass and watched the mist form. Not dead yet. Not beautiful, either. Scrubbing herself in the bathroom did not improve anything.

She could not find the car keys and would not look, walked down the road to the church, limping slightly. Imagining herself running away, slowing down to resist the impulse. When in doubt, turn tail. But then, running away was a practice she had adopted too often and it always involved coming back. Isabel made herself think, rooted her thoughts in memories.

What was it Mab had said so sadly? You only know your own strength when you learn to keep on loving someone who does not love you. There was a frost, dampening slowly in the face of the winter sun which swelled behind cloud, more a presence than a reality. Her mouth felt dry and, at the back of her throat, a lingering taste of wine. One step proceeded in front of another, towards a telephone.

She could not remember the neighbours' names; she could scarcely recall her own. It was a miracle that Andrew's card was in her purse. Isabel steeled herself to tell lies.

In the town-centre branch of Dixon's, as soon as it opened its doors, George carefully avoided the sales assistant who had been so dismissive of him last time, although there would have been a certain sense of triumph had he encountered her and proved he could pay for the dictaphone. It was a matter of pride for him to have brought with him in a separate paper bag exactly the right sum, down to the last 99p. The woman behind the counter took the cash without any sign of being impressed by the nonchalant ease with which he presented it. She must have mistaken him for some executive. He was shaken by sudden irritation that she did not want to engage him in conversation: why did he want to buy it, who it was for, how thrilled the recipient would be and how amazing it was for anyone to spend all this money at once. Then he looked around at cameras, computers and ritzy telephones coloured pink and green, and felt himself shrink. He was glad there was no one else in the shop to negate the effect of his own purchase by buying something far larger, and, in the end, was so anxious to leave he almost forgot his parcel.

Where to put this possession, to save it from prying eyes? A problem, that. He walked around town, aware of carrying the equivalent of contraband, wondering about it. The exercise of spending money made him curious and confident. He stepped boldly in and out of the shops, no longer intimidated, looking at sweaters, socks, radios, shoes, items he would only ever consider buying in the charity shops where he was more at home. He felt, in a strange way, content, superior, relieved to be free of the kind of indecision which must surely accompany the buying of goods at such prices. There was a moment of unhappiness when he paused outside a jeweller's and wished against every other wish he could have bought her something pretty, but then he felt the shape of the recorder against his chest, solid and safe, felt, yes, he had done the right thing after all.

Strange, when he was enjoying himself the presence of people receded into the background: even the noise was forgiven.

He felt rich. A big spender. A fully paid-up member of the human race.

By the time George had finished dreaming and failed to discover anything better to do with Serena's gift than carry it round with him, probably until Christmas when he would present her with it, he was late, way outside the normal routine of arrival, and he even felt satisfaction in that. He sat inside the car, making sure he could work it. He said hallo to it twice, then said goodbye and erased it, delighted.

Perhaps by Christmas Isabel would have gone. Gone and long forgotten. Fed up and out of the way. He had an enormous capacity for self-deception: it came from being a dreamer. He could put things out of his mind and on to a different planet by a sheer effort of will, had made himself suspend belief about Derek's plans, just by blotting them out. The refusal to think could be made to last for days: it was a cue to survival, but when he got to the house, he knew. He could almost hear the sensation of his dreams exploding around him like the sound of tinkling glass.

George saw from the gates the signs of the posse of the sheriff's men. One police car, Doc Reilly's Volvo, Robert Burley's Ford still hot from two hours' drive, Andrew Cornell's car which he recognized from his own careful habit of noting vehicles, Uncle Tom Cobbley and all. Not a posse, a jury, waiting to find him guilty. Instead of going into the house, which he knew he would have to do sometime, but not just yet, he reversed the car down the road, left it and walked away across the fields.

If there had been an ambulance he would have faced up right away. As it was he wanted to preserve the residue of hope for an hour, paced into the valley, counting his steps, breathing with deliberate regularity. He stopped beneath a tree and tried the recorder again. "I didn't do it," he repeated, his teeth chattering. "I didn't do it."

John Cornell looked at the auction room and wished his son could love him with half the intensity with which he loved his son. No method of loving could be identical: any way would do, as long as it carried acceptance and fair judgement. Such as son recognizing that father was not entirely without heart. Or seeing at some point that he admired a boy with such high and naïve principles of honour, even if it meant a dearth of bloody common sense sometimes. It was just as well that one of them had been a cynical opportunist for most of his life: but hardly the same thing as the crudity of theft that Andrew suspected. Andrew had far too much fine taste for his own good. Antique furniture was not worthy of veneration: it existed to be acquired and no commodity was worth that much respect. Business was business: buy cheap and sell dear. Looking after a dog was more important.

The telephone he held in his hand was cold to the touch. He

supposed it was efficient of the police to phone anyone in the business as soon as ever to tell them to look out for anyone flogging large items the day after they were nicked. Routine procedure, but it was this assumption that all thieves were congenital idiots which led to so many of them getting away with it. For Christ's sake, that stuff was long gone. What troubled him most was the idea that his son might suspect he had something to do with it. Perfidious he might be. Pragmatic to the point of brutality. But dishonesty on such a scale was self-defeating.

"Tell them," he said to the disembodied voice at the other end, "that if they want to borrow stuff, I got plenty in store they can have. Really."

Borrow it, keep it, what was the difference? It was only money.

He wanted a word with that son of his. About the young woman; about her mother and her aunt.

"How is she?"

"She keeps asking about the cat . . ."

Serena sat on the single chair, close to the fire, with her handbag over her arm, smiling politely. She reminded him of the queen, posing for a photograph to put on a stamp. Privately, and with difficulty in keeping his estimation from becoming obvious, Andrew Cornell found Robert Burley quite ridiculous. There had been a conspiracy of efficiency and quiet voices before he arrived, a decent aura of shock and respect between the time when the faint voice of Isabel had caught him unawares and he had told her to wait where she was and he would come and collect her, bringing a phone. Then he arranged the arrival of Doc Reilly, whom Andrew considered she needed, along with that of the police, all huddling together, pooling God alone knows what theories and information, murmuring names and instructions while someone else arrived to add to the mess with fingerprint powder. And yet R. Burley acted like a conductor. The sort, Andrew thought, who would reduce an orchestra to anarchy before the end of Act One.

"I don't understand how this could have happened," he was saying for the tenth time, looking at his sister with an expression supposed to be sorrowful, but, in reality, merely full of sorrowful recrimination. The look given to a destructive idiot one is bound to forgive. Andrew wondered how many people in the world considered Isabel to be a fool. He did not; Doc Reilly did not; only her brother knew better. I must ask him, Andrew thought, if his father was also a bully.

"It must have been someone who knows the house," Robert stated with all the authority of an expert. "I can't believe you didn't hear a thing."

"Not at first, no." Isabel was mild. "But I did, finally."

Robert did not appear to register that her passivity was brittle and artificial, too calm to be genuine. "And you saw them but you can't even remember what they looked like? Amazing. Even the one who tied you up?"

She winced. "Not very well. Faces get distorted in candlelight . . ."

"Colours, too," Andrew added.

"One with a big nose," Isabel said, deliberately vague. "One with a big beard. One with . . . Oh, never mind." She stopped and stared at her feet. Slipper socks; most unbecoming. Whatever else had been seen in the kitchen was not going to be mentioned. She was confused, speaking like a person with retarded intelligence, but some things she could force herself to forget.

"Which one hit Mother?"

She was even vaguer about that, her voice lower. "I don't think any of them did. I think she fell."

The voices echoed in the room. It was a fat little policeman, without uniform, who was doing the fingerprinting. He had taken to making his reports to Robert, obviously sensing a natural leader, Andrew thought ironically. What a clean house this was, the fat one remarked now; very few sets of prints, and probably none from the burglars.

"Of course it's clean," Isabel volunteered. "I've cleaned it top to bottom." She looked at Robert, a hint of mockery in a voice that was otherwise toneless. "That's what I do all day."

Your prints, said the man, chattily, Mrs Burley's, of course, and those of a third party. All prevalent in most rooms; all three in Mrs Burley's bedroom. Would the third party be the gentleman called George whom all of them had mentioned?

"George?" Robert demanded. "George? He walks the dog. What would his prints be doing in her bedroom?"

"A word about George," Doc Reilly began, apologetically. Needs must, he supposed, hardly a breach of confidence, and hardly any choice either, other than to communicate to his inspector friend in the corner what little he knew about George. The inspector, thin and sallow, stood apart from them all, listening.

"He could only have gone into her bedroom to pry," Robert burst out, desperate to cast blame. "And where is he now? Hours late."

"I need this man George to get his prints for elimination," the fat man said, fussily. "Where is he?"

"And I need tea," said Doc Reilly, irritated beyond his belief.

On cue with that observation, George appeared on the

threshold, flanked by that damned dog. He seemed to have shrunk and he looked on the verge of tears, regarding the emptiness with dismay.

"Hallo," he said, eyes on Serena. The rest of them need not have existed.

She crowed with delight. "George, darling!"

"She's OK, George," Isabel said sharply. "She's probably the only one who is."

He shook his head from side to side, the only part of him he seemed able to move, confused and slow.

"You'll be needing some more coal for that fire," he remarked finally. They all seemed to expect him to say something: it was the best he could do.

The shadowy, thin policeman stepped forward. "George Craske, is it?"

"That's right."

"And what do you know about all of this, George?"

"All what?"

"Twenty thousand quid's worth of burglary is what, what did you think I meant?" The voice seemed to gloat.

"Leave him alone," said Isabel.

George shrank further. It seemed to Isabel, from the outside, as if the fat and thin officers closed ranks on George, ready to surround him, with Robert on the flank waiting to move in and kick. There was fear in his eyes, along with unshed tears. It would be like this watching a gang forming, she thought. Assessing their chances, lowering, ready to charge.

"Not exactly new to you is it?" the thin one said unpleasantly. "Got form, haven't you, George? One for rape, three or four for theft from an employer. That's right, isn't it?"

"Jesus Christ!" Robert shouted. "And you've been in my

mother's bedroom. Christ almighty, Isabel, did you know about this?"

She shook her head, oddly unsurprised by the information, which did not seem to her to be of the greatest relevance. They had all known there was something odd about George: why be amazed now? She shook herself, desperately trying to gather energy for something that was more important than her own fuzzy exhaustion.

"Look," she said levelly, "I can tell you one thing for sure. George would never have anything to do with this, never in a million years." The earnestness of her announcement created a momentary pause. She was surprised to find such certainty, such animation in herself.

George moved slowly and knelt by Serena's chair. The isolation of it in a room otherwise unfurnished added to her air of a royal presence, with him the courtier.

"Are you all right, Mrs Burley?"

She nodded, emphatically.

"Are you sure now? Who hit you? Did they hit you?"

She looked at him with adoration. Touched her own forehead, and then touched his brow, as if the action of so doing would transfer the contusion from her own to his and it was an injury he would willingly accept. It was a little like a blessing. The sight of the contact made Robert squirm. Doc Reilly coughed. The thin policeman did not care for it either.

"Who do you mean 'they', George? Do we know how many you mean by 'they'? I mean, how many you showed around in the first place? Your friends, she said they were. From the first time. She can't say much else, can she? Which you must have known, if anyone did, I suppose. She can't say what your friends looked like either. Very useful."

It was a quiet, taunting voice, grating on the ears, each word a fresh graze. Robert came closer, swearing under his breath, ready to pull George away from the vicinity of the regal chair. It was too much for George. He punched him in the soft part of the gut and, in the same moment, all the men were on him in a pack. It was a decorous and swift manhandling, as if rehearsed in deference to the women. No further blows struck, simply a restraint against which George struggled briefly before he stopped and stood limply, with his hands pinned behind him. He allowed himself to be patted down by the fat copper, who seemed to be out of breath, jerky with excitement. Those precise, rather feminine hands, which seemed designed for powder, prints and other unpleasant minutiae of life, found the dictaphone. That was all there was. He held it to his ear, shook it, turned it over, and then depressed the switch. They all listened to the sound of George's voice, speaking uncertainly at first, then louder, repeating himself over and over.

"I didn't do it," said the voice. "I didn't do it."

Silence fell upon them like a stone into water, the ripples going wide.

Serena's harsh shout of laughter jarred. "Lovely, George," she cried. "How clever you are! You clever, clever thing! Just what I need!" Then, in a lower, more confidential voice, "I liked your friends, George. When are they coming back?"

"Give it to her," George muttered. "It's hers."

The thin one almost purred with satisfaction, dying to state the obvious. "If you didn't know about this burglary till you got here this afternoon, Mr Craske, how did you know you didn't do it?" He nodded at Robert. "We'll take him with us, sir." He spoke like a man offering to remove the rubbish.

"Stop it!" Isabel shouted. "Stop it now! Listen to me, this is crap." She moved to put her hand on George's shoulder. "George would never be involved . . . You can't possibly believe a word she says. Friends? What friends?"

It was the first time she had ever touched him. Beneath the sweater his skin was boiling hot, his eyes, for once meeting hers in a way he normally avoided, looked at her as if he had never seen her before.

"George," she began, shaking him. George, she wanted to say, I don't like you, but I know you better than them.

Robert elbowed her aside.

"Do you know something, Miss Isabel?" George said over his shoulder. "She always seems to hurt herself with you around, and she never did before. At least you haven't bitten her. Yet."

No one heard but Isabel. A blush covered her face from chin to scalp, her mouth opened and closed in a resurgence of her so far suppressed shock, and, in that moment, she lost all pity for him. The pity was for herself.

He was ushered away. A slow shuffle beyond the door, the procession continuing down the corridor, three bodies in reluctant embrace.

"See you tomorrow!" Isabel yelled.

Another door slammed.

Serena struggled to her feet, sat back. She began to cry. A low pitched, keening noise at first, which rose into a howl of despair. Isabel could not bring herself to touch her. It was Andrew who hugged her and tried in vain to stem the flow. Isabel watched them with complete detachment.

Then, choosing the moment, the lights went out.

The sobbing died and Serena gazed at the light of the fire as if it were a new discovery. Then turned her gaze to the dying light outside. "Electricity," she said. "Must pay it."

The winter of this discontent was depressing. A different, shivering kind of darkness by ten at night. The light of a summer evening seemed remote.

"Do me a favour, boy. Stay awhile."

It was not like John Cornell to plead. He made it sound so gruff that the request seemed not really to matter, but it was still a plea.

"What's the matter, Pop? Feeling my age?"

"I'm not as old as that Serena Burley. She must have had her kids late on, mustn't she? Not good for a woman, that. They've got too independent by then. Start young, that's the answer."

Andrew smiled. To be honest, the cluttered comfort of his father's small living room was welcome relief. Being concerned for Isabel, which he was, did not make any difference to the fact he had been glad to get out of the house and leave her with her brother. He had been rather too helpful, he gathered, becoming *de trop* in the face of blood being thicker than water; found himself dismissed. A sense of loneliness had driven him to his father's and he was more than content to stay. At least this old boy had a tongue in his head and was not a hypocrite. Andrew found himself driven into approval of his dad by the sheer effect of contrast with another man. He poured them both generous measures of whisky.

"If I drink this and then another, which is what I feel like doing," he said, "I might have to stay the night."

"That'd be nice," his father said.

They sipped companionably.

"Pity about what happened up there," John said. "I should have liked the chance to buy that furniture. Sometime, when no one else had any further use for it."

"I know. So would I. I feel personally insulted by someone

stealing stuff and then wasting it. Don't worry, Dad. I know you wouldn't have jumped the gun."

John grunted, obscurely pleased. "You know who chose most of it, don't you?" he said. "It wasn't Serena who had the eye for a bargain in the seventies. It was her sister, the lovely Mabel. She was the one with the eye, and never did seem to resent the fact that she was buying the stuff for her richer, well married sister. Well, anyway, she and her brother-in-law, they were the ones with taste. He found stuff wherever he was, but Mab had a gift for knowing what was good. Plain as a pikestaff, clever as a monkey, mad as a hatter. I had a fling with her, once."

"Did you?" Andrew was amused. He restrained his avid curiosity. Despite the mellow mood, Papa was quite capable of refusing to tell a story just to keep him in suspense. "What was she like?"

"Straight up the wicket when it came to sex, but quite impossibly possessive. Seething cauldron, that woman. When I told her it was no go she wrote me a filthy letter."

"Significant letter writers, these women," Andrew remarked drily.

"The habits of childhood," his father said. "We all wrote letters. Telephones never quite became second nature. What's going to happen up at that house?"

"I don't know."

"Alzheimer's," his father said dreamily. "We used to call it senility. Your grandmother had it, did I tell you? In the days when there was no question of sending anyone away. Probably poisoned my attitude to women. Made me guilty as hell when you stayed put to look after me. You know what it does? It makes the person who's got it an absolute monster. Not a sweet little old thing, except in appearance, but a bundle of harm.

Completely selfish. Completely irresponsible and quite incapable of love. If I ever get like that, boy, do us both a favour and shoot me. I'm not a good man, but I don't want to be as bad as that. Not without enjoying it."

He paused, extended his glass for a refill, chuckled grimly. "Old granny wrecked us. You'll have heard tales of sweet eccentricity. Not tales of a wilful bitch who used the last remnants of her brain to manipulate. Fixed on survival. No one mattered."

"That bad?" said Andrew, lightly.

"Oh yes, make no mistake about it. It's the form of insanity that drives other people mad. It'll do that to your Isabel."

"She's not my Isabel. She's her brother's sister and her mother's daughter."

"God help her, then. God help her brother too. He was a nice little boy once. Adored his mother, but she was never there. Mab didn't like him much. There's nothing so destructive as duty. I don't want duty from you, never did."

"What do you want, then?" Andrew was grinning.

John pretended to consider, also grinning "You aren't that bad a business partner, I suppose. Otherwise, a bit of grudging admiration would do. The mutual kind."

Andrew nodded, as if sealing a deal. They were going to get drunk. His father got up and went in search of cheese and biscuits. A long time since lunch.

"By the way," he said. "Something I forgot to tell you. That little runt Derek, the one you never liked. Doc tells me he lives at the same address as that George you both told me about. Handy, isn't it?"

"Shit," said Andrew.

It reminded him of something else. In his pocket was a pencil torch he had found in the Burleys' backyard.

How fickle you are, you dreadful old bitch, Isabel thought, and how nice it is to indulge the disgust. There she sat, head of the table, Serena the queen, face decorated by a crazy black eye about which her daughter could not even feel shame. Laughing as Robert cut up her fish and encouraged her to feed scraps to the dog. And there she was, regardless of the betrayal of her lovely friend George, lapping up the attention Robert saw fit to give her. She did not even notice that he was acting like a politician, paying exaggerated tribute to someone's very important baby.

Isabel detested sitting in the kitchen. She congratulated herself on the amazing job she was doing in blotting out what had happened in it. The effort was debilitating, but survival depended on making it.

"Nice," Serena was saying. "Very nice, but too hot."

"Blow on it, then."

"She can be very sweet, can't she?" Robert said. Oh God, when could he go home?

Isabel could see his mind whirring, evading conclusions. He had regaled Isabel with recent experiences of typical old folks' homes, working himself into a lather. It was still out of the question, wasn't it, he pleaded? Look at her now, happy as a sandboy, and what a shame it would be to deliver all that insurance money over to the state. She felt monstrously tired, almost beyond fatigue and into a light-headed state in which the only thing that would weight her to earth was the effort of pretence and the food she did not want to eat.

"We've got to decide what to do," Robert stated portentously.

"There isn't much to decide, is there? Apart from the fact that you'll go home tomorrow. You must. All your responsibilities." The irony was lost on him.

"Yes, but we'll have to get someone in to help. Stay overnight. The police think these men might come back. That's quite common, I gather."

"Robert, exactly who do you think would be prepared to stay overnight in a deserted old barn like this? Nurses from a nursing agency? Then we would have two and a half women guarding the place as opposed to one and a half."

"I take it you're prepared to go on? With a better security system, of course. Good girl!" He could scarcely keep the relief from spreading into his voice like sugar dissolving in tea.

That was not quite what she had said, but she could not think coherently. She could only think of sleep; not having to move or make any decisions whatever. The lethargy would have made her agreeable to suicide; she was aware of it and powerless. Words happened of their own accord.

"Oh, yes," she said. "The worst has happened already. It can only get better. Besides," she added, without looking at her mother, "we probably deserve one another."

Robert had been good at practicalities. Such as getting the lights turned back on by dint of a combination of telephonic persuasion and cash. He had also sorted out the post. Got Serena to sign her cheques like a lamb. So useful to have a man round the place.

Robert had a dim memory of bedrooms in boarding schools, a memory he resented. The one allocated to him here was scarcely different. Cold sheets, so chilly he remained curled for half an hour, gradually easing his toes further and further down until he lay almost straight. Thinking of his daughter. George in his mother's room, no, not thinking about that. Fretting his head with thoughts of money and rage at burglars, not quite as keen on the desperation of the underprivileged as he might have been. Wondering if Isabel was having an affair with that Andrew Cornell bloke and that was why she was so biddable. Could be the answer to a lot of problems if they got together. And then, a man who dealt in antiques, now was that coincidence or not? Surely it was; his sister was not clever enough to conspire.

Somewhere way beyond the middle of the night he decided it was perfectly proper for a real man such as himself to have a real hot-water bottle. Fuzzy from the half sleep which is all that was possible with icy-cold feet, he fumbled downstairs. Poor Isabel, he thought for the first time, she must have done this. Halfway down he paused, wondering what it must have been like to hear ghostly music in the distance.

He saw her at the bottom of the stairs. His mother, standing by the front door, wearing all her night apparel and a pair of white gloves. Her pose was ambiguous; she could have been beckoning someone in or waving them away.

She drooped in disappointment, like a sad flower. Such a nice party. He regarded her with longing, then with despair. Thought of all the times when he had been favourite, and she loved him with such intensity and then left him to those play-ground boys. He could not bear to watch. He backed away, lay in bed listening for her until he slept and, with the advent of morning, told himself that he, too, had been dreaming.

This time Serena sat on the black-and-white tiles by the front door and looked out through the glass, in case they came back. Such a disgrace to have let people in through the kitchen. The kitchen was for the sort of painful person who volunteered to do the washing-up at the end of a party, like Mab. Everyone else pissed as a parrot, and her at the sink, smiling up from the suds like a sainted martyr. For all Serena knew, she was still there. Last night's lot seemed to leave a hell of a mess and have taken half the food with them when they went. In a coach.

The truth was, she was not at all sure of what had happened, although she did remember being put to bed with half her clothes on, tsk, tsk, drunk again, she supposed. The people from the party had stayed on, including her own son, which was surprising, because she could not recall him being much of a party animal. Poor little boy, the one she had missed most of all. Other boys hurt him at school, and she had not looked after him. Mab said playgrounds should be fun. Her son, big boy now, had told her they were hell.

It was sad for him to be afraid of playing.

It all made her contemplate the strange and charming magic exerted by a convivial crowd of people. She drew a smiling face in the air, too lazy and tired to leave her miserable daughter a message to that effect. She wanted to say that they should do this kind of thing more often and, if the child really wanted to persist in the lunacy of wanting to preserve her mother's miserable life, all she had to do was arrange for similar injections of spirit at regular intervals. Rooms should be cleared to make room for lots of men, without their boring wives. They could have parties for the fire brigade.

Of course once she got hold of that fucking recording thingy darling George had brought it would make life so much easier. It would save her from writing down her daily list of words, in the same way she had done in a small vocabulary notebook in school in order to learn at least twenty new words a week. But the words she remembered best were the ones that were forbidden, also the shortest: fuck, cunt, bugger, shit and damn. Words that sounded like exclamations, easy to expel in a series of gasps.

She had worked out on paper various permutations that did not sound as good. Tunc, rebugg, tish and nadm, to say nothing of raft for fart and palc for clap, not as satisfying at all. They lacked a certain resonance. There were no replacement words.

Serena sighed impatiently. So many tasks, so little time. Her room sailed over the house and she doubted if it was still attached after all this junketing. She had to go and unlock the door in case it snowed. Duty was a terrible thing.

She followed her usual route, hands outstretched, ready to touch the pictures and the chairs, the sofa, the clock, the table, the candlesticks. The dark was not really dark when it was occupied. There was a kind of light dancing around things.

Once she got away from the glass it was blacker than the inside of an oven. She felt, all of a sudden, as if someone had cut off the last joint of every finger, leaving little stubby knuckles waving at air, nothing to touch at all.

Nothing to direct her feet.

She clung to the door and waved at her own reflection. Beckoning for someone to come and show her the way back to bed. Footsteps came and went and she could not move for terror.

Chapter Eleven

AN OLD LADY with a worn-out mind was a mixture of animal, vegetable and mineral. She had to be made to ingest all those things. That was all there was to it.

She's significantly worse than when I last saw her, the psychiatric nurse told Isabel.

"Quite some time ago, wasn't it?"

"Three months. You could have called us before," she said defensively. "There are far more critical cases than this."

"I'm sure. What do you mean by worse?"

"Memory loss, worse. Lack of social awareness, worse. She bothers less with the façade. No greeting today."

"You aren't a man, you see."

The woman ignored her. "Lessened ability to perform ordinary domestic tasks, rather more eccentric about appearance, less physical coordination. Suffers slightly from persecution mania, which I don't remember noting before. Claims to have been bludgeoned by the cat."

Isabel was silent.

"But still compos mentis in flashes. Busies herself, fairly careful in her movements. Conspicuously clean."

"Early toilet training never forgotten," Isabel quipped. "And yes, she loves a bath. Absolutely independent about that. It's the only time I'm grateful for the fact she can't bear a locked

door. She plays with toys in there, floods the place. Great fun."
Stop burbling.

"The burglary must have upset her," the woman suggested with grave professional concern.

Isabel tried to prevent herself snapping. In another situation, she told herself, I might like your cheerful countenance and pity you for your impossible job, but at the moment I loathe the sight of you. Mother is not upset about the burglary. I am. It is me in pain, not her.

"The local authority can provide various aids. Rails, handles for the bath. Day Centre, twice a week?"

They can also piss in the wind. Isabel accepted the Day Centre suggestion and the offer of home help as occasional babysitter, both designed to give her a respite. All problems can be cured by tinkering. She lied to Robert on the phone, said there was more. New locks, a security system loaned by the police. There was. Mother had watched the installation of it, carefully. Hidden in the hall cupboard, once turned on it would detect movement beyond the kitchen. But as long as Serena wandered at night it was impossible to leave it on. The police had been called out and cancelled in time twice already.

"She's sort of on the cusp," the nurse said, not without admiration. "Extraordinary case. She seems to keep the worst at bay by sheer effort of will. Tells me she writes everything down."

"On the cusp of what?"

"I don't quite know. Complete change, or breakdown? She swore at me, you know."

"That's nothing different. She has a penchant for rude words."

"Funny, isn't it, what we retain? Admirable, really."

"Fucking disgusting, really."

Isabel had the feeling that while Mother had passed a test, she herself had not. She no longer exuded that air of compassion; nor was she gentle; not actively unkind, but not particularly patient either. She was like someone who, resigned to a sentence of imprisonment, has decided to play by the rules, albeit resentfully. The home help appeared the next day, equally resentful, easily intimidated by both of them. Isabel used her presence as an escape route. Looked over the promised Day Centre, where there was not a single person in sight among the crocks lined up against the wall, and left in a hurry, despair, failure and revulsion dogging her heels. Stocked up with animal, vegetable and mineral, came home and locked them both in. She bought a tapestry to keep her hands busy and stop them itching to slap. She bought soap, shampoo, gel and facial scrubs, scoured herself nightly, trying to eradicate the lingering odour of shame.

The Day Centre would not work. Without quite defining why, Isabel was sure of it and took no steps to warn or prevent disaster. Allowed them to take Mother, resplendent in hat, skirt, with three cardigans adding to her breadth, plus ghetto blaster under one arm and handbag carried like a cudgel under the other. Watched, without much sympathy, when the car came back three hours later, the woman driver resembling a person who had endured three rounds inside a boxing ring with unfair opposition. Ghost-coloured, she was. Mrs Burley had caused mayhem. Loud music, blaring. Telling them all they were a load of old farts, or was it tarts, and why didn't they get up and dance. Tried to haul them out of wheelchairs. Fought all the way home, wanting to drive the car back. Had them all over the road.

"Perhaps she got a bit overheated," Isabel suggested, smiling sweetly.

"It was nice," Serena announced, refusing to get out of the passenger seat. "Very nice."

"Nice for you," Isabel said, pulling her out without any attempt at persuasion. "Not so nice for them." She scowled at the driver, challenging. "Same time on Thursday, then?"

"I'll have to check . . ."

"Of course you will."

Perhaps, Isabel reflected, four days after the emptying of her mother's house, it is me who has made her worse. Why on earth did I ever think I could make her better? I offered comprehensive care to someone I loved, thus taking away what little responsibility there was left in her; maybe the downhill path would not have been as swift without me. I am silly. Silly and sullied. There were times when a jumbling of words seemed a useful saving of any kind of analysis. She did not speak to her mother; she hissed at her.

And then there was George. Sitting on her conscience like a heavy toad, his absence filling the house, even though it was a relief. In the early afternoons Serena set out a tray for tea. It took a full half hour, all her movements indecisive, looking at cups and saucers, moving in and out of awareness of what they were for. Then sitting beside them with her gaze fixed on the back door, waiting with the dog. Waiting.

Isabel could scarcely bear to touch Serena. She did not want to touch anyone, or to be touched. Not on the hand. Not anywhere on the skin. Especially when the van came up to the back door. Andrew and another greeted by Serena like honoured guests, while Isabel quailed, heart in mouth. Impossible to imagine the dancing men would come back, not in daylight, not so soon. How easy it was to terrify with an act of kindness. By the time she had stopped shaking, Andrew had explained himself. A spare sofa and a couple of armchairs, he said. My father thought you could do without a dining-room table for a while, didn't use it much anyhow, did you? But the living room, that nice room with the fire, well, pity to waste it.

They were not the family of sofa, chairs and rugs that any-one present would have chosen, but they were clean and they were adequate. They sat in the vastness of the drawing room like forlorn creatures seeking warmth, comic caricatures of the real thing, refugees from an alien culture, speaking to no one. Isabel was aware that gratitude was in order, spoke it, but could not feel it.

"What's happened about George, Andrew? Do you know?"

Of course he would know, sooner than she. Via the all-male network that was morally obliged to tell her last, in case she got upset.

"They had to let him go. On bail to return in a couple of days. Pending further inquiries. Condition of bail not to come here."

He watched her closely, wondering why exactly she had become so brittle and what it was such news might provoke in her. Anger? Amazement? Relief? Robert Burley was reported to have expressed the first two, while she seemed indifferent. He wished she would open her arms instead of hugging them to her chest, let him melt some of this fierce and secretive resentment.

"Oh, I collected the post," he said. Three letters.

"Mine," said Serena, grabbing them with the speed the dog took a titbit.

Andrew watched. He felt as if his fingers had been bitten.

"Mine," said Isabel, seizing Serena's wrist, squeezing hard until Mother's fingers succumbed and she gave a sharp shriek of pain. Her protest was not coupled with surprise. It was as if such treatment had become commonplace. Andrew did not like what he saw, Isabel hugging rage and fear against her ribs, her face as sharp as a beak.

You can go home now, George Craske, for a day or two, and bad luck to you. Don't shake my hand, will you? Come back the day after tomorrow, or we'll come looking.

What have we done to you? Nothing, in any obvious sense. Oh, they could have been violent, but then George's own experience of the police, admittedly not recent by any manner of means, had never included rough stuff. Persistence to the point of tears, yes, violence as such, no; he had never even feared it. All they had done before giving up in disgust was to use a kind of malevolent chumminess to turn his life inside out and leave the raw nerves of it exposed. About those previous convictions, Georgie Boy? You were a cook, weren't you? Yes, for a works canteen. Could do with you in ours, Georgie. Three works canteens, wasn't it? Two arrests for thieving from your employers. Then there was that girl in the third, amazing you could get another job, wasn't it, but I suppose way up north they might not be fussy about someone who can actually cook what real men eat during the night shift. Is that right, George?

He could feel himself beginning to weep. Felt grateful for that little hostel room where anything of value was already gone and there was never any point in saving things, not like his other rooms in olden, golden days, stuffed with items he might just need later: packet soup, tins, foil containers, napkins, towels; things which even he could see no logical reason to steal.

I had a hungry childhood, he said. Not much of an explanation to the supervisor in the last set of kitchens. He'd taken a shine to her and been ignored, ain't that right, George? Like Isabel Burley, is it, George? Like the teapot in your car? We know you're a thief. The question is, how much of one?

"No!" he shouted. Although, perversely, it calmed him. At least they had got something totally wrong. Reassuring, that. Don't touch me.

So why did you rape her, George? Why do that to the poor girl? He could still hold on to the way they had not got their facts quite right, because it had not been a girl, not as such. A mature woman who'd given him the wink, put him on the day shift to be under her eye, although the crowds and the noise drove him witless. He couldn't talk to her, couldn't explain. Whichever God allocated vocabulary had been unkind to him. Can't talk, George, that's your problem. Haven't got the words.

You told her a lot, George. Actions speak louder than, don't they? She came and found me after dark. A pound of bacon in my bag. There'd been an argument, end of shift. Waiting in line to be checked out, leaving me last. They had music on in there all day. Wasn't a man worked there didn't shout and scream. Pay was awful too, we were expected to steal things. See? She did see. She was a nice woman. I hit her with something and found myself giving her one. Last time I ever gave anyone one, if you take my meaning. Never again, I swear, and never on a kitchen floor. Although, God knows, my life's been spent in kitchens. Poor cow. She was going to shop me and I thought she liked me. Thought it would put things right, and it went too far.

Women are a bit difficult, George, aren't they? You did hit

her quite hard. I mean, no one could have said she was consenting. Not what with being unconscious at the material time. I suppose she moaned in appreciation, did she, George? Brutal rape, it says here. You even pleaded guilty. Your sort of bastard stops at nothing.

Don't know what you mean, George said. He didn't. The translation of ethics from one offence to another made no sense to him. Couldn't they see? A petty thief and a haunted, limited man did not automatically meld into other forms of dishonour. They did see. They believed him, literal men that they were. Questions about friends were met with the same confusion. Questions at the hostel, indifferently conducted since everyone was bored by now, seemed to reveal a welcome, if friendless, inmate who cooked. Not a skill common with burglars.

So that was what he was. A harmless little rapist with a connection to a burgled house. The sort of face and boyish hair for whom some mad old lady might invent the friends which a sweet motherly woman like that might wish him to have.

Not the violent, claustrophobic man who walked into the ice-cold air in search of Derek. Derek, who would survive any questions, the reformer's dream, because he was never short of the words. Derek would hit a princess and walk away with an explanation about a cupboard door attacking him on the way out. Derek made shit smell of roses. He had no scars. Mr Milk Froth. Pimply, purply rat-haired fuck of a cunt, was he.

The one thing they had done was give him back his dictaphone.

The warden looked at him with sorrowful opprobrium, told him his room had been searched. He knew, did he not, that his tenure in it was temporary, dependent on him not being charged with another criminal offence. Sod off, George told him, I've not been charged and I won't be either. Have you seen Derek? The man looked at his watch. Oh, he'll be away at his work, now. They brought back your car and he borrowed it. That's what I want to see him about, George said, neutrally. The warden was proud of Derek. Kept himself smart. He did not know that he was facing in George the only criminal he might ever meet who had accepted what he had done and was sorry for it.

George was hungry. He supposed, quite irrelevantly, that the only bonus of a couple of days in police cells was not spending money on food. Not that this kind of hunger was the same as the desire to eat; he did not want to give himself that kind of comfort, slow himself down, stop him jogging past the neat little houses into town.

Fog was wreathing around the old church hall near what used to be the railway station. It added anonymity to the innocence of daylight. George knew he would find Derek there, because a sense of justice informed him that that was the way it should be, simply on account of the fact it was his turn for something to go right. He had told himself that all he wanted to do was ask Derek why? Why steal the furniture and drop him in it? Why pick that particular house and not another?

Fate was kind enough to deliver him Derek without allies. Everyone else gone, and him left in charge of the shop. The boss at home, nursing stiff legs and business was slack, anyway, the way it was as soon as people got a sniff of Christmas. Seeing Derek, whistling at the back, ignoring the creak of the door, George paused for a moment to wonder what anyone would ever want with all this stuff. To live in such confusion: a warehouse full of furniture was something disgusting when he considered how futile it was and how empty that room of Serena's had been. Furniture with numbers on, waiting to be possessed, made no sense.

Derek, still whistling, pushed his bantamweight against a table, getting it lined up with the next thing. Gave it a wipe with a cloth, totally absorbed when George hit him. So much for questions and conversation.

It could not end there: Derek was too quick, too strong, to be stunned by a blow on the back of his head. He pretended was all, falling across his table until George tried to drag him off, then whirling round and pushing a foul-smelling rag into George's face. Hitting him below the belt, encountering rock, opening his mouth to speak, his wet, red lips forming an O. George smacked him in it, followed through to the ribs. Trust Derek to raise his hands to protect his pretty face, serve him right. He was soft in the stomach; all his power was in his head, that filthy little brain of his.

He butted George, catching his forehead with agonizing accuracy, so that George saw redder than ever. Kicked away at Derek's shins, so that he fell among a pile of chairs, screaming. One of the chairs seemed to explode into a series of legs. George took one and hit Derek in the lower part of his face. He used the wood like a hammer. More than once. He was not counting.

Something crashed in the corner of the room. The furniture was closely and unsteadily stacked, the floor uneven. The shiver of breaking glass from a capsized wardrobe door stopped all other movement, so shocking was the sound. Without thinking, George dragged Derek in that direction. There was blood on his hands. There was the dim thought that if he placed Derek and wardrobe together, the damage might appear accidental, provided no one looked closely. Derek's jaw hung crooked, broken, teeth smashed. There would not be much by way of words coming out of that gob for a while.

Or ever? George listened for the sound of breathing, heard the rattling. He had his heel poised to stamp on the jaw, hesitated, stopped. Didn't particularly want him dead.

Someone would be in soon. No one left junk like this unguarded for long. He took his car keys from Derek, which felt, oddly, like some kind of theft, taking something out of someone's pocket, and it was then he began to see the enormity of what he had done, the sheer, bloody-minded stupidity of it. It was not even as satisfying as he had imagined, this transitory sweetness of revenge. Five minutes ago he could have defended himself against the world. Now he could not. Ten minutes since he could have said he was still a free man. Now he could not. There was a set of overalls hanging on a hook in the back office. Huge, made for a bigger man than he, covered the blood nicely.

Then he was out of there, remembering the car but wanting to run. Back to the hostel. Looking at the wreckage of the room. Took his spare sweaters and the old boots that no one else had wanted, stuffed into a polythene bag. Left an old envelope from the hall on his bed, bearing the legend, "Gone to relatives." Chance would be a fine thing. If his relatives existed George did not know them. The message seemed sadly dishonest, so he changed it. "Gone home." People could impute whatever meaning they liked to that. He felt uncharacteristically clever as he walked out into the darkness, a clever fool with the mark of Cain branded on his forehead.

Into a car which smelt of Derek and the sense of nowhere to go.

The trouble with kindness was that it had to be first earned and then repaid. Isabel did not like these kind of debts. It was death to self-respect to begin and go on owing someone something. She could not accept that as her due. There was a nagging feeling which made her feel that she owed Andrew something, just as she owed the world, as if she still had to explain herself, justify her existence. Muddled it was, but she could not accept generosity with grace, even on behalf of someone else. She did not want victim support, either: it made her feel like a victim. She wanted the whole lot of them out of her hair, but tea must be made, biscuits produced, the situation talked about, as if the theft of belongings had been the most important thing about the invasion. She shivered. She was always cold. She made all the right, hospitable moves and would not let anyone around her settle.

And when they were gone she looked at the letters. A formulaic, citizens' charter type letter for Ma from the Electricity Board, an inventory of things stolen from Robert, and a letter from Joe. Mother waved from her new chair by the fire, struggled to get up. The sight of paper coming out of envelopes seemed to enrage her.

"Darling!" she yelled.

"Don't darling me." Isabel plonked into her lap three of the largest books with torn pages, sufficient to weigh her down into her seat without doing damage. Enough to get several minutes' respite while the poor old sweetheart worked out a way to get them off her knees and on to the floor while darling daughter retired to the kitchen. Perhaps a letter from Joe would change the universe. Give the greyness a tinge of pink, if that could be imagined. Lift the afternoon fog. Stop everything from being animal, vegetable and mineral.

Sweetheart,

No word from you and I do miss you! What do you do all day? Life here is busy, busy, busy! But there is a window coming up soon, a whole free weekend, so do you think you could get away, just before Xmas? Or I could come nearer you! There must be hotels in your neck of the woods! I don't suppose you'd want to bother your mother, and I wouldn't want to bother her, of course, but on the 16th, 17th (or thereabouts, depending on you), I'm all yours!

Issy, I know I'm slow about a lot of things, but I have been thinking about you . . .

A series of pictures rose into her mind in a rising tide of panic. What would he think of this place, the patrician grandeur of it, the lack of any kind of amenity he held dear? The second image was Aunt Mab saying out loud, this one is not worth his salt, my niece is worth, far better, my niece is the price of rubies. She shoved that image away along with the first. Thought instead of Joe climbing all over her like a man faced with the Matterhorn, protesting allegiance to no other cliff face. The shivering of cold began again. All those bloody exclamation marks. Shallow, Mab was shouting: men are as shallow as puddles. Isabel finally felt nothing but a lethargic sadness. A fog of melancholia which mirrored the garden outside. Until she heard her mother shouting. Torn books had a use after all. They were fuel for the fire, which sparked and caught the edge of Serena's long corduroy skirt. The hem was smouldering into a half-hearted flame.

Isabel seized her under the shoulders, hauled her upright where she stood uncertainly, grabbing the mantelpiece while her daughter stripped the skirt from round her middle. Plumped her gasping mother back down in the damn chair, chucked the skirt on the fire, knelt at her feet and checked her legs for damage. Nothing. She could have used that big, heavy skirt as a fire screen, or blackout curtains. Sitting in suspenders and heavy stockings beneath faded silk drawers, Serena looked ludicrous. She spoke urgently, reached out her hand. The shock was not going to kill her. The screams were more rage than fear.

"I need to talk to you," she said. "Tell you things. Like I didn't ever. Got to tell you things."

"There, my sweetie," Isabel crooned, looking with something like pleasure at the image of her mother, knees apart, thighs pressing against suspenders, old-lady knickers, all of it resembling some dreadful parody of glamour. "You just sit still. It's so good to see you without your dignity," Isabel crooned. "Get some idea how it feels, do you? I hate you: do you know that? I hate you."

Andrew found his father's little helper. There was a sharp smell of blood, urine, faeces, marking the spot where Derek had begun to crawl in a circle. Whichever way he looked, there was a view of wooden panels, legs, a forest of inanimate things offering nothing but impediment. Derek could not pull himself up with his hands: if he took his hands from his face, his face would drop apart. Andrew stared at the face. It recalled a previous fascination with surrealist paintings.

Andrew had nursed an invalid, was no stranger to the stench of human excrement. He knew how to control revulsion. Ambulance, yes. Turn the man on his side and clear the airways to ensure he did not choke, yes. He knew that his footsteps going away to the phone would create desperation. He did not hurry.

He had always disliked Derek with peculiar intensity.

Compassion for him now did not mean the same thing as liking; nor did it defy his instinctive conclusions. It was a small town, after all.

"In a minute, Derek, in a minute. Going to be all right in a minute. The ambulance is on its way."

Derek had such sweet blue eyes. His nails, spread in a fan across his blood-streaked cheeks, looked dirty and pale. A film of varnish clung to them.

"You fell into the chairs," Andrew said evenly. "And then, half dazed, you staggered into the wardrobe. Raise one of your little pinkies if you understand." The fingers remained still, the look desperate.

"This piece of wood," Andrew continued, holding it up, then throwing it away, so that it clattered and echoed, "has nothing to do with anything. Just as George has nothing to do with anything. If it was George, you get tied in with a burglary, or why would he hit you? Not that he did. Of course. Not George's style, is it? And you had nothing to do with any burglary, of course. It would never cross your mind."

This time the index finger raised itself in a kind of salute, which Andrew acknowledged. There was the comforting sound of the phone ringing.

"You'll be all right, Derek. Dad's got an insurance policy against accidents on the premises. Only accidents, mind. Not assault."

Derek closed his eyes and attempted to nod. The effort was alarming, an audible movement of bone and the granular sound of torn cartilege.

"One last thing," Andrew mentioned evenly, standing up so his feet were level with Derek's head. "Did any of you buggers touch Isabel?"

The tortured face, swollen to twice its size, looked at him in blank denial. Enough, Andrew thought. Enough. I have implicated myself in sufficient violence for today. First Isabel's, then my own.

It was not Isabel's house. Her house was in another place, another time zone, almost another climate. Circling round her mother, who had taken that evening to following her like a shadow, behaving like a hungry cat rubbing round calves in an orgy of cupboard love, Isabel made herself feel homesick. For the metropolis, for useless Joe and the sound of sirens, alarms and other punctuation marks which made her life seem crowded. Knowing that the rereading of his letter to her might implode this self-induced longing, she consigned that to the fire. Along with Mother's damaged petticoat. There was no protest from the owner, only a cry of admiration, reminiscent of fireworks, as the remnants of it burst into flames and flew up the chimney. When Isabel traversed the dark corridor to the kitchen, Mother was her shadow, talking aimlessly. When Isabel went upstairs to the lavatory, Mother went too, hanging about until she had finished, like a person lost. Chatter, chatter, chatter. Worse than the deafening sound of the music machine she had confiscated.

What was she talking about with the stream of words she produced in response to enforced silence? Things, Serena said. Things. There were snippets of ancient grievances Isabel recognized from previous tellings hitherto ignored. About darling Aunt Mab always washing up. About parties. Each room visited created a pause, a change of subject. She was suddenly affectionate, wanting to touch. She stroked the living-room walls as she might have stroked a cat. Patience wore thin.

"Got to tell you things, darling. Where are my letters? I need my letters."

Isabel doused the fire. "You didn't write letters, Ma. You used to. Oh yes, you used to do that a lot. Then you wrote letters to people abusing them, didn't you Ma? I found some of the drafts on the floor. Some you sent, I suppose, others you forgot, left in the desk. You wouldn't want Doc Reilly or George to see those, would you, Ma?"

She kicked the coal. "You probably got this wonderful idea writing letters to my lovers. Jealous cow," Isabel continued, talking to herself. "Probably just as well they got posted."

"What letters?" Serena asked, head on one side. The bruise above her eye was rainbow-coloured, could have been the result of an extreme application of cosmetics. "Letters," she repeated with wonder. "A, B, C. See?"

"And all you write now is a list of favourite words. I saw those too."

Serena tapped her forehead. "Words, darling. I need them to tell me things." She looked slowly about herself, as if expecting to find them littered all over the floor. Words she wrote but never said out loud, because they were rude.

They were back in the kitchen. The security system was so simple a child could work it, the man said. Serena had watched with avid curiosity while it was put in place, enjoying her view of the broad back of the man who installed it. She had examined the keys for the new locks with apparent indifference; she examined them again now. Let her get out, then, if she wanted, Isabel thought. I don't give a shit what happens to me. She felt as if she was being followed by a cloud of flies. Tomorrow Serena could have back her music.

"Isabel, darling?"

"Yes? What?" Cross to the point of fury.

Big eyes, hooded lids ready to burst in that lined face. "Why do you hate me? What have I done?"

Fucking nothing. Bitch.

"Isabel? Can you take me down?"

"Down where?"

"Down into the snow. I don't know. I don't know the way."

"What snow? What way? Say what you mean. Follow the lights."

"Oh, yes. Good-night then, my lovely cat. Good-night."

Chapter Twelve

SERENA HAD A CERTAIN STEP, slow, quick, quick slow. She could do it in a kind of dance, as if she measured indecision with every set of steps. The music acted as a design for movement. Slow, over the difficult stairs; fast down the smoother corridors, like a waltz, or a polka needing a partner at every turn.

Without George she was rootless. She went round the house, slow, slow, quick quick slow, looking for him. Looking for someone. It was a big house; the empty ground floor echoed to the sound of footsteps. When they stopped Isabel wondered where they were: when they began again she wanted to scream. Poor soul. No cat to trail round after her, no man to mouth kisses, poor Mummy, who had to make do with her daughter and a daft dog.

Serena liked the sound of her own steps: she put on her boots and stamped; she made as much noise as an army on the march, except at night, when she tiptoed. She wanted to talk all the time. Isabel stayed silent, wanting to punish. She took refuge, in her bedroom, in the corridors — so that she would know which way to run when the footsteps came towards her — and, finally, in the bathroom. The floor littered with towels. The place smelled of Mother.

Can your mother wash unaided, she mouthed to herself? Oh, yes, all but the teeth. She likes to wash, morning and night, but in here, and everywhere, she leaves a trail of mess.

A week after the burglary, Isabel squinted at her steamy reflection. The face was not her own. An alien cast of features, set into a skull wrongly shaped for too long a neck, blurred back at her. Get into your car and go, she told it. Why not? Pride? A lack of confidence about that outside world, as if she were as incompetent in it as this old cow with her marching? She gave herself a wan smile. The distortions in the mirror were not entirely the premature ageing and brutalizing of a face. The glass was smeared with fingerprints. It could almost have been writing, someone writing in the steam. I DIDN'T DO IT, on one corner. She looked closely.

There was a banging on the door.

"Can I come in?"

"No."

"Yes! Yes! Yes!"

Isabel was mesmerized now, less by her own reflection than by the writing and the thought of fingerprints. George's fingerprints in Mother's bedroom. A fact forgotten. Cunning replaced impatience. Curiosity replaced a sense of futility.

The thin policeman had been back, keeping an eye on the house. Isabel felt oddly brave about the prospect of the burglars returning. There was safety in the possession of a mobile phone and the simple alarm. Burglars with big pricks were not as intimidating as an animal, vegetable, mineral old woman who had come to behave like a malevolent ghost. And nothing was as frightening to Isabel as herself.

"Come down to the kitchen, Mother."

Isabel got pen and paper, squashed Serena into a chair facing

her writing implements. As a version of *Playschool*, this sometimes worked, although daylight and writing did not always go
together in Serena's mind. Writing was for after dark.

"Write it down, Mummy. Go on, write. You haven't done
your letters."

The therapy was not going to distract this time. Oh, how
she detested her, pitied her, failed to recognize her. She wanted
to guide that large hand, fuelled by that deficient mind, across
the paper. Make her mother write once, and once only: I am
sorry for what I have done to you.

"I don't want to do this."

"Yes, you do. Get on with it."

One hour to go until the social worker arrived to take her
to the Day Centre, probably the last time they could manage. It
had never been a long-term project. The waiting between
respites seemed interminable. Isabel had a sullen ambition to
get inside Serena's room and Serena's bloody-minded mind.
There was no privacy left to violate in this house. She had begun
by vowing to respect her mother's desire for that precious commodity. Left her desk alone, left her room alone.

Serena cocked her head. "I heard my cat," she announced. "I
did, I heard her."

"Where?"

"Down the cellar."

Isabel was seized with malice. "Go and find it, then. I won't
stop you."

Serena could fall down all those steps, those damp and list-
ing steps, fatal to old limbs. The door could be locked against
her resurrection. If she were to choose her fate, it was surely
better than burning to death.

"I shall, but only if you come with me."

Serena spoke with a calm deliberation that sent a chill through Isabel's spine. She was not mad, merely a stranger. A stranger with a terrible instinct for truth, bent to the task of forming words on a page with the slow patience of an industrious, dull-witted child. She seemed to guess how much Isabel loathed her, relished it. Don't do it, said the words. Don't.

In an all too brief Day Centre respite, Isabel drove to the shops for food and bits and pieces, and, on impulse, stopped by the church on the way back. Maybe Mab's grave would provide some inspiration. She would tidy it up again at least, a sop to conscience for the fact that the increasing untidiness of the house was becoming a matter of indifference. The days were so grey, the ration of light so mean, the barren lack of order seemed less accusing and Isabel remained constantly tired. The ghost of Mab might lift the resolve with earthy advice, remind her of duty and honour, and postpone the business of going home.

The graveyard was like a stage set of what a graveyard should be before dark: damp, lifeless, peculiarly verdant, even in winter. The black slate of memorial stones shone with the perspiration of damp. Isabel changed direction to amble down avenues of graves, fascinated by the grim tranquillity of this car park of the dead and the manner in which they were commemorated. No Mums and Dads here; all inscriptions conventional and respectful, but small control over violent pink granite, a headstone shaped like an aeroplane, a weeping angel holding a guitar. Something in the hedge caught her eye. Lurking beneath the holly was a phone. At first she thought it was a deliberate joke, part of the mementoes, a piece of wit left in case Grandad in the adjacent plot should wish to phone home when he was feeling better. Then she recognized the phone from the living room of their own ravaged house. Stuck with a label, an old phone, nothing newfangled about it, thrown into the hedge by a passing thief and looking forlorn. Isabel touched it, gingerly, left it where it was. Moved on to the graves of Mab and her father, quickly looking over her shoulder. Nothing; an innocent afternoon in the middle of the week when no one but she was visiting the avenues of the deceased.

Someone had improved on the tidiness of her father's grave. Sprigs of holly from the hedge sat in a tin on the neatened gravel, giving the thing a festive air; the letters of his name were free of the misty cobwebs that adorned Mab's less fulsome inscription. Isabel stared at the holly leaves, waxy and shiny, sharp. The holly bears a berry... as red as any blood... The lines of the Christmas carol stirring in her mind, making her want to hum the rest of the words she could never remember. Her father had a fine singing voice, she could recall the sound. He would sing at parties; once he had serenaded her on her eighteenth birthday in front of fifty guests and all she had felt was embarrassment. A strict and loving man, resented, ignored, adored; far too demonstrative for a teenager obsessed by masculinity of the more youthful kind, hellbent still on them and the approval of that distant, amused mother. Isabel had never credited him with his own personality: he was provider, ruler, more absent than present, loved madly on the first day he came home before his attempts to exert control made him irritating. Darling, distinguished Dad, a slippy kind of memory, perhaps because his wife never discussed him.

Isabel was saddened by her ignorance of him, puzzled and alarmed by the recent attentions to his grave. Someone had tended it before; she had known that and had failed to question it when she had given the same attention to Mab's miserable patch. There could be a sort of contract cleaning service for graves, as far as she knew, although it seemed a strange service to be provided by strangers. She no longer remembered what she had thought about the disparity before, other than it creating another notch on the guilt scale for not thinking about it at all.

Grazed nerves made for vivid imagery. Kneeling on the edge of Father's plinth, she could imagine a disembodied arm extending from Mab's grave, sticking up out of the earth, twisting and busily plucking at the weeds. Tidy, organized Mab, unable to tolerate mess for long. It was, after all, Mab who had rooted the family here; she may even have found them the house, or maybe they had dumped themselves so close because she had been vital to the arrangements. Isabel was surprised by how little she knew of any of this. How little she would ever know now. How strange and sad it was that it was her mother whom she had sought to emulate when, all the time, Mab was the one worth copying.

She stood up in sudden disgust. Maudlin, macabre and escapist. The dead were dead: they did not matter in their graves. Nor talk to themselves, as she did, nor suffer the chattering teeth that afflicted her as she ran back to her car, flung herself inside for the flimsy protection it afforded, pitched the thing back up the track as if it were a jeep and the holes in the road did not matter.

A light appeared in the window of the neighbours who lived next to the church and faced the parking space. A curtain twitched. Look at the way she had parked her car, that girl; look at the way she drove it. She was just like her mother, both of them nutty as fruitcakes.

"What does she think she's doing?" Sal said to George. "She took off like all hell was behind her. Seen a ghost or something? Only for a minute I thought she was about to come through the window. Like her mother nearly did the other year."

"She wouldn't do that. Not normally."

"You all right, George? Sure you don't want another bit of cake?"

She half wanted him to go, half to stay. Her old man had never been keen on George. It was a trifle embarrassing to have him stay so long, sit about talking as if he were waiting for something. He was nice enough, always had been, but awkward company. Sal was puzzled, but since he seemed so ignorant of the burglary that had brought Isabel to the door, and then the police with questions about what she had not seen, he was less than rewarding.

"No thanks, Missus. It was lovely."

"Look, there she is, Mrs Burley, being brought back home. That's three afternoons this week someone's taken her out and brought her back. Gets shorter each time, though I'm glad someone does that. I don't think her daughter looks fit to look after her."

"No," said George. "I'm not sure about that either."

Sal was a mixture of window-hopping curiosity and a curious lack of observation, aided by hardness of hearing and the constant companionship of her television set. George often wondered why people who lived in the middle of woods and fields still found their greatest acquaintance with nature in wildlife programmes. As long as he had visited here, for post and cake, Sal had always been indoors, wore the pallor of a woman who never went for a walk.

"Don't you want to take the letters, George?"

"No, leave 'em. Nothing important, I'll be bound."

She didn't question why he hid his car round the back instead of parking on the road. George was grateful for that.

"Going to snow," said Sal, affecting a country wisdom learned from the weather forecast. "You can tell by the sky."

"I hope not," George remarked.

Indeed he hoped not. He was becoming afraid of the cold.

Passing the church Andrew Cornell realized that he still had the habit of prayer, learned by rote early on and preserved entirely for addressing an amorphous and anonymous God on the subject of the weather. Such as, why are you allowing it to snow? Please don't. Offering some form of atonement to the deity if he would listen. Perhaps the deity realized that, although the blossoming skies and first flakes of white might curtail his errand of mercy as he made his way to Serena Burley's house with a television in the back of his car, the errand was not actually done from the purest of motives. What motivates a man to feel concern for a woman unless it be lust of a kind? No, it was not disinterested kindness. He simply did not like a day to pass without seeing Isabel's face. Even though she sent him away, denying his attempts to lighten the load, even though that face was as pinched as a shrivelled berry, the rest of her as spare as a winter twig, and what she exuded was a bitter sap. He wanted to help because he wanted at least a sight of the girl he thought he could perceive beyond the smothering blanket of her responsibilities. No, he conceded, it was not selfless; otherwise he would not also want her to look back and see him.

The snow was light and damp, uncertain snow, the same as the last week of purgatorial English weather, teasing with bitter cold, daring a citizen to go about his business. The solace of these days for children was the prospect of Christmas; for Andrew, long conversations with his father. What that man knew astounded and sometimes disturbed him. Made him realize that his own habit of secrecy was an inherited feature. We should have been spies, his father said. The things we have in common, son, are a matter of blood and cannot be avoided. Father was wise, in his way; a man to be trusted, enjoyed, but not always liked for his perspicacity.

There was the same form of greeting from Serena, ecstatic, fluttering, but fading into a fixed smile and a constant patting of his arm, as if to ensure he was solid flesh. A contrast to Isabel's greeting, friendly enough, relieved even, but not sufficient to make him feel his presence had been sorely missed. The television was produced, with magnetic effect on Serena. Andrew fixed it in the living room: cops and robbers blared from the screen, loud, dramatic music. He noticed a new fireguard around the fire, ash spreading on the replacement rug, dust on the mantelpiece. Serena sat, apparently content, blinking at the screen through unwashed glasses.

"Why didn't I think of replacing the telly?" Isabel asked, wrong-footed again. "Should have done that first, shouldn't I? Why am I so stupid?"

Don't think about it, he murmured: I had one spare.

They took up independent residence in the kitchen. There had been a nursing chair by the fire he had admired before, now relegated to a corner. Crumbs on the table, dishes in the sink, the dog restive for attention. Isabel watched Andrew taking in the details, felt herself afflicted by a sense of inadequacy.

"It was my mother wrote those letters, you know," she told him, not wasting time. She was beyond making polite conversation and this was the first thing she could think of, however irrelevant, to offer as an oblique excuse for the sloppiness that was evident all around her.

He shook his head. "I don't think so."

He no longer did. It no longer mattered. He wanted to tell her about Derek, ask her if this little man, last seen sweetly silent with a wired-up jaw in a hospital ward, resembled one of the burglars; wondered if the hint of revenge for the theft of objects to which she had been so clearly indifferent would make any difference to her desperate malaise. He decided not.

"I hate her," Isabel said. "That's what's making all this so difficult. I would be brave enough, competent enough, if I didn't have that at my back."

He reached over the table and took her hand in his. There was a perceptible flinching, but she did not pull away, smiled at him briefly and apologetically.

"You could go," he said. "Just go. Someone would pick up the pieces; someone always does."

"No. It may seem mad, but I can't just go."

"Look," he said, "I can't help you if you won't let me."

"You help a lot, Andrew. I don't know what we would have done . . ."

"Only it occurred to me that if you could perhaps see the woman she was, the one she used to be — and I don't mean a woman who might have written malicious letters when her mind was unhinged by the menopause — well, you might find it easier." He was flustered.

She let her hand remain as it was. "What do you mean?"

"Discover what she was like. Go through her things. Try and remember what it was you loved about her. Look at her all over again. She was magnificent: my father says so, everyone says so, I knew so, so did you. If you're so determined to stay, you need . . . justification. If you haven't got a vocation, you either look after someone out of love, or a relic of that love. You can't do it without respecting her for something. Seeing something. Does that make sense?"

Not really, he could tell by her face, and even to his own ears his words were pretentious and silly. What could he know?

"Explore this house. I would," he said softly. "How closely have you really looked? Look for clues. Attics?"

She shook her head. "Small. Empty."

"Cellars?"

"Cold and cluttered. Things get shoved down there because it's easy."

Something stirred in her even as she shrugged. The same curiosity that had stirred earlier in the day. The challenge of a task. Finding something more in the mother who had betrayed her, spat on her devotion, then and now. Looking for something that would justify the veneration for Mother which she had carried around for a lifetime. Looking for redemption for them both.

Andrew looked out of the window uneasily. The snow was falling thick and fast, hectic globs of white, fighting each other. Tomorrow was auction day: he could not afford to be marooned out here, although the thought was in other ways far from unpleasant. There were duties, as well as hopeless causes. She caught the direction of the glance, translated the anxiety.

"Oh damn. Is it settling? Look, you'd better go. Don't worry about us. We've got enough of everything."

She wanted to say, come back soon. Talk to me about something else. Tell me about your father and the way we were, alleviate my inward-looking life by allowing me to listen to more than these footsteps. She liked him; inside the barrier which had erected itself, she liked him plenty, but there was no room for such a suggestion, because she could not feel herself worth liking. Silly and sullied; his attention made her less excited than afraid of what he saw and what he might find. A body which had currently lost possession of whatever it had been that passed for a purpose in life, or a soul. Not a lot to offer anyone. Which made it a mixture of sadness and relief to see him go.

The snow brought warmth, acted as a draught-excluder. She could feel the weight of it grow on the roof and gather round the windows, a shroud for her own abandonment. It lent a peculiar sense of safety; no burglars would begin to traverse this. The house would become anonymous beneath this blanket, so would she. Snow calmed the nerves, took away choices. It was easier to be this kind of prisoner when the snow fell with such gentle finality. Closing them in with greater inevitability than they did themselves, blurring everything except resolve.

Mother complied, snoozing in front of the fire, paper round her feet, head dropped on her chest, the television set chirping news of snow drifts before going on to drama of a less believable kind. Good.

Isabel went upstairs into the realm of her mother's bedroom, where she had rarely been except to check for excessive mess and lack of hygiene. On the whole Serena managed it well, changed her bed sheets with great ceremony and sufficient regularity, brought back down from there cups and ashtrays and most of the detritus she had taken in. Apart from barbed wire and such, Isabel reflected, but there had been nothing else beneath the mattress: one sly visit had ensured it. One must allow as much privacy as possible; the Alzheimer's leaflet said so. She was the guardian of the manor, not the owner of her mother's life, and she followed the advice.

There was a huge Victorian wardrobe, walnut-veneered, a piece of furniture successive generations had found invaluable, unfortunate, grotesque, useful, arrogantly space-wasting — large enough to house a small car — and finally magnificent but not yet a work of expensive art. Andrew's auction would sell it for more than it cost and less than it was worth, Isabel reflected with a smile of congratulation for new-found wisdom. But she was interested in the contents rather than the design. He would look at it from the opposite viewpoint. He thought she did not listen, but she did.

Inside, the level of organization was astounding. Isabel began at the lowest drawer. The first two revealed silk underwear, vests, chemises, nightdresses of uncertain age, folded into creases that had become permanent. They were all scented with lavender bags, sprinkled with pot pourri which exploded against her nostrils with a stale, sweet smell. She remembered her mother's clothes, the finest kind, simple to the point of being stark, deep navy blue, cream, camel, black, enlivened with crimson, white, searing pink. No patterns, no flowers, no glitzy buttons, but a love of stripes to offset the effect of long, lean lines. Suits, tailored in Singapore, worn to perfection on that statuesque figure which went in and out in all the right places, legs reaching waist via dimply knees, the line from then on leading to a fine set of shoulders and a face of laughing splendour beneath a hat.

Hats were another thing. Hats for country and town. Hats of velour with crooked feathers. Delicious hats of yellow straw, trimmed with navy ribbon, fit for a garden party or a colonial lawn. A turban for a 1940s gown. In the hanging compartment of the friendly compactum were three evening dresses, shimmering, while on the other side there were three suits, suitable for all occasions. Heather tweed with pleated skirt, still fresh, smelling of mothballs, a swanky number in white and one in brilliant red, which Isabel recalled her wearing. The bottom compartment held shoes. There were labels on the drawers, such as "Keep for further use", or, "Coloured stockings to go with particular outfits" and, by the shoes, a reminder, "More shoes in chest in cellar. Also his".

Most of these clothes, and even the shoes, would not fit Serena now. She had thickened round the middle; her feet had broadened. She wore, on a regular basis, a medley of the same few things in various combinations. The daily decision about what to put on first took longer and longer, as if she were persuading these remaining serviceable clothes to aspire to the elegance of another age.

The dressing table revealed costume jewellery, again never worn now, but not extravagant. Large lapel pins, a dozen sets of earrings, diamanté, pearl — all paste. Plus another notice in smaller writing, "The rest of this in chest in cellar".

The cupboard by the bed contained a carrier bag full of old diaries and letters. The letters Isabel did not examine: the sight of letters made her shiver. The diaries she decided she must approach with caution. The pages were closely covered. A glance at one, fifteen years old, revealed nothing more than pages of reminders, businesslike records of obligations and appointments and that alone relieved the daughter who was beginning to feel like an intruder, although she had begun from the standpoint of considering her mother deserved no better.

Isabel sat on the floor and allowed herself the long delayed luxury of tears, which she had forbidden herself in the last few days, afraid that tears would be the beginning of falling apart. It was not the reminders of former glory that affected her so much, but the painstaking way in which it was categorized. There were salient reminders of another life more varied than any Isabel herself had known, but what was more impressive was the effort to keep it in order. Serena's memory must have been fading when she wrote these painstaking labels, trying to make an inventory of personal possessions before they, too, escaped into the fog. And for all that the tally was spartan. Serena was not a hoarder. She could have kept far more than this, written a dozen more labels, given more evidence of the spoiled life Isabel was convinced had been hers.

Isabel went downstairs to the cellar, led by Mother's writing. She did not check to see if Serena still dozed: the television sound was a reassuring murmur. Snow had begun to gather outside the back door.

Her forays into the cellar had been minimal so far; the gloom of it had not attracted the spring-cleaning fervour that had so polished and improved the house. There were the stone shelves she had used to store food before Robert's visit with his family: that, as far as she was concerned, was the major use to which the cellar had been put in party-giving days. It had been the anteroom of parties, beer and wine kept in there, boxes for glasses, large dishes that had no use except when feeding a multitude. Serena's liking for cooking extended to highly decorated mass catering where attention to detail in the cooking was less important than the finished look of a buffet where food would only be snatched by chattering guests. In the first room, where a cobweb-clad bulb illuminated brick walls, there was nothing but junk: two boxes of Christmas decorations, the cheese press, empty bottles, curtains and old blankets otherwise used as floor covers for painters and decorators. Broken chairs. There was a door from the front cellar to a further room at the back. Not a secret place: the door was always open on account of being impossible to shut, but she had never ventured there where the light scarcely reached. Not for the sake of finding more rubbish.

The hinge creaked in protest. There was a small window, set into the base of the house, source of a sudden blast of air and giving a surprising and comforting illumination from the whitening world outside. Not enough to see much more than the dim outline of more broken objects. There was nothing that announced itself as a chest of belongings that would reveal either treasures or answers to God knows what. Isabel shoved a hand through her long, lank hair. It was corny being down in a cellar looking for something which those thorough burglars were unlikely to have missed.

She moved back to the relative familiarity of the first room, stirred the old painting clothes with her foot. Strange, she seemed to remember there had been more of these once, and they had been neatly folded. She had looked, in the early days, to see if there was anything worth retrieving. Some impulse of automatic tidiness made her pick one up and begin to fold it. The blanket smelled of turpentine. She halfway liked it down here. The cellar was not a sinister place: it was an extra pantry, no more nor less, full of clean, cold air, as if the damp that made the steps shine penetrated no further. The silence was soothing.

Something dropped from the blanket. Oblong, shiny, black. Familiar. A dictaphone. She bent to pick it up at the same moment that the door above her slammed shut. She froze. There was no preliminary to this sudden sound, no footsteps. Then only a slight hesitation before, one by one, the bolts went home and the light went out. Isabel raced up the slippery steps, skidded, fell, clawing at the walls, landed on her hip halfway up.

Staring upwards, all she could see was the frame of the door outlined by the light from the kitchen. She scrambled up again, carefully this time, until she was behind the door, kicking it with one foot after another until both feet were sore. There was no sound whatever from the other side. Isabel felt an absurd desire to hit the wood with her head, instead pounded it with the heels of her hands. Silence. Not even a whisper of breath. Then the presence of the dog, snuffling round the doorframe, whimpering in protest, until, in a burst of sound so close it was shocking, there was music. Loud music, fit to drive away devils, big-band sound, inviting someone to dance.

"Mummy!" Isabel screamed. The scream became a wail. "Mummy, Mummy, Mummy!"

George envied the warmth he could see through the windows. It was no fun camping in a car, sheltered and hidden in the furthest outhouse, but at least it was quiet. Couldn't go on indefinitely, though, not with this snow. The belfry of the church was better, so easily accessible it made him wonder why others did not use it all the time. It was where he would have retired later tonight, but the road was dangerous now.

There were many reasons he had given himself for watching as he did, none of them complete. Underlying them all was the pull of the place, like a hawser to a ship which strained to escape a harbour wall in uneasy seas. Then there was the fact that he must hide somewhere. Indifference to whether or not he had killed Derek did not stop him being terrified of the possible consequences, nor was the terror equal to the shame. Prison walls, crowds — he would rather die of cold first. Then there was her, the mistress of his celibate heart, whom he could not leave. Impossible to try, impossible to consider. She was in danger, poor lamb, far worse than his own. She was imprisoned by a girl who would hit her, abuse her, had done so already, the author of all her misfortunes, and his own.

Even George knew, as he painted lurid pictures of his own muddled motives, that there was something slightly wrong with the scenario: it was Isabel, after all, who had made some attempt to defend him and he was grudgingly grateful for that, but it was also she who blacked her mother's eye, looked at her with that weary contempt, pushed her about the house and threw her clothes in the fire. People were always locking their doors against the world when the danger really came from within. Serena looked so tranquil, asleep in her chair, so innocent.

But now what was she doing? Suddenly nimble, radio in one hand, appearing in the kitchen where he had seen Isabel descend the cellar steps, purposeful. Shifting the dog away from its station by the open cellar door by kicking it roughly, shutting the door, taking a breath, fastening the bolts. He could not hear, but he could feel the bolts, imagine the sound heard from below. Look, Mrs Burley, my lovely, he found himself saying, this is not quite fair. Very cold down that cellar. You might not like that child of yours, but it strikes me she's all you've got, and if you hurt her they'll take you away. She isn't so bad, is she? He heard himself pose the question about the hated Isabel and it shocked him. Perhaps it had been lurking there all the time, perhaps the cold had got into his bones, perhaps it was a sudden and complete empathy with someone, anyone, under lock and key. That was a terrible sensation: terrible.

The snow was gentler now, a steady fall of delicate flakes as he moved round the side of the house and stood a few feet distant from the site of the little cellar window, almost obscured even without snow. He willed Isabel to think of it. If he had managed to crawl in there, then she, lithe, agile thing she was, could manage to get out; he remembered the way her body could twist and turn. He stood, oblivious to the cold and his icy feet, which he had tried to keep dry, concentrating his mind, trying to influence hers. Lift the window towards you, he said, pull it out; it's rotted away from the wall. If you were a thief, you would know exactly what to do. There's a way out, silly girl, find it. Furtively, he ran there. Moved the snow, tugged, ran back.

The music faded away, along with shuffling, triumphant footsteps, moving in time with a waltz. The dog remained against the door. Isabel could hear the animal breathe, fancied she might even feel the warmth of her if she sat with her back pressed against the wood. She tried, but the step was cold. The dog whimpered, and that was a comfort. Isabel put her head between her knees and wept for the mummy who was not there. She could have been ten years old all over again.

Mummy had left the frame of light around the door. Kind of her, so kind. For a minute Isabel almost succumbed to the same hysteria she recalled following the departure of the burglars, felt again that revolting sensation in the mouth, the helpless humiliation. She could sit in this cellar and laugh herself warm. No, this was incarceration, not violation. Survivors choose survival, Mab had said, until they have no choice.

She was standing now, with her arms across her chest. She could feel her knuckles supporting her bosom. She took her pulse; too fast but getting slower. A sign of recovery. But I am a damaged bird, trapped in a cage. Not bird as in bimbo, bird as in dark-feathered crow, with wings, and beak, capable of survival. Why does she do this to me?

Only the curious survive, said Mab. Isabel touched the wall

surrounding the door. At this level, it felt dusty, but not chill. Perhaps it was here George had spent a night, or more, whispering to the dog once he had slipped through the kitchen. The dog would stay there all night. She had never been kind enough to the dog, who had been her idea in the first place. Dogs took a long time to die, bitches longer.

How long would she take, in the absence of any surplus flesh? Why does she do this to me? It is nothing as simple as hatred.

There was greater warmth by the door, but it was still cold, with the whole weight of the house pressing down on top of her. No one would arrive in the morning. She would have to preserve enough energy to shout in the afternoon, or the evening, unless Mother relented. Which she would not. Isabel tried to talk to the dog; the response was anxious snuffling. Keep warm, then. Terror feeds on paralysis. Move.

The echo of the fading music remained in her mind; along with school dancing lessons — not the balletic kind but the enforced tuition in how to do the waltz, the quickstep and two Scottish dances, redundant now for most social occasions. Isabel descended the steps again. She put the dictaphone on a stone shelf, safely, and she could feel to pick up one of the decorating sheets and fling it round her shoulders like a stole. She remembered her mother's garments, silk stockings and all, as she moved across the cellar floor like a person on a very small, uneven dance floor, controlling a reluctant partner. Slow, slow, quick, slow, that was it; move aside, please. I am the most beautiful girl in the room. Isabel could remember an eightsome reel, the Gay Gordons and the Viennese waltz. Her mother would have danced them better, in better clothes. The air was cold against the skin. Why should she, generous soul as once was, do this to me? Amazing, she must have been, in her evening gowns.

The dancing grew more hectic, then slowed when the sweat hit her eyes. Blinking it away, Isabel realized that the darkness had been an illusion. The detritus stored was all dimly visible. Dancing was comfort; it had the effect of blocking thought and provoking it. There was light in this darkness. There was the window and George, not a man of stealth, might have used that rather than the door. Thought had acquired her mother's rhythms. Slow, quick, quick, quick.

Took her time, she did. Ages and ages until he saw her slithering out, black against the white, clutching at the ivy on the base of the wall, hands pink, her face a pale blue. George wanted to cheer, restrained himself, followed her as she stumbled back across the route he had already followed, her arms hugging herself. At that point he would not even have minded if she had seen him, but she was hellbent, noticing nothing, not even the footsteps already partially obscured but still visible. She was a brave brute, really.

He was several yards behind when she reached the kitchen door, peered through the window. Serena had gone to bed: the dog pawed at the inside of the door, for once barking madly. No good waiting there, my girl, neither of them can let you in. Isabel moved down the contours of the house, first invisible, then visible, punching the glass on the french windows with her fist wrapped inside her sweater; she was going to hurt herself getting through there. Big panes of glass, tinkling. He winced.

George had seen the burglar-alarm box on the wall and suddenly remembered it. The house might suddenly reverberate with sound, but it did not. She was, in a manner of speaking, safe inside, probably, if she had a thought left in her head, turning it off. He felt in an odd sense almost triumphant for her. That was a cruel thing to do, Mrs Burley, darling: you mustn't do it again.

Perhaps Isabel would go upstairs and hit the old dear. No, he did not really think that, could not, somehow, imagine it. Hitting people came from heat; it was not something done by a body shivering with cold. There were lights in the kitchen now. She might let the dog out, and the dog might run towards him.

George went back to the car. The snow sighed into drifts and ceased to fall. The silence was the way he had once liked it.

Chapter Thirteen

IT WAS THE ACTION of climbing back into the house, standing still in the sudden warmth and listening to her own heartbeat, which told Isabel the truth of the situation. The panic, the cathartic sound of breaking glass, the onset of pain which came with the heat from the dying fire, the contrast between life out there and life in here, the futility of screaming into silence, all revealed to her what she was in this house. In her mother's eyes she was, quite simply, an intruder, with no more business on the premises than any burglar. A burglar was preferable; a burglar had discernible, even admirable, motives. He simply wanted surplus things, things which were going begging. His needs were simple: it was the demands and expectations of a daughter that were outrageous. There was no particular dislike involved. Serena did not have love left for anyone who carried all those obligations of blood. She was not rationing it; it was not there to be rationed. There was no malice, simply a vacuum. Isabel had the utter calmness of the survivor, coupled with a crazy desire to laugh. If it were me apprehending an intruder, she thought, I might lock them out of the way, let them grow cold or hot, deal with the problem in the morning. If I remembered. But then, if I were mad, I might not remember; even less would I care who they were. I would not pity anyone who destroyed my peace and privacy.

My mother might have been locking out the nuisancy ghost of the cat.

It had been, in a fierce kind of way, sweet out there in the snow, which had sunk into her indoor clothes. Fear created its own perspective; the release of it brought a dizzying clarity of vision and the opposite of fear. When Isabel opened the back door for the dog, she nearly envied her brief, lazy, leg-raising interlude in the snow. Petal hesitated in the yard, sniffing, reluctant to return, but, as always, followed the stronger instinct: to obey shouted orders. A little like myself, Isabel told her, touching with still-cold fingers the warm ruffle at the back of her neck. Bum life for a bitch.

Finding herself on the brink of understanding was fine, but it made no difference to the next step. A reluctance to catch the train in the morning in order to get to a job she did not like did not alter the necessity of stepping aboard the carriage. Isabel the burglar went upstairs, as she was obliged to do, whatever Serena had done to her. Because it was necessary.

Do you love me, Mummy? No, of course not. Why on earth should you? But I loved you. I just didn't realize you had become the child, that's all. I was asking for the moon and no one owns that.

Serena slept, her profile lit by the bedside lamp with its paper shade so browned and frayed by clumsy handling, the survival of it was miraculous. And how long was it since she had stopped using the right bulb, unable to differentiate between one hundred watt and sixty? The curved lines of the lampshade beams stood out like the veins in a wrist, the parchment was as pock-marked as Serena's brown-spotted skin; the two could have married into a colour scheme. White sheets, a face furrowed against the pillow, all of it sloping into the pristine cover, leaving on the one side a profile like a skull, under it the bulk of facial flesh. One hand was under the pillow, the other arm held the blanket close to her chest. In repose she was as beautiful as living daylight, the hair abundant curls of luxuriant grey. No rollers tonight. Her eyes were wet, blinked open and then closed again, the moisture making the pouched skin beneath shine like dusty leaves in rain. If there was any idea in her mind that she might have killed, humiliated, terrified this daughter of her flesh, there was no sign in this innocent sleep. There might have been no knowledge either. Isabel could not love this lump of body and skin, but neither could she hate it.

Her position looked less than comfortable, twisted somehow in slumber so that she sprawled all over the bed at an awkward angle which Isabel wanted to straighten up. She stopped herself. Mother, Serena, whatever this stranger was named, could sleep in whatever position she pleased until she met the undertaker. Or whatever God it was she may have worshipped. I do not know you, Ma, I do not know the first thing about you, not even the way you sleep.

Her right palm was extended over Serena's neck, fingers flexing, twitching. There was an instinct to strangle her mother, as well as to stroke. Place long, thin fingers on that fatty neck, feel free to slice into the folds over the larynx, end that life. She could have killed Serena for her single crime of not knowing how to love her.

Blood fell on to the pillow. Isabel's numb fingers were webbed with blood which hung in icicles from tiny lacerations not yet discovered, pumping indoors, frozen outside. For a whole minute, she let the blood drop on to her mother's forehead, where it lay like bright red pebbles before shifting into rivulets along the deep-set lines of her brow. Isabel regarded the blood with disinterested fascination. She sat by the side of the bed until some sense of survival made her raise her arms, reverse this flow. It was a strange way to pray, arms straining out of sockets like this. She linked her fingers, stretched; drops of blood fell on to her hair, mess, more mess.

Serena opened her eyes again, sightless blue. "Please," she murmured. "Please. Let me go."

The eyes closed slowly. Isabel sighed.

"Don't worry, darling. Love where you love. I know it isn't me. It isn't your fault you are what you are." She leaned closer. "And, by the way, George is here somewhere. He left you a message. Lots of love, get your rest."

Her mother lay sleeping, bloodied. They did this, Isabel remembered, to the huntsman who has caught his first stag.

In the bathroom, treating the cuts to her hands and arms with shaky efficiency, Isabel could only feel enormous relief that the blood on her mother's forehead was not blood she had drawn. She trembled in the aftermath of that temptation.

In the morning, long before Serena awoke, Isabel found the chest in the cellar. Inside, there were two large teddy bears, plus three small parcels, tied in polythene with a dozen elastic bands each, making them difficult to open. One contained earrings, the second her father's cufflinks and the third a ring from a cracker. Otherwise, there was nothing inside but paper.

"Thank God the snow's melted," Andrew observed to his father. "Fickle stuff."

"It's just getting ready for the real thing, shouldn't wonder. Been playing about for a week. Wish I was God. In command of the weather."

Doc Reilly nodded. On a morning like this they allowed

themselves a little sherry, poured into smeared glasses taken from the display cabinet that flanked the rostrum in the chapel. An electric fire alleviated the cold of that part of the room. The rest of it was fairly empty. Buyers had collected their goods; compensation offered and accepted for breakages. There was little left except a few rugs: the place almost homely. In the town centre, Christmas decorations had appeared on lamp posts. The lights did not extend as far as this, although John had entered into the spirit of the thing by pinning tinsel round the rostrum. For the last auction before Christmas he might wear a Santa Claus hat, if they did not have to cancel, which seemed likely.

"How are you going to manage, John? You've got no one to hump the stuff."

"Nope. Bob's worse than ever, I doubt he'll come back at all, his brother's pretty useless and Derek had that . . . accident. There's only my son and heir, and although he's wonderboy, he can't carry a wardrobe all on his own. Besides, he's got other things on his mind, haven't you, Andrew? Still, it's not the end of the world. We never take much, this time of year. They're all out there buying in crap as if there were no tomorrow."

"Derek getting better, is he?" Doc Reilly asked.

"Far as I know. He isn't getting worse and he isn't dead, so he must be. Not saying much at the moment. That won't last. Silly bugger."

"Very apposite, I must say, calling him that." Doc Reilly's shoulders heaved with gentle mirth. Yes, they are a pair of conspirators, Andrew thought with affection. The liking was tinged with a healthy suspicion. They have a common cynicism: they know exactly what they're talking about, so much so that they keep what they know from one another and admit it at the same time. The best form of communication was hints, winks and silences. Canny rather than crooked.

"Well," said Doc Reilly, heaving himself upright and looking at Andrew expectantly, "as the elder statesmen of this parish, what are we going to do about it? I mean, do you want us to tell Isabel?"

"Tell her what?"

"Oh Christ, she don't know the half of it. I bet she doesn't know whose act to follow now. She's got her aunty's common sense, her mother's looks and her father's sensitivity. They all loved her, after their fashion, but it was Mab who was the control-freak. Ruled that bloody household whether she was in it or not. I don't know what happened before they came to live here, I can't guess, but she'd already done a good job undermining Serena's authority. Edward Burley would always listen to her first. She even dictated where everything went. No wonder Serena enjoyed having the place to herself these last years."

"Is that so?" Andrew murmured. He felt vaguely uncomfortable talking about it, although he wanted them to go on.

"I can see Mabel, now," his father said, dreamily. "She knew she was dying a long time before she let on to anyone else. You told me that, didn't you, Doc? She knew for more than a year. She was well capable of doing a bit of dividing and conquering before she went. A great letter-writer. She could have made sure her niece didn't marry too young, she always disapproved of that. Also made sure she got out from under by giving her money. Mab was good at arranging lives she couldn't own. Only she would never do it by a direct route."

"This could be nonsense," Andrew said.

"Of course it could be. It's nothing more than pure, bloody-minded speculation," Doc Reilly replied. "It comes from me,

John here, my wife and a couple of patients. But that's the best we've got."

"None of this helps the present," Andrew remarked.

"Nope," the doctor agreed. "Nothing does."

"What's happened to that poor bastard George?" John Cornell asked.

"No one knows. He didn't return to the nick as ordered. They're looking for him."

"And will those burglars really go back?" Andrew wondered.

"There's no telling." John was looking at his feet. "Well, two of them might. Not in this weather. And if they do, they'll trip over an alarm."

They would not trip over an alarm. Not even a man trap. The alarm was an exercise in uselessness, unless the house was empty. Robert's promise of security, augmented by the mobile phone in Isabel's room. There was no point turning it on at night unless Serena was locked in her room, and that was impossible to contemplate. Because there was a connection between switching the switch and the arrival of two policemen after ten minutes, she was, intermittently, fascinated by it, although it was something which faded in and out.

"Come away from there, Mummy. See what I've got."

Isabel was sure that what she had would please, she was learning fast. The teddy bears had been greeted with pleasure, the Christmas decorations seemed to have the effect of making Serena imagine there was going to be another party. They spilled out on the kitchen table, dusty and dated and varied, the nicer rubbish from the cellar. Would there were more of them, since Serena clearly found them both curious and delightful. Dust did not bother her. Tinsel could furnish a room. The decorations made her tranquil and had taken hours out of the day since their discovery. Serena chose one golden foil device to hang against a window frame, took it to the living room, placed it with enormous care, changed her mind, tried another, with all the consultative care of an interior designer. Isabel was similarly tranquil; it could even be said they were cheerful together: there was an element of both resignation and courtesy about them both. Isabel had taken her behaviour right back to the beginning. Or near the beginning, when she had first begun to comprehend the need for alternative language. She cooed at Mother as she might at any frustrated child. She cajoled rather than ordered. She reversed the flow of Serena's chatter by chattering herself, not incessantly, but frequently. Serena kept touching her arm.

"Now look, Mummy. I did tell you about that switch, didn't I? Naughty switch. I know it brings out the fellas, but they won't be pleased to see you. And there's another reason. I've got the feeling Georgie is out there looking for you. If he wants to come in, even though those nice policemen say he mustn't, that's OK by you, isn't it? We don't want to set bells ringing, do we now?"

She must have repeated the words a dozen times. Some of them might sink in, especially in this mood; most of the words were true. Mother could somehow tell when she was being told a lie. Whatever she received by way of wisdom was filtered through an imperceptible net. The whole difference in approach came from the release of the need to be loved by this childlike lady who only happened to be her mother. If she treated her like a robust but delicate stranger who needed care, it was all so much easier. She was not a daughter any more: she was simply someone with a fierce sense of responsibility for someone who was helpless. There were two of them in need, after all. Who loves you, darling, if not me? One needed to give, the other to take. It was a neat, workable equation.

Isabel was not entirely sure how this conclusion had come into mind. It had percolated for a while, she supposed. Solidified when she remembered herself standing in the chill of the cellar fumbling round in the dark with that dictaphone. George knew about love and how simple it should be: he had even recorded it.

"I love you, Serena B. Whatever happens to me, I'll always be that way. I hope you find this. It's for remembering words with."

A few weeks before Isabel would have been insanely jealous of George, indeed had been. For knowing her mother better than she ever would and meaning so much more. It did not matter where he came from and what he might have done. He had the password to her mother's affection and that was all that mattered. He was a good man in his own way, capable of mistakes, possibly violence. That gave him and Isabel something in common, she thought wryly. And if Mother was going to screw up her life, had done, would continue to, she did not see why George should be put on the same bonfire.

"I like this green tinsel best, don't you, Mummy? But I like the glass balls best of all."

"Balls! Oh very funny," Serena giggled like a girl who has just discovered how funny the word bottom is.

"Not those kind of balls, Mummy. Honestly not."

Glass baubles, light as air, turquoise, silver and blue, to be dusted and handled with care. Isabel's mind went blank at the prospect of Christmas, apart from a calm conviction that she would still be here, but not for much longer afterwards. She would do what she could, but nothing was definite.

"What did you do with these, Mummy darling? Hang them on a tree?"

Serena was not able to tell her how the house had once been decorated. Isabel, who had avoided Christmas like the plague, could scarcely remember. The day itself had always featured Mab, she recalled; Mab had also starred in the preparations, doing the boring bits Mother loathed.

The radio played softly, not bothering either of them. Twigs painted white, that was what Mab did, she had whitened or silvered winter twigs, fixed them in chicken-wire inside a huge silver vase, hung the turquoise, silver and blue baubles from them and placed them above the fireplace. Serena had always wanted more colour than this conservative arrangement, but Mab's taste prevailed. The thought filled Isabel with curious unease, and yet the idea appealed. Mother's preference now was a series of fat little Santa Clauses, highly coloured plastic, suspended on frayed scarlet ribbon. Things from the market, plastic flowers, bright and artificial. Who cared about taste?

The sky was the pink of optimism when she went out into the garden on one of the most peaceful afternoons of her life. She was not a daughter any more, she had no allegiances, no rights, but there were aspects of the place she loved. The colours of it, the determined grandeur that stood proud over the desecrations of time and neglect. There were ghosts on the tennis court, cavorting among the moss. The lumpy lawns, which she had earlier regarded as a shame, retained the right to be a lawn, but only just, while the kitchen garden had long since relinquished identity. The orchard where she had walked with her nephew. She was not really out here to collect twigs; she was walking in a widening circle with open eyes. Wondering where poor, daft George was and how cold he must be. He might have lived for her mother; she did not want him to die for her. The dog went ahead, found the car in the last outhouse, scarce big enough for a car and certainly not designed for anything better than pigs. He must have pulled the rotten door across, leaving enough space to enter and exit. There was a residual warmth about the place, a smell of exhaust fumes, but of himself no sign. Isabel found a clean tissue in her pocket along with a Biro, and wrote, "Come in the house, G, Serena needs you, Love, Petal."

Words were everything, they were all a person needed to get on in life. He might not come because he was cold; he would come if he were needed. He must have watched them long enough to know all other visitors were temporary. He might be watching now. Watching her usher the dog away home, the dog taking two steps forward and one back, yelping the way it did so rarely and only then for those worth affection. The pink sky had turned grey. No red sky at night, to be shepherds' delight. There had been red in the morning, shepherds' warning. The day had begun as it died, ominously cheerful.

She wanted to tell Andrew all this, because her clarity of vision now cast him on the side of the allies, and, even if he were not, then in all likelihood he would do as she asked. It was not much to ask. Since he was likely to arrive anyway, on one of those carefully contrived errands that so often coincided with early evening, Isabel felt she did not have much choice. Depending on which of them arrived first. There was no master plan about any of this: she was not a planner. It seemed important to follow instinct, like the dog did a scent. That was the only thing the dog was good for.

Inside, it was warm again. Colourful with the tinsel, while Serena tinkered and one of them waited.

Do what you like with my life for now, Ma, Isabel said. Not with George. She was hanging more tinsel over the drawing-room window where the snow had drifted in and Isabel had done her best with damaged hands and cardboard. They were somehow, waiting on those damn fish and chips.

Isabel noted, with some satisfaction, the dog nuzzling round the cellar door. Seven o'clock, dark as midnight, and the snow had begun to fall again. Serena came back into the kitchen, took up a knife, looked at it quizzically, and began to peel a potato.

"Too cold," she said. Isabel laughed. "Yes, and when it's cooked it'll be too hot."

"Who else is coming? People?"

"I don't know."

Serena's face puckered.

"Now, now, sweetheart. No feet stamping, please. Be a good girl."

Serena wandered away into the pantry, looking for something more interesting than the potato. It had all been sweetness and light and now she was bored. Isabel's thoughts drifted, hung between anxiety and a strange contentment. She hardly noticed her mother sidling out of the kitchen, back to her fireside, did not mind. Serena in the vicinity of the kitchen sink was more hindrance than help. The dog at the cellar door grew more agitated, looked at Isabel in dumb appeal, pacing around her legs, telling her something.

"Yes," she said. "I know, yes. In a minute. These things take time."

She went to the pantry for the frozen fish, wishing there was more than frozen vegetables. Maybe a cheese sauce would do something for tasteless cauliflower.

Serena appeared at her elbow, giggling. She had moved so quietly all day, the result of slippers rather than boots.

"You know what I've done?"

"Stabbed a spud?"

"No. I turned on that thing. People coming. Soon, I think." Serena grinned with enormous satisfaction. For a moment Isabel was back to wanting to hit her, then she shook her head in furious amazement at what this wandering, wavering, determined intelligence could achieve. Serena was in search of a party, therefore switch the alarm on and call the police, simple. It took ten minutes, driving at speed. They were already looking for George; they would be here any time now. She opened the back door and heard, sure enough, the distant whine of an engine.

"Mother, you're an idiot. Go and put your hat on."

If there had not been the question of that poor simple-minded fugitive down in the cellar, Isabel might have seen how farcical it was. There was time to wonder if the coalhouse fire, which had been the spur for her coming here, had been merely the result of Mother's desire to attract large men to the premises. Lights appeared in the backyard. Serena was tidying her hair with busy fingers, watching through the window.

Isabel stepped quickly to the cellar door, the dog getting in the way. She called down urgently. "George! Stay where you are, for God's sake. Don't go out. They'll go round the side. Stay where you are."

As the first burly officer blinked in the light of the kitchen, Isabel was in the act of closing the cellar door behind her.

"Good heavens," she said gaily. "What are you doing here?"

Andrew appeared behind the third officer. He saw her raised eyebrows and shrugged.

"Coincidence," he said. "They overtook me. What goes on?"

They might have been less patient about the whole débâcle and their wasted time and the hazard to their vehicles bumping up this track if Isabel had not been such a pretty sight. Hand over mouth, fluttering eyelashes, enormous eyes wide with worry to have caused so much trouble.

Andrew watched what he could see was a performance. He wondered why it was she would not step away from the cellar door. Amazing to see a police officer simper. They searched the house anyway, just to be obliging. One walked around the outside of the building quickly, hugging himself against the snow which began again in earnest. They might have stayed longer but for the twittering of Serena as she followed them about, the obvious, delicately protested mistake and the fact there was, by now, a man in the house with a proprietorial gleam in his eye. They lingered in the kitchen long enough to warn the young lady that if George Craske should by any remote chance appear, she was not to let him in on any account.

She said, of course not. Wicked George Craske. Sorry about my mother's busy fingers.

George sat shrouded in the painting clothes, conscious of the smell cutting across the more unpleasant smell of his own body, bathed in the hot flush of sweat that had turned to ice on his skin. This was prison without the crowds; this was humiliation and despair; he had never felt weaker, or more profoundly ashamed. Tears dripped down his face; no sobbing, simply tears, turning to icicles on his chin. He could hear the reverberations of noise in the house: the sound of many feet, voices which he could not distinguish. He waited in misery for the light to shine on him, to discover him like a rat in a trap. Men to bundle him upstairs, banging his head against the crusted walls as they went, himself unable to fight, limp like a corpse.

When the silence fell, it covered him. There was nothing to do but wait and hope.

"What was all that about, Isabel?" Andrew asked.

She turned to him, put her arms around his waist and buried her head in his neck. Was this a performance too? Let it not be. He squeezed her gently; it was the body of a greyhound, slender and deceptively strong, the flesh warm. If she kissed him, he would know she was acting, but he would let himself be fooled. He was disappointed as well as relieved when she did not, simply remained close against him until she sighed an enormous sigh into his shoulder.

"Go and keep Mother company, would you?" she asked, withdrawing from him, no longer the flirt. "I've got to get George out of the cellar."

He held her at arms' length, looked at her questioningly. It was a look which said, "Do you know what you are doing?" but he did not accompany it with words. It was a satisfying thing to have her judgement unquestioned, a novel experience.

Serena was trying to attract Andrew's attention, pulling at his sleeve. The departure of all those lovely men had left her at a loose end. Andrew was the only one left.

"Come and see my decorations," she demanded coyly.

"Of course," Andrew said gravely. "Delighted."

Isabel opened the cellar door, put on the light and got on with peeling potatoes. After counting she added several more and put on the radio, loud. She could see the snow falling outside the window, and wished she was making a more ambitious meal. Never mind, they could have candles. Give the place that party air Serena craved. No one would be going anywhere tonight.

George emerged into the warmth of the kitchen blinking like a mole. Shrivelled with cold and the more corrosive effect of anxiety, he stumbled in and smiled at her. A proper smile.

He was dirty and the smell of him overcame all other odours in the kitchen. Isabel considered the immediate offer of a bath, then decided that this was the kind of implied insult that would offend him. It could wait.

"Could you lift in that coal for the fire, George? Just outside the door. Thanks ever so."

As if nothing had happened. She was the Janice, he the friend. Each to his proper place.

"Can't let the fire go out," he said.

"Oh no. Never do that."

He stood awkwardly, looking round the kitchen as if he had never seen it before, nodding with satisfaction. The dog stuck her nose into his crotch: he fondled her big head absently. Order had been restored in here. Isabel continued peeling potatoes.

"Is she all right then?"

"Yes, George, she's fine. Oh, you know. I lost my temper with her from time to time, but I've got better at it. The dog's been missing you as well."

He nodded, easing slightly. He was not in a position to judge someone for loss of temper. Then his legs seemed to buckle and he sat abruptly on the edge of the table, arms folded across his chest, like a drunk pretending to be sober.

"Oh dear, George, take a chair. I don't think you're looking after yourself properly. Have some tea."

She thrust it in front of him, along with biscuits, continued with the supper so that she would not watch him eat chocolate-chip cookies with the same speed the dog ate dinner. He was temporarily restored, his complexion turning from yellow-white to pink. There were the dark marks of exhaustion beneath his eyes. The health was fair, she decided. George would last a long time out in the cold. Far longer than she would have done herself.

"Thanks," he said.

"No bother, George. Sorry about all that row, earlier. Ma set the alarm off. Why are the police looking for you, George?"

He grunted. "I beat up one of the burglars. May be that."

"Oh, I see. You'd better stay here, then. They won't be back for a while."

There was a comfortable silence.

"Do you know what, George, I think I'll poach this fish rather than fry it. What do you think?"

"Fry it."

The dog's head on his knees was like a hot-water bottle.

"And I think I'll put some masking tape over that bloody alarm switch."

"Good idea."

Another pause. The sound of waltz music drifted down the corridor.

George cleared his throat. "I used to come back and read to her at night, you know," he volunteered. "Sit on the bed and read to her. Nothing more than that. I wouldn't, you know. I mean, I couldn't."

"Shame," said Isabel.

"What do you mean, shame?"

"Shame you had to go home, you silly bugger. Shame about people talking. There's five bedrooms."

"She'd tell me things. About her husband loving you and that sister of hers best. About places they'd been. Wonderful places. She didn't want to come back." He looked down at the big-eyed dog, communicating with it. Isabel waited, heart aching with a dull remnant of the old, sad jealousy.

"Talking and dancing stopped her wanting to kill herself," George added. "She hated it, you know. Hated it like poison. Losing the words. I kept on taking away the knives and things. Perhaps I shouldn't have done. People should die, if they want."

The fish sizzled in the pan. The smell of frying food made him salivate.

"You did everything for the best, George. That's what we all try to do, isn't it? Don't let her break your heart."

She began to set the table. Four knives, four forks; he counted them slowly and audibly, suspicion dawning.

"There's Andrew as well, George. Don't worry about him. Now, will you go and tell them supper's nearly ready? You'll just have time for a wash. Trust me, OK?"

He did. It filled him with wonder.

Chapter Fourteen

$\mathscr{T}$RUST ME.

Bob said it was utterly mad and Dick agreed, but the one was in pain, the other halfway loco, and both had taken the appropriate anaesthetic after going to see Derek in hospital.

There had not been any significant sympathy for Derek. Neither of them liked him all that much, at least not enough to feel desire for revenge on his behalf, but he was a horrible sight. Bob was the family man, so he took the grapes, a touching tribute for a fellow human being who was required to take sustenance through a straw. Dick remarked on the sensitivity of the gesture. Both of them looked the souls of concern as they crept towards his bed. A couple of concerned drinking companions. Nothing very much was said: they were merely inquiring after his health. From Derek's supine position they loomed over him, looking by turns avuncular, sinister and, finally, dangerous. In the sterility of the ward the blood and sweat smell of Dick, exaggerated by the heat, wafted towards Derek's busted nose like a lethal perfume. They promised to come back. He put up two fingers.

Purpose achieved, they were still shocked. Shocked into the fourth round of Carlsberg, which deadened pain nicely. This is the last chance, Dick said.

Last chance for what? Well, we aren't going to get as much as we should for the big lot, and I reckon that old bird must have some jewellery somewhere, stands to reason, doesn't it? And you want that clock. Doncha? And she's got a cellar. We never looked in the cellar. Booze for Christmas. We forgot those candlesticks.

He was right. Bob had dreamed of that grandfather clock in his waking hours, wanting something to measure the reaches of the night.

That was all, Dick said. Jewellery and the clock, nothing else heavy.

Why now? Bob asked, thinking how he might never work again.

Because Dick had a van that night, and if they waited until Derek was better he would not have a van, on account of a couple of days before Christmas he would be laid off, you bet.

You want the girl, Bob said, admiring the nerve.

No, I don't, plenty of girls and that one's too thin, believe me. Dick's jowled face was turned in the direction of the plump bums lining the bar.

Bob jeered. After a week, they'll have that house on a trigger. Bristling with alarms.

Na. They'll be feeling safe again. We could go anyway. Just to have a look.

What about the snow?

What about it?

It was a real party. Andrew remembered Serena and the fireworks, the way the sight of them had transformed her face with joy. Sensation was what she wanted, to wallow in it and forget her constant puzzlement. Lights, music, the distraction of sound and visual stimulation. Around the kitchen table, by candlelight, there was one interruption for the telephone. Robert Burley calling: was everything under control? In the background, he could hear jazz, male laughter, Serena's high-pitched giggle. In the foreground his sister sounding breathless.

"Who's there?" he wanted to know. Isabel almost mentioned George, bit her tongue in time and sounded carefree enough to worry Robert profoundly.

"Oh, just a couple of people. Mother's having a lovely time." Mother, centre stage, not worrying about words, pulling faces towards the phone, making them laugh at her, enjoying it.

"Don't forget the alarm system." Robert's answer to everything. Lock the trouble out.

"Never. Wouldn't dream of it."

For a moment, she was sorry for him.

There was nothing to be kept at bay but the snow, which stopped and started, started and stopped. George decided he would regard this as his Christmas. Isabel, his friend Isabel, had already told him he could have Robert Burley's room for as long as he wanted. He had one task, she told him, one only. He must teach the dog to bark. She said this gravely. He was slow to see the joke, but when he did his laughter was cataclysmic. His face was shiny after a bath and his giggling was of the infectious kind, a neighing sound that was funny in itself, sparking unconscious mimicry. Isabel no longer minded that she had never made her mother laugh as he now did: that was someone else's privilege. Hers was to provide the fish and chips and pudding with tinned cream as if it was a feast.

It was a feast. Andrew had put coloured paper round the candlesticks; when the candles burned low, it caught alight. Brief flames. Shrieks, like a children's party. Food consumed with nothing left over for the dog.

No one asked George questions, but he told them about

where he had lived. Andrew told George that perhaps they could talk about a job, when all the fuss had died down. George took that as a literal assurance that the fuss would die down, and in this semblance of family, holding Serena's hand beneath the table, there was nothing that was not possible. Andrew wondered at himself, offering work to a man with such a record, purely on the basis of his own and Isabel's judgement of a good heart. How spontaneous of him. Perhaps he was losing his respectability, growing to like rogues and act without analysis, like his father.

Then Serena said she wanted to dance. The wine that Andrew had produced along with the sherry had been consumed. George did not like it, took a little, Serena copied him, Isabel and Andrew drank the rest. There was not enough for excess, sufficient to oil the mood of loud relaxation. All of us against the world, and the world cannot get at us tonight. Nor any other night. Why not dance?

"How very old fashioned," Isabel murmured. "Like a 1950s film. Waltzing in front of the fire. Andrew, I don't know how to do it."

"Slow, slow, quick, quick slow. . . Or is that a quickstep? Just shuffle."

Serena had forgotten how to dance. She could manage a fairly rhythmic movement with energy, with George holding her at arms' length, as if they were dancing the tango. Which, in turn, they tried, like a quartet of clowns, with exaggerated, pouting faces and dramatic gestures. That made them weak with laughter, and they managed better when they moved to rock and roll. Anyone of any age could jig around to that. It was all deeply, gloriously silly. No one in that company was wiser than the most foolish.

The hours blurred into bedtime. Serena faded first. George took her to bed. A little later, when she and Andrew went upstairs by common consent, they could hear his voice reading to her, and, later still, his movement from her room into the one that had been Robert's. George was an oddball, but a gentleman.

Andrew sat on the side of Isabel's bed. The rooms were no longer cold: the house seemed to have generated enough heat for an army.

"I haven't an ounce of passion in me," Isabel said, cheerfully.

"I could tell you a story," he suggested. "Or I could just lie beside you, quiet as a mouse."

"That would be nice." She yawned. "I'm worried about George. One of these days he might realize that he isn't as important to her as she is to him. No one is."

"It can wait. Am I important to you?"

"I don't know yet. You have to wait too." She hesitated, trying to remember something, but she was slightly tipsy, on a range of sensations which included a novel feeling of calm which came from having done something right, entirely by accident.

"Tell me something," she asked, sleepily, as she lay on the bed and pulled a blanket over her clothes. "If you were to write a person a letter, would you use exclamation marks?"

He considered the question. "Whatever for? I thought you only put them in to show that someone was shouting."

"That's all right, then."

At about four in the morning Serena left her room and went downstairs. The key for the door was easy to find and the alarm was silent. She looked at the snow, first from one window, then the next, shaking her head at the marvel. It had snowed on and off while they danced; something so comforting about the snow; in the morning it would be different. The living room still held its warmth; she hummed to herself and turned two brief pirouettes, which made her dizzy. She looked at the dictaphone in her hand, puzzled over it and threw it away. No energy, these young things, going to bed when there was so much else to do. Such as get out when the going was good. Quit when you were ahead.

Serena tried to write a message in the condensation on the window. It was going to say, Love you really, darlings, you don't need me, but the phrases were too complicated and her arms were tired. She managed to scrawl "luck" before she forgot the import of the message or why she was trying to write anything. Did she mean "lick" or "fuck"? The snow outside was mesmerizingly white.

She had difficulty opening the back door, because of the unfamiliar key, but the sheer desire to paddle her feet in the white stuff prevailed. She liked the sound of her awkward footsteps over the yard. The fresh snow creaked beneath her feet.

The drive was unrecognizable, a carpet of white. She made for the gates, where the road dipped and the snow was deepest. It was all unutterably perfect, warm and welcoming as cotton wool. Then she lay down and listened to the silence. She crossed one hand across her bosom and, with the other, conducted the music of the stars.

The van proceeded over the fields because there was no choice. This was an even worse example of insanity than either of the other two expeditions. It was imperative to go on because there was nowhere to turn. It had become an exercise in survival. They would not stop at the house, not for anything. They would simply use the gateway to try and get the vehicle round and then go back. Get out before they were really stuck. The taste in Bob's mouth was sour, stale beer. Regret that he, the leader, should have let himself be led. Dick said nothing about anything. He made muttering noises to the engine, words of encouragement which sounded more like threatening prayers. His breath smelt of anxiety. In between other noises, he whistled between his teeth.

There was less snow through the woods. Dick exhaled a sigh of relief. He turned into the gates and began to reverse back. The wheels spun, encountered an obstruction and the van bumped forward, violently, rocking them in their seats. Bob moaned: it felt as if he had been stabbed in the back. Dick gunned the engine, swearing. The wheels spun again and they bounced back. He wasn't a wimp like Derek; he was a good driver when he was desperate.

The ground floor of the house was illuminated like a Christmas tree. Worse than the town centre at five in the afternoon and far more welcoming, it beckoned all strangers.

Bob could see tinsel at the kitchen window. "Fuck this for a game of monkeys," he whispered. "Get us out of here."

"All right, all right, all right."

Halfway through the woods Dick began to shake. Bob did not understand. It was easier going back. In the light of the moon, they could follow their own tracks. Dick shook like a man in the throes of delirium tremens. His teeth chattered as if they would break.

"Whassa matter?" Bob shouted. "What now?"

"We hit something, Bob. I know we did."

"Snow, you daft bastard, only snow."

"No. A fox. Something, I felt it move."

"Fox? Dog? For Jesus' sake, stop crying, Dick. Whatever it was, we probably did them a favour."

May God have mercy on her soul.

Robert Burley blustered. He had brought his son to the funeral, for the good of the boy's education and so that he himself would have a hand to hold on either side. Also because he feared there would not be enough of them to give the sensation of a crowd. He vowed to include in his will a clause in favour of cremation. That way, he would save his relatives from having to hang around in the cold. The thought of a funeral in summer did not enter his mind. The two did not go together. The old died in the winter.

Or they were murdered by neglect. Nothing much preyed upon his mind other than a dull sense of being thwarted by the lack of something tangible to blame for the whole sorry condition he was in. His mother had somehow outwitted them. Blackmail in death as well as life, a continuous process.

He wished, irreverently and again with a maddening sense of being beaten by a short head, that he had steered his mother's liver-spotted hand into making a will. He could even have done it without her: he could forge her signature well enough. He had always been able to. Anyone could copy her hand, cramped though it had become. Mab had taught her to write: Mab had taught them all.

Ashes to ashes. Half the insurance money, under the rules of intestacy when it should have been all of it, because the whole thing was Isabel's fault. There was not the same right in law to charge a person for negligent management of an adult as existed for a child. You could be imprisoned for being drunk in charge of a vehicle, but not for being drunk in charge of a demented old lady. His thoughts were a medley of angry colours, trying to find an outlet for the channel of molten sadness which filled his gut under his suit. Trying to turn it into rage when he knew there really was no room for anger.

He shoved himself in front of George and stood on Mab's grave without thinking. George had no business here. Robert regretted his action, but still he did it. He could not change. He felt betrayed. Quite a crowd, a respectable number for a funeral, including neighbours and friends he had never seen.

"Where were they," Robert hissed to Isabel, "when we needed them?" She did not move. Her imperturbability was another irritant.

"They were trying to manage their lives," she said. "Like you. Like I should have done. As people must."

Isabel listened to the wind that buffeted the graveyard beneath a leaden sky. Whispered her own variation on the prayers. Goodbye, Serena, wish I'd known you and what made you tick. I'm not going to let you wreck me more than you already have. Do you hear me? Robert's son detached himself from his father, uncomfortable with the pressure on his own, small fingers. He moved to Isabel and put his hand in her pocket. She smiled at him and pulled a soon-this-will-be-over kind of face. He found a packet of forbidden bubble-gum nestling against the lining. The coat was not black like everyone else's. It was a brilliant red, Mab's favourite colour.

Mother, Isabel thought, what a monster you were to die in this fashion, simply to tar me with the brush of fecklessness. You picked us up and dropped us, left us squirming in the mud, George and me. Extracting the last ounce of drama and guilt, the way you always could. You got the house full of men in uniforms again, didn't you? You wonderful old cow.

She winked at the boy to indicate it was OK to chew the gum with such loud concentration, and turned her head. He should not have been here as his father's prop. Weeping was a private business. She thought she would weep for ever and ever, until all the fluid was gone from under her skin. The sense of loss and unfinished business was a bottomless pit, a fountain of endless tears.

It was a short but convoluted route, Andrew said, between wishing someone dead and wishing against all wishes that they were still alive.

Back at the house (back at the ranch, as Robert's wife playfully labelled it), Joan neglected the supervision of funeral meats. Easy-peasy, sausage rolls and stuff. Not a wicked woman, simply a shrewd one with a life to conduct. She was looking at how Rob and she could really dance the light fantastic here, even with only five years left on the lease. Tennis on the tennis court; chairperson of local committees; devotee of local causes, homeless kids from town staring at Laura Ashley curtains.

She should have been a vicar's wife was Andrew's unspoken verdict. One of those people who believed there was nothing which could not be fixed. But she was right. The house needed children. The nice old punchbag dog was the first part of the furniture. People died so that others might be able to live. In the style to which they wished to become accustomed. Robert said she was cynical; pregnancy always brought about an advanced stage of pragmatism, Isabel said looking through a smeared window pane, good luck, get on with it.

"Where do you live, Isabel?" John Cornell always wanted

details. Even when mashing a sausage roll between stubby fingers and carrying a large whisky. Always suss out the opposition when they look weak. He found it difficult to imagine why any youth, his own son included, found this pale and puffy-faced, big-eyed girl such a hot item.

"A flat. In a block." Isabel seemed to have difficulty in placing it, put a hand to her brow and laughed uncertainly. "Caretaker and carpets, all that stuff. He's probably installed his relatives by now. You know what families are," she added.

"It'll only be a bit dusty, I expect," said Doc Reilly, kindly, kneading the toe of a well-worn shoe against the dustless boards of the drawing room.

"It wasn't pristine before. There was blood on the walls when I left."

That mystified him.

There was less dust than she would have expected, but then Isabel could scarcely remember how long it was she'd been away and how little she'd thought of her home in the meantime. An apartment, like she told the good doctor, in a block, with a view of the sky and security provided by a caretaker aided by electronics. Autumn when she had left, winter now. Washing lay fusty in the machine, the windows were grimy and the air was stale. She looked with disinterest into the cupboards full of clothes and hung up her bright red funeral coat. Flung her single suitcase to the back and began to clean.

In the life that had preceded the departure, the silence would have unnerved her. She would have left the dirt and flung herself at the telephone, worked her way through every contact in her black book, looking for attention. Now she liked it. The prospect of a quiet phone was not frightening.

Six-thirty in the evening, the ideal time for a man to call upon his mistress, even if she had sent him a letter kissing him goodbye.

Nothing new in that. Isabel enjoyed the occasional tantrum. Joe knew that as well as he knew how she could be twisted into compliance, like any woman without much will of her own. All that fiery passion turning into sweetness, the contrasts he loved, even when they hurt. He stood at the door armed with a bottle of wine and a bunch of roses. Clichéd, he thought, but foolproof. Rang the bell and yodelled her name. The door opened on a long safety chain.

He proffered the roses and the wine in their unromantic carrier bag, puckered his mouth into a kiss. A hand reddened with housework stretched through the doorway, plucked the bag from his fingers and retreated. The door slammed in his face.

"I love you, Isabel!" he shouted.

She could hear the exclamation mark. Tough luck, boy, I'm busy learning how to like myself. Somebody's got to do it.

She looked at the label on the bottle. Not bad.

Andrew arrived in the new year. The city streets were covered in slush and the January sales clogged the pavements. It confirmed what had been formulating in his mind. For all his years of discontent he enjoyed the lack of anonymity in small-town life. He would never want to hide away in the wider streets of a metropolis, even if he felt at ease in Isabel's flat with modern furniture he would never have chosen. But he knew he would never persuade her back unless she wanted to go. There was nothing tentative about her greeting or her smile; nothing much of the flirt, either. He looked at her expressive face and her gestures, searching for clues to what she might become. Never a writer of letters.

There was news he could impart and news he could not. No, no burglars found and no clues. Yes, George was as well as could be expected, using muscle to shift furniture, caretaking for Andrew's father, with whom he got on surprisingly well, by the use of very few words. An interim arrangement; something better would turn up. Andrew had corresponded with Robert, without success, about George keeping the dog. Furious letters, in a desperately familiar hand. Andrew did not mention that. There seemed little enough point.

Isabel had taken the silver candlesticks and that was all. They suited a glass table as well as they had suited polished wood. She had found beeswax candles, looking like sticks of honeycomb and smelling sweet. The room was soft with the scent of affection, understated and unmistakable.

If he were the someone to love, it would have to be on her own terms. There would be no dynasty. Let the body howl for that fulfilment. There were a number of things she was going to be and do before she was at risk of losing her mind, but there was one negative. She was brave enough and strong enough to vow it now.

She was never, ever, going to be some child's mother.

Look for FRANCES FYFIELD'S next book

Without Consent

∞

In bookstores everywhere!

Read on for a sneak preview from
this absorbing new novel . . .

CHAPTER ONE

Listen, Bailey said.

Once upon a time, there was a girl, going out.

Dressing for the party, she had felt she was worth a million dollars. Somehow that phrase meant more than the sterling equivalent of the day – the last of her life as she had known it – and she might have been worth more. Coming down for a moment from the quarrel with her mother, the third this week, and putting a jacket over what her father called her itsy-bit skirt and the skimpy top, wearing it as if she would never part with it, rather than shed it as soon as she got there, she had a sudden surge of rebellious love for her repressive parents. They weren't so bad, some of the time. For a brief moment, she knew that she was safe as houses, because she had this room to come back to and this number to call, although the only reason she was worth so much to herself was the fact that after three weeks' diet, her waist was where she wanted and her ribs stuck out. Not a milligram of surplus flesh, although, if she ate as much as a bread roll, her stomach came out like a balloon. The answer was not to eat.

'Bye, Mum. Bye, Dad . . .'

'Let's see you,' he called. She stepped into the living-room, pretending great haste even though she was early. The jacket was buttoned. She had on a prim little choker round her neck, which would go from throat to handbag before she had reached the end of the road. The make-up would go on in the bus.

'Very nice,' he said, reassuringly, thinking nothing of the kind. Why did this child have to look so fierce and why on earth was she so addicted to black? Why did she go about with that girl who was so much older and prettier? One quick peck on the cheek, given and received in an overpowering atmosphere of multilayered perfume, and she was off before Mother came out of the kitchen. Because Mother was harder to fool.

Later on, when they picked her up after the police had called, she stank of booze. The itsy-bit skirt was torn and stained. The child whimpered, but did not hug; could not bear to touch. Her thighs were scored with scratches; there was detritus under her nails. She was scantily dressed; it was presumed she had been stripped prior to her foetal curl in the gutter where she was found. A few bruises.

No knickers, no jacket. In the presence of her parents, she said she had lost them. That was all she uttered, apart from sobbing. Even after hours with a sympathetic woman in a nice little house with pictures on the wall.

'Well?'

Helen West, Prosecutor, sat on Bailey's sofa, still listening. They did this sometimes, a kind of dress rehearsal for tomorrow's challenges, both occasionally mourning the coincidence of their professions. Senior police officer, experienced Crown Prosecutor. It was not a relationship she would recommend, but she was stuck with it, like the fly which had fallen into her drink. Bailey had a creased face and a fine way of telling a story. He animated his narrative with verbal cartoons and embellished the whole thing with gestures, but as soon as he said, 'Once upon a time', she knew the story was going to be doctored with his own opinions and recounted in a style he would never use in front of a judge.

'Drugs?' She questioned crisply.

'Negligible, from her demeanour. I'd guess not.'

'Booze?'

'Plenty.'

'Semen?'

'Saliva, yes. Here and there; not there. Semen, no. Several

abandoned condoms around, but a lovers' trysting place. Bodily fluids also in the gutter. And no, she isn't a virgin. Not quite.'

'That's not enough,' Helen said.

Bailey watched the graceful figure of his betrothed cross the broad expanse of his living-room and thought of his ex-wife, for whom his traveller's tales from the police force had always taken second place to what they should do with the bathroom in preparation for the first child. He might as well have been out to stud. Oh, silence, he told himself, don't fall into clichés as if you were obliging someone on the psychiatrist's consulting couch. That woman had her needs, you had yours, which coincided at the time and might still if the child had not died. A child who would be the same age, give or take a year or two, as the girl in the story. He found himself repeating, what a pity, the trite words hiding a multitude of sins. His stomach growled. The last year of his life had seen the development of an ulcer.

'The way you tell it', Helen said, settling easily into the big fat settee he would never have possessed in his married life, 'gives me all the clues to the verdict. Silly little seventeen-year-old goes out to party, as described to parents, to whom she lies habitually, about dress code, about everything. Goes shimmering in there, dressed in nothing.' He was silent.

'The bloke for whom she's wearing all the glitz does not pitch. So she salves her disappointment by drinking a bit more and then a bit more and ends up in a scrum with a stranger. She doesn't have the faintest idea what a half-naked, flirtatious girl risks.'

'She wanted love.'

'She had love, the silly little bitch. She wanted attention.'

Helen took a sip of coffee. One bottle of wine in an evening was enough. He could continue, since it never seemed to effect him; she would not. There was a level of control in her he both admired and resented. She was a beautiful woman, after her own fashion. The kindest he had ever met, easily the most imaginative, the most elusive, the most measured. He wondered if she had agreed to marry him for the same hormonal reasons which had affected his wife. Helen was in her late thirties, about a decade his junior.

'Her parents are howling for blood. They insist she was raped,' he said. 'Someone must hang, they say, namely the boy with whom she left. Spotty little oik, who says he tried to kiss her, but she shoved him and ran off. He says she had other fish to fry. Someone she was meeting; someone older.'

'No case,' Helen said. 'Not even if she swore it was him. She could be a victim; she could be a cock-tease. Unless, of course, he caused the scratches. But I'd bet she did them herself.'

'Right. Her own skin beneath her fingernails.'

'And tomorrow, how come *you* have to explain to mum and dad why the evidence is insufficient?'

'I don't. Ryan does. He asked my advice on diplomacy.'

She made a mocking gesture, using two fingers to point a gun at her head, and pulled a sympathetic face.

The lovely Ryan was not always her favourite man. Bailey's bag carrier when first they had met, progressing since then, onward and upward. Capable of being outrageous and treated by Bailey as the son he never had. There was a fidelity between the two of them she accepted, because she had no choice. Personally, she doubted Ryan deserved it, but there it was: a mutual devotion without rhyme or reason, just like any other kind of love.

'Ah well, early night, then.'

Bailey moved to sit beside her, put his arm round her shoulder and felt her rest against him, willingly. They were easier together since their decision to marry; she joked it had probably caused the ulcer, but it had altered something, although he was not sure how. In a moment, he would clear the last of the glasses and papers from the table. In Helen's flat, litter remained at least until morning, perhaps the same weekday of the following week. One thing they had proved: compatibility need not involve a common domestic attitude.

'Tell me, love, do you always regard this subject with such a bold and jaundiced eye?'

'Do you mean sex cases? Rape? My current, almost exclusive stock-in-trade? Yes. But drunken teenagers don't raise my heartbeat. Oh, I'm sorry for a kid like that; something happened to her, but you can't make a case out of *naïveté* betrayed.'

Would they make love tonight or not? The idea rarely lost its appeal, except when she was tired to her bones. Perhaps she would let it happen, perhaps not. If she did, would that be rape? The idea was laughable. Rape was the exertion of force; Bailey had enough power over her already, although she did her best not to let him know.

He was sound asleep by the time she reached him.

The night light was a pale darkness, glowing through the window. Bailey lived so high above the ground, there was no need for the curtains he despised. From the front windows of her basement flat, Helen could see the feet of people walking past, sometimes peering down, but at the back, there was nothing but the garden. She missed her home, especially the solitude of her garden, and then, when she was in it, she missed the light of Bailey's vast attic. When they were married, they would live in exactly the same way.

His sleep made her perversely sleepless. He would wake if she touched him and his sleep was the unfeigned unconsciousness of the just, the result perhaps of a pragmatism she could not share. He believed in fate, and telling himself that you could only do the best possible with what you were given. No 'if onlys' for Bailey. You did what you did, apologized if necessary, and then you slept. Soundly. Did he really want this marriage, or was it his version of courtesy? In Bailey's eyes, a relationship as long as theirs would have to be honoured somehow. Loving Bailey was one of the best things to happen in her life, but she had a mortal dread of being owned and knew she could still throw it all away. Out of fear.

Failing to sleep opened the floodgates of all those things left undone or badly done. Cases swimming before her eyes. Visions of her previous married life, plus visions of all those odd and brutal couplings she read about on paper and which filled her waking hours with speculation, making her feel like a voyeur.

They should not have been talking about rape before going to bed.

Something had happened to that little girl. She wondered what it might have been.

'All right,' Aemon Connor said, in tones which combined both aggression and resignation. 'That's fine. That's absolutely fine. If you don't want to, that's fine by me. You frigid little cow. Was a time you couldn't have enough of it. Don't worry about it. I can always get someone else.'

Brigid whimpered in the darkness. He was refusing to hear it; he had listened long enough and conversation never cured anything. She complained it hurt; so, if it hurt, why couldn't she use her imagination? He could tell her what hurt, all right, and that was a mammoth state of arousal with nowhere to go. She was his woman, remember; his wife, even; what a joke, when she just wouldn't do it any more.

He lay on his side, him fuming and her still snuffling, opening his mouth to speak. He could not stop talking.

'I could get someone else tomorrow. And then where would you be?'

There was a long silence, until he felt her fingers moving timidly to touch the back of his head.

'Changed your mind, have you?' he muttered. 'Thought you would.' Forcing himself inside was difficult enough, even without listening to the sounds she made or noticing the passive resistance which seemed second nature. The process was brief and noisy. He held her down by the shoulder and in the aftermath of climax fell into a deep and suffocating sleep. Later, having eased herself from under the bulk of his huge drowsy body, she felt for the marks of his hands and wished herself dead.

The bathroom to which she tiptoed was splendid. There was a power shower among the black marble tiles and a bidet with gold-coloured taps which she used religiously, especially at times like these, to wash away all traces of him.

She had no idea how to live outside this house. It was her home and her prison, and living in such a place represented the pinnacle of all achievement. She liked this bathroom best; she had made it her own, and she could hide behind the door after doing her duty as a good Catholic wife. She could also sit and lie here too long in contemplation of avoiding it. Praying to God and occupying the bidet at the same time seemed faintly obscene, but Brigid imagined God would forgive her that, at least, since he demanded so much of her otherwise, and was supposed to forgive a great deal more than her husband. Dedicating the act of sex as a penance for the holy souls also seemed indecent, but might ensure a blessing in advance. Maybe Aemon was right and she should have been a nun.

You used to love it, he'd said. He said that every time, taunting her. There was a muffled shouting from outside, her name called, 'Brigid, Brigid . . . where are you?' sounding as if he was lost. God help us, he was awake again after insufficient drink to anaesthetize. She touched the lips of her vagina, swollen like cocktail sausages, almost screamed, reached for the lubricant from the cupboard and answered him.

'I'm here, I'm here, in a minute.'

He hated to wake up and find himself alone. It was an insult to his manhood: it gave him nightmares.

Aemon and Brigid, happily married.

In a neat little terraced house, light showed from every window, as if the occupant owned shares in London Electricity, or could not stand the dark. Around three a.m., a solid form could be seen, balanced on a ladder, silhouetted against the window to the left of the door, painting the ceiling of the living-room. Anna was in a sweat. The radio played softly only because she was a considerate neighbour. What she really wanted was a house pulsing with vapid, heavy-beat noise, amplified to fill her head. Anything to block thinking and aid the manic activity which had continued since early afternoon.

Ceiling, two coats, a small area, quickly covered; the whole place a bit of a doll's house. Walls could be finished in an hour, possibly tomorrow. The washing-machine hummed in the kitchen; third load today. Curtains hung damply; she would paint round them. The carpet had already been shampooed. She was doing things out of order, but perfect decor, logically created, was not the object of this exercise. The achievement of cleanliness was.

The ladder wobbled; Anna clutched, swore, saved herself from falling, and watched the paint tray fall to the floor, face down. Scraping the white ooze from the ruined pile with desultory energy, she realized that bending over made her dizzy and she could not see straight. All that white, glimmering against the unsteady light of the naked bulb which swung from the ceiling; her eyes were no longer able to comprehend colour. Or the fact that there might be someone outside, looking in.

She might as well paint the carpet, too, and be finished with it; the thought made her smile. All this work had done the trick; she was so tired she could scarcely put one foot in front of the other, and at last the place smelt of nothing but emulsion.

Anna held one hand in front of her face, watched its tremor, and delivered the now-familiar lecture. You can cope, girl, you can cope; it's all the rest who can't. Talking to herself, out loud; that was another thing to be cured, but not yet. The hand trembled; the burn marks on her arms were fading; her legs had the substance of jelly. She could sleep now.

As Anna tried to ignore the spots in front of her eyes while sticking the paint roller in a bucket of water which suddenly seemed red instead of white, the phone by Superintendent Bailey's bed bleeped without apology. He did not need to look at his watch to know that it was shortly after three; he always knew the time.

'Bailey. What do you want?'

It had been a joke on regular squads that Bailey always sounded as if he had a woman with him. Probably had too; the man had been a bachelor a long, long time. Going out and staying in with a lawyer from the Crown Prosecution Service was seen as another lascivious eccentricity which went with his good suits. The wearing of the one on his back and the other on his arm, bordered on some undefined treachery. The men who claimed to know him longest were placing bets on this marriage. Ten to one, it would not take place at all, five to three it wouldn't last a year. They had different kinds of faith in Bailey. The existence of Helen West did not exactly do him any favours.

The voice on the other end of the line appeared to hide an element of amusement. Sometimes, in the comparative regularity of his newish role, Bailey forgot that working for Complaints and Discipline was still, potentially, a twenty-four-hour shift.

'Islington. Sorry to disturb you, sir, but we've got a problem. Allegation of rape.'

'Against whom?'

The officer sounded as if he was reciting from a reading primer for under fives, spelling the sounds as he spoke.

'Detective Sergeant Ryan, sir.'

Bailey paused for a moment's palpable shock.

'I can't investigate allegations against Ryan,' he said. 'I know him.'

The voice coughed. 'That's the problem, sir. We've tried everyone else on the complaints rota, but everyone knows Ryan.' He paused for effect. 'Everyone.'

Bailey knew what he should do if he were going straight by the book. Get up, look up all other available numbers, tell this sergeant who did not yet have a name to continue his exploration down the list, because yes, he knew Ryan. Far too well. Knew him as a man of flawed intelligence, deliberate blindness, sexual fecklessness, indiscretions of all kinds. A man lacking in imagination, dogged in loyalty, but finally, in the last two years, emerging from a chrysalis, abandoning frustrated youth in favour of some degree of wisdom. Bailey had tutored him, forgiven him, covered up for him, believed in him, right up until that recent point where the belief was justified and Ryan had suddenly taken off and learnt to think, wonder, take responsibility and ask real questions. He had grown, shed his juvenile prejudices like unwanted skin, and learnt the art of patience, the way Bailey had always hoped he would. Looking at Ryan as he was was like looking at the man Bailey himself had once been. What retrograde nonsense was this? Stupid, stupid bastard.

The pause was long enough for the sergeant to cough again. 'Sir?'

'On my way.'

Bailey was precise. In the same way that he knew the time, he knew where to find his clothes. Helen stirred, listening. Bailey knew she couldn't quite fathom his absurd loyalty to Ryan any more than he could himself, and felt a flash of annoyance that the phone call should make him peculiarly, defensively embarrassed, as if she could guess that this was more than his paid duty. He touched her shoulder and left without a word of goodbye. Singing in his head as he went for the car, not Ryan, not Ryan, please. Not just as he was making good. Not Ryan and rape.

With that good-looking boy there would never be the need.

*   *   *

Bailey made himself drive slowly, although the instinct was to race and the sheer emptiness of the streets was an invitation to speed. Emptiness was a relative concept in London. There were always people. In these God-forsaken early hours there were simply fewer, plying the night-time trades, some of them innocent, some not. The factory making dresses for tomorrow's market, the loading of goods, the post-midnight clearing out, the parties which never stopped and the increasing numbers of those sleeping rough. He regretted that his duties no longer really included this twilight zone of all-night pit stops: conspiracy, danger, chat, street light. The night isolated people, made them more truthful. You poor old man, he thought to himself ruefully, they'll make a gardener of you yet. Set you to trimming roses in distant suburban police stations, or polishing the commander's shoes. Instead of this loathsome business of pruning, examining the varied complaints against officers of his own kind.

Oh, surely this was a storm in a nightclub cocktail? He knew in his bones it was not. Ryan, you bloody fool. What now? You always had a weakness for women and they for you. Bailey found he was thinking of the girl with something akin to dislike, already formulating disbelief in what she would say. He shook his head. This would not do.

The back of the station yard was lit with orange light, as if to reduce the white paint of the cars to a sickly cream. Bailey went to the back door. Better than going to the front and possibly running the phalanx of waiting relatives, supposing there were any. The interior corridor was a similar warm and oppressive yellow. He was met with the distant courtesy his role demanded. Everyone knew Ryan, a convivial and popular character, while several more knew Bailey, who could not be thus described. No chance, Bailey thought, of an incident like this failing to enter the history books.

The duty inspector was embarrassed, a symptom rarely apparent on ruddy red features such as his, unless he was talking about his daughters with the boastful and nervous pride he reserved for their achievements. The existence of a family made wild men tame, gave them different perspectives; it had done that for Ryan, albeit slowly. However many years he had taken to fall into respectful love with his own wife, he had still done so although only after he had led her a merry dance, and she him. Boys will be boys, and girls retaliate. The rape story was told, dispassionately, the voice avoiding judgement.

'Decent enough girl. No record, works in a shop. She knows Ryan on account of being a witness in one of his cases. Seems like she went to a disco with a girl who got into some kind of trouble on the way home, and she's giving evidence about what time they got there, what time the girl left, that kind of thing. Anyway, Ryan takes the statement and they get along fine, and he goes back to tidy it up, and they still get along fine. Then, according to her, he meets her for a third time, purely social. He starts to pester her. She lives with a bloke. She and Ryan – Shelley Pelmore she's called, sir – go out for a drink. On the way home, he suggests a walk in the park and he rapes her. Or, at least, he tries. Penetration, but no ejaculation.' The inspector coughed apologetically. Another source of ridicule for Ryan. Didn't even make it, poor bastard; couldn't keep it up.

'Obvious signs of resistance. Sir.'

The police service was an army with a self-appointed officer class, so Bailey understood. Respect had to be earned and in the eyes of this man, he had not earned it yet.

'Now why on earth would he do that?' Bailey wondered out loud, making light of it. The inspector caught his drift, laughed briefly.

'See what you mean, sir. Usually he only has to ask nicely, although everyone says he's quietened down. But then why do politicians go with tarts, even when they've got groupies and their fragrant wives at home, sir? Dicing with death, someone's idea of fun.'

'Do you believe her?' Bailey tried to get the plea out of his voice. The cough was repeated.

'Can't say, sir, can I? I haven't met her, wouldn't know if I did. They were seen together in the pub. He says they met by accident, chatted, that was all, gave her a lift, went separate ways.'

'Who reported it?'

'The boyfriend. Found her on the doorstep. Brought her in. She's in the rape suite up at Holloway. We can't deal with her here for obvious reasons. Ryan's in the detention room.'

'Well, come with me, will you? I can't see him alone.'

Another long hesitation.

'Oh, one more thing, sir. When she came in, she was wearing Ryan's jacket . . .'

He would need a witness to ensure fair play – no hidden intimacies between himself and an old pal – and also because he needed someone to stiffen his own backbone when he saw Ryan. Bailey might as well have been looking at the victim of a car smash, one who was resigned to being told that apart from being blind for life, the legs would have to be removed as well. Ryan's handsome face was puffed; he had not avoided the disgrace of weeping, which had made his eyes red and his skin blotched as if it was bruised. There was a smell of drink, not overpowering but noticeable, and the different, overlying smell of perspiration and soap. He sat on the bench in his shirtsleeves above creased cotton trousers. On their entrance, he placed his hands behind his back, guiltily. Bailey had the distinct impression that he had been biting his nails. He swung round on the other officer, almost falling into him.

'Has he had a shower?'

'Sir, yes. At home, before we collected him.'

Ryan's face had opened into the beginnings of a smile before Bailey spoke. Then it closed into sullen lines and he turned his eyes to a long examination of his hands. Nails bitten to the quick, Bailey noticed. In as long as he had known the man, Ryan had never bitten his nails. Not even in the long reaches of the night when nerves turned men into anxious boys.

'Has he been examined?'

'Not yet, sir . . .'

'For Christ's sake, that should have been first.'

Bailey swung on Ryan with the anger of a parent trying to prevent himself from slapping a child out of sheer disappointment.

'What have you got to say?' Bailey barked at him.

Ryan shifted. His voice was surprisingly firm.

'Nothing, sir. Nothing at all.'

And he turned his head to the wall.